Alien voices? No, that was madness . . .

I bent my knees into a *demi-plié*, forcing my heels to remain on the floor.

Sharp pains shot from my knees into my brain. It felt as if someone drove daggers directly into my temples, again and again in rhythm with my elevated pulse.

I collapsed onto the floor, pressing the heels of my palms into my eyes. The moment I stretched my body flat on the floor the pain stopped. But the memory remained. I cowered there for many long moments, whimpering.

Alien voices? Nanobots inside my body. *Alien voices!*

My mind looped around and around the problem. Could it be? Could the mad surgeon with his miracle procedure have done more. Much, much more?

The nanobots repaired damage. The doctor had hinted that they could even recognize new damage as it occurred.

Was the leap to recognizing *potential* damage too far?

From there might they not need to discourage behavior that *could* lead to potential damage?

No, I reasoned. That was madness.

Madness. Had the nurse used that word?

From "Alien Voices" by P.R. Frost

THE FUTURE WE WISH WE HAD

EDITED BY
Martin H. Greenberg
and Rebecca Lickiss

DAW BOOKS, INC.
DONALD A. WOLLHEIM, FOUNDER
375 Hudson Street, New York, NY 10014

ELIZABETH R. WOLLHEIM
SHEILA E. GILBERT
PUBLISHERS
http://www.dawbooks.com

First Printing, December 2007
1 2 3 4 5 6 7 8 9

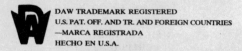

DAW TRADEMARK REGISTERED
U.S. PAT. OFF. AND TR. AND FOREIGN COUNTRIES
—MARCA REGISTRADA
HECHO EN U.S.A.

PRINTED IN THE U.S.A.

ACKNOWLEDGMENTS

Introduction copyright © 2007 by Rebecca Lickiss

"A *Rosé* for Emily," copyright © 2007 by Esther M. Friesner

"Waiting For Juliette," copyright © 2007 by Sarah A. Hoyt

"Boys," copyright © 2007 by Dave Freer

"Trainer of Whales," copyright © 2007 by Brenda Cooper

"Good Old Days," copyright © 2007 by Kevin J. Anderson

"Kicking and Screaming Her Way to the Altar," copyright © 2007 by Alan L. Lickiss

"Alien Voices," copyright © 2007 by P. R. Frost

"Inside Job," copyright © 2007 by Loren L. Coleman

"A Small Skirmish in the Culture War," copyright © 2007 by Mike Resnick and James Patrick Kelly

"Dark Wings," copyright © 2007 by Lisanne Norman

"My Father, The Popsicle," copyright © 2007 by Annie Reed

"Destiny," copyright © 2007 by Julie Hyzy

"Cold Comfort," copyright © 2007 by Dean Wesley Smith

"The Stink of Reality," copyright © 2007 by Phyllis Irene Radford

"Yellow Submarine," copyright © 2007 by Rebecca Moesta

"Good Genes," copyright © 2007 by Kristine Kathryn Rusch

CONTENTS

Introduction

Rebecca Lickiss

I remember watching the lunar missions on TV. Men landing and walking on the moon, collecting rocks and dirt, jumping around and having fun in their lunar buggy. It was exciting, thrilling, breathtaking, and inspiring. I remember one night looking up at the moon and thinking someone was up there, looking back at me. Probably they were busy elsewhere, or whatnot, but let's go with it.

Then and there I promised myself that someday I would live on the moon. It didn't seem such an impossible dream. All the science fiction that I read clearly implied that the future would hold wonders of technology that would revolutionize our lives, change the way we understood and interacted with each other, and help us to achieve the ideals of freedom and equality and prosperity that would make the world a better place. After all, why would anyone go to the trouble of getting to the moon, and then stop?

Sadly, but I'm sure not surprisingly, I don't live on the moon, and there's very little chance I ever will. Someone, somewhere along the line didn't keep the implied promise of the future.

You know that future: the one where we all have some form of flying transportation, flying cars or jet-packs, and no one has to cook or do any of the boring housework that *everyone* hates. Everyone is smart; probably, we're all scientists. Everything is all shiny chrome and sleekly aerodynamic.

Well, here we are in the future. Shiny chrome and sleek aerodynamics come and go as design fashions. We didn't get our flying cars, but the entertainment possibilities today are staggering. We have music on demand, and we're able to hear music seemingly minutes after it has been recorded. Also, there are some home theater systems that rival small theaters, without the overpriced snacks. Phones everywhere we go, which is becoming annoying.

It is interesting and exciting in its own way, but not exactly what I was expecting. Probably not what you were expecting either. Everyone had their own expectations—their own idea of what should and shouldn't be. Which is why we get what we have.

Gathered here are sixteen stories of what this future we have now, and will have tomorrow, might have been. Could have been. Maybe still will be. Or maybe even one we're glad is not.

I hope you enjoy these stories as much as I did. I hope they make you as nostalgic for the future that could have been as they have made me.

A ROSÉ FOR EMILY

Esther M. Friesner

" 'Newfangled'?" Marjorie Bedford echoed, as if repeating the outlandish word would somehow make it go away. She leaned her forearms on the massive mahogany desk that was hers by right of being Paradise Purchased Properties' top saleswoman. Behind her, floor-to-ceiling windows framed a glittering panorama of New York City from a very expensive height. "Did I actually hear you call the Carème 6000 Mequizeen 'newfangled'?"

"Would you like me to call it a 'contraption' while I'm at it?" Emily June Newcomb replied tartly. She tossed back her golden hair and added: "I'm willing to throw in a couple of complimentary 'goldangs' and maybe a 'consarn it' or two, if you insist, but 'yeehaw' costs extra."

"I assure you, Ms. Newcomb, I didn't mean to insult you," Marjorie said hastily. "I was simply . . . charmed by your colorful choice of words."

"Bullshit, ma'am," Emily said without raising her voice. She didn't have to: a woman with her celebrity-level good looks was *always* heard. "How's that for colorful? I know what you really think of me and my

3

family. I just wish that when you were showing us the house, I wasn't the only one who noticed the way you kept giving Mama and Daddy those condescending little smirks every time they *ooh*ed and *aah*ed over all the fancy tricks that deathtrap could do. It was like you were at the zoo, thinking 'What *clever* little monkeys. Why, they're almost human!' Instead of the fruit basket and bottle of swill you gave us as a moving-in gift, why didn't you just buy us a welcome mat that said *Hicks With Money*?"

Marjorie felt her cheeks heat with the intense blush of an amoral wife caught by hubby 'twixt the sheets with the pool boy. (Which indeed was how Marjorie's last-marriage-but-one had ended.) *Damn this girl,* she thought. *How* dare *she? How dare she be so bloody right, the sow?*

"Ms. Newcomb, aren't you being a trifle harsh?" Marjorie's teeth gritted together only a *little* when she smiled. " 'Monkeys'? 'Deathtrap'? And calling a bottle of Moët et Chandon 'swill'? Tsk. I do apologize if you've misconstrued any of my words or actions. It was a privilege and a pleasure to deal with your parents."

"I know," Emily returned. "I saw the check Daddy handed over at the closing. We know a family or two back home who could live for a year on the commission you earned. And before your mind flashes into *Beverly Hillbillies* reruns, 'back home' for us was neither the backwoods nor the boondocks. Not *all* small Southern towns are drenched in hot-and-cold running possums."

Marjorie's fingers curled, her hands knotted. She wanted to squeeze Emily June's slim, white neck like a toothpaste tube. "I *thought* you'd come to see me about the problems your family's having with the Carème 6000, Ms. Newcomb," she growled. "But if your sole purpose was to berate me for what *you* think is my attitude towards your family, congratulations on your fabulous ESP."

Emily opened the Italian leather briefcase in her lap and yanked out a stack of papers. "You want me to cut to the chase? Here's the scalpel." She slapped the rustling pile onto Marjorie's desk. "The house you sold to my parents is unsatisfactory and the Carème 6000 Mequizeen kitchen unit contained therein is a danger to life and limb. We want it removed and destroyed. We also want payment for acute psychological damage, loss of self-esteem, and being the victims of hate speech. The figure we want is *here*." She pointed to a long line of numerals on the top page. "That's if Paradise Purchased and the Mequizeen Company settle *now*. If this goes to court, I promise that figure will swell up like . . . like a tick on a hound dog." She showed her teeth, then *very* deliberately added: "Hoo-ee."

Emily June Newcomb was no lawyer, nor had she gone so far as to retain one. Yet. Still, the legalese in the papers she'd dropped in Marjorie's lap was flawless. Two of the attorneys on payroll with Paradise Purchase Properties read it and wet themselves.

Stupid bitch should've gone to law school instead of to work for her daddy, Marjorie thought bitterly as she stood in the throng of reporters gathered on the Newcomb lawn. *Then she'd be someone else's headache.*

It was a headache that centered on Marjorie's wallet. She shuddered, recalling how very opposite-of-pleased her boss had been when she'd brought the Newcombs' complaint into his office. At thirty-five, well-spoken and dead sexy, CEO Joss Parker was the sort of man the Trump wannabes of the world hated and envied with a white-hot passion. It wasn't just that his career was an apparently effortless, Fred Astaire-like dance across the walls and ceilings of life. What galled his rivals most was that he then sold the apartments containing said walls and ceilings for a pretty penny. (More accurately, for an unsightly seven-figure sum.)

What galled *him* was the thought of needlessly parting with money. His first reaction to the Newcomb threat was dismissive. "Let them sue. We've got better lawyers than any— What sort of business is Newcomb in, anyhow?" He flashed the boyish grin that had caused many a supermodel to drop her La Perla undies at his bidding. "Oil? Black gold? Texas tea?"

Marjorie pursed her lips. "Sir, trust me, you *don't* want to mention anything even vaguely connected with that old TV show around the Newcombs, especially their daughter. Boone Newcomb's money comes from insurance."

"You mean the little skank is a *second* generation conman?" Joss turned stern. "If she wants to ride the fake personal injury pony, I've got private investigators who'll yank her out of the saddle before she can even *look* at a neck brace."

"Boone Newcomb *owns* an insurance company, a very profitable one. He specializes in insuring the *incredibly* wealthy. He and his daughter have contacts with—"

"—*our* target market." Joss shaded his eyes wearily. "If we don't give that bitch satisfaction, she won't just take us to court, she'll badmouth us to her daddy's clients. I might as well cut her that check right now." He gave Marjorie a hard look. "Your commission from the Newcomb sale won't *quite* cover this, but it will be a start, and I'll take the remainder out of your next sale."

Marjorie's jaw dropped. "*My* commission?" For the first time in her life, she understood Abraham's feelings when he'd received the initial directive to sacrifice his son Isaac.

"You were the person who sold them the—" Joss's manicured finger skimmed through the documents before him. "—*hostile and unsafe domicile.* It's only fair that you make amends." He was grinning again, but there was less Charming Little Man-Child behind those pearly whites and *much* more Big, Bad, Commission-Devouring Wolf.

Marjorie made a stab at fiscal self-preservation: "All right, Mr. Parker," she said sweetly. "I'll make the necessary arrangements with Accounting." She turned to go, then paused and turned at the door. "Do you want me to alert Legal too?"

"Legal?" Joss echoed. "We're settling this out of court."

"Yes," Marjorie purred. "We're settling with the Newcombs out of court, but I don't think that Mequizeen, Incorporated, will be willing to do the same when they sue us for defamation."

"*What*?"

She framed imaginary headlines with her hands: " 'Real Estate Tycoon Affirms Mequizeen's Carème 6000 Unsafe, Generously Offers Reparations to Victims of Robotic Death-Chef.' Mequizeen will be *so* pleased."

Joss Parker looked stricken. Marjorie had presented a plausible scenario, every syllable laden with grief. In his gilt-swaddled world, grief was for other people. "We'll make the payment to the Newcombs through a third party," he suggested, eager to make everything go *his* way again. "They won't care, as long as they get their money."

"You forget, they also want the Carème 6000 re-

moved and destroyed. That is *not* a common piece of
kitchen equipment, sir. Remember when Mequizeen
first put it on the market? 'The Kitchen of the Future
Is Yours Today!' Every Carème 6000 installation was
a major publicity splash. Some sites still have their
own corps of dedicated *paparazzi,* watching and
waiting."

"For what?" Joss asked. "Dinner?"

Marjorie laughed dutifully at her employer's sally.
"Waiting for something to go wrong. Horribly, dra-
matically, photogenically wrong. Sir, do you remember
the old cartoons where the main character finds fully
automated model house? At first it's wonderful. Push
the big red start button and the house does everything
for you, *especially* the kitchen. Turn the dial, punch
the keypad, throw the switch, and robotic mechanisms
make you any dish you want, from pizza to *pâté de
foie gras.* But then, this being a cartoon, hijinks ensue.
Next thing you know, the main character's being
kneaded, floured, tossed, sprinkled with mozzarella,
and shoved into the oven. And *that,* sir, is what the
paparazzi are waiting for and hoping to capture happening in real life."

Joss closed his brilliant blue eyes and pinched the
bridge of his nose. He looked pained. "So it will be
virtually impossible to comply with the Newcombs' de-
mands without attracting unfavorable media attention
to the Carème 6000?"

"Yes, sir."

"But if we don't comply, the Newcombs will sue us
and most likely win?"

"Yes, sir. Sorry, sir."

"Marjorie, you'll have to excuse me: this is my first
encounter with a lose-lose situation and I can't say I
like it. As a matter of fact, as we speak, my brain is

racing to find a way to distance myself from it as fast as possible. I think I'm gong to fire you, for starters."

"Sir, I wouldn't do that," Marjorie said quickly. "It would leave me with no motivation to give you the solution you need."

"Solution?" Joss perked up, eager and attentive.

"Yes, sir. As in lose-lose turning into win-win for us, whereas for the Newcombs . . ."

"Tell me more."

Which is how Marjorie wound up on the Newcombs' lawn, rubbing elbows with a mob of reporters, waiting for their hosts to appear. She'd presented her employer with a *plan*—a plan of simplicity, a plan of brilliance, a plan that would defang the Newcomb's threatened lawsuit and save her commission. It was perfect.

Now, if it would only *work*.

While they waited, the press reviewed the briefing download Marjorie had sent to their PDAs, along with the notification of the event itself. None of them could figure out how *hate speech* could have anything to do with a fully automated kitchen either.

"It's like saying your bathroom's gender-biased!" an AP stringer declared.

"Mine was until we got one of those automated seat-lowering devices installed," said a female colleague. "My husband is *not* trainable." The other women in the crowd made sympathetic noises.

"Maybe the refrigerator made a nasty crack about the Polish sausage," a would-be wit suggested. "Or the Italian bread, or the French dressing, or the—"

He could have gone on in the same vein at painful length, but luckily for his companions, at that moment the front door of the great mansion opened wide. Boone and Betsy Newcomb stepped out on the wide front porch, regarding the clamoring reporters like a pair of overweight asthmatic antelopes tapped to be keynote speakers at a leopard convention.

Boone Newcomb was a simple, sincere soul. He welcomed the media with the air of a man who has been dragged into a situation that scares the scrapple out of him. Nonetheless, he'd been raised with certain ideals, among which was the firm belief that John Wayne was right: *a man is obliged to accomplish what a man is required to achieve.* Or words to that effect.

He was still greeting the news corps when Marjorie broke a path to him through the mob. Boone smiled. "Why, Miz Marjorie, it's good to see you again. I'm truly sorry that it's taken something like this to bring you over for a visit. Betsy and me, we took a real shine to you, and that's a fact. We meant it when we said you'd be welcome to come by here any time."

Marjorie's smile was a brittle grimace. The look of apology in Boone's eyes was real. This whole ugly business hadn't been his idea; she'd wager her next sales commission *and* her realtor's license on it. "I'm sorry too, Mr. Newcomb," she said. "I hope that I'll be able to make up for it once we've settled this little . . . mix-up."

" 'Mix-up'?" Emily June Newcomb stepped out onto the porch from her lurking post behind the great double-wide front doors. "I'd hardly call endangering *and* belittling our family a 'mix-up.' "

Marjorie had to hand it to the younger woman: Emily knew how to make an entrance. Cameras clicked and whirred; reporters swarmed forward. The undercover crowd-control personnel that Marjorie had so wisely placed among the newshounds subtly stepped in to hold back the tide, but it wasn't easy. Emily June Newcomb was eye candy of the first order, and she

spoke with a ferocious intensity and passion that prac-
tically screamed *sound bite*! Marjorie could almost feel
the sudden, almost erotic thrill that coursed through
the media mob.

"Well, I suppose we'd best get started," Boone said.
He did not sound happy or eager. Marjorie couldn't
blame him. *Chez* Newcomb was pure Neo-Greek Revival, a displaced Southern plantation-style abode with
a nice patch of pricey landscape surrounding it. Now,
thanks to Emily, only a few select reporters were
being allowed inside to witness the trial of the Carème
6000, leaving the rest of the pack to trample the costly
vegetation outside.

(For the sufficiently well-heeled, ownership of a substantial patch of greenery in the heart of New York
City was no longer a pipe dream. The Newcomb place
was part of Eminent Domains, an upscale housing de-
velopment that came into existence when an agenda-
toting D.C. *somebody* did an end-run around the elec-
torate and decreed that unless Central Park became
privatized, the terrorists would already have won. It
worked like a knee-jerk charm before you could say
"bulldozer.")

Boone conducted his unwished-for guests through the
front doors and onward to the kitchen. Marjorie heard
the collective gasp of awe from the reporters when they
crossed the threshold. Though posh digs were same-old
same-old to her, even she still felt a *frisson* of wonder
whenever she encountered a Mequizeen-equipped home.
The high-tech cookplace was a monument to sleek, un-
derstated opulence, cool practicality, and preprogrammed culinary expertise. The room itself glittered,
but looked relatively bare, presenting an array of
smooth, shining surfaces. Nonetheless, that smooth
shininess reminded the human hindbrain of the sur-

face of a tranquil prehistoric lake. You just *knew* something was lurking below the surface; something big, with teeth.

"Ready, Mr. Newcomb?" Marjorie asked, taking charge as she stepped up to the control panel. Set into the wall nearest the door, its thin chrome frame embraced a small, flat keypad and a blank display screen.

"Ready as I'll ever be."

"Wonderful," she said, not really meaning it. Marjorie hated putting the Newcombs through this media circus, but what choice did she have? It was them or her commission, and besides, their miserable brat had started it! *And why?* she wondered, not for the first time. *For the money? But her parents are rolling in it! What in the world does Emily June Newcomb hope to achieve by putting Mr. Parker's company and Mequizeen through the negative PR wringer?* She was damned if she could figure it out.

You know what? she told herself. *The hell with figuring out Miss Emily's motive. I'll worry about that after I've rescued my livelihood and Joss Parker's corporate bacon, not before, so let's get cooking!*

Marjorie girded her loins and grinned resolutely into the crosshairs of the cameras. "Hi, everyone!" she chirped. "We're here today to help our good friends the Newcomb family learn what a wonderful convenience the Carème 6000 by Mequizeen can be once you *fully understand* it. Mr. Newcomb here is an intelligent man. He's been alive long enough to know that new and exciting technology always requires a little getting used to, and there's no shame in that. Isn't that right, Mr. Newcomb?" Boone only nodded. Marjorie thought it was amazing how the man could stand perfectly still and yet give the impression of squirming like a hooked nightcrawler.

As much as she sympathized, Marjorie had no choice but to proceed. "When I got my first Mequizeen, I just about starved to death before I got up the nerve to touch it." *As if I could ever afford anything this expensive!* she thought. "Sometimes *new* is just another word for *scary,*" she went on, showering charm alternately over Boone Newcomb and the reporters. "And sometimes you get *so* scared by something new, you convince yourself it must be dangerous, because if it wasn't, you'd be kind of *silly* to be scared of it, right? Well, we at Paradise Purchased Properties care about our clients' happiness, even *long* after the papers are signed, and how happy is a family that's scared of its own kitchen?"

The reporters chuckled. *Just like I wanted them to,* Marjorie thought. *I'm making the Newcombs seem like frightened children. Boone and Betsy both look like they wish they could crawl into the freezer and hide.* She felt a momentary twinge of guilt, then she glanced at Emily and the twinge vaporized.

"People, *please,*" she gently chided the reporters. "How can you make fun of a man whose only desire is the safety of his family?" With impeccable timing and delivery, she distanced herself from the derision she had just incited. The reporters were abashed, Boone and Betsy gazed at her with pathetic gratitude, but Emily looked rightfully suspicious.

Marjorie turned to the business at hand. "So, let's make our valued Paradise Purchased Properties friends happy by showing them—*and* you—that the Carème 6000 is nothing an intelligent, forward-thinking family can't handle. I have personally worked out a demo that will prove it's a modern marvel of efficiency, *safety,* and courtesy. Mr. Newcomb, if you would—?" She handed him a small, folded slip of paper.

Boone Newcomb's apprehension grew perceptibly as he scanned the page. " 'Scuse me, but what's all this?"

"The menu," Marjorie replied suavely. "The Carème 6000's built-in voice recognition software doesn't let anyone but its owners give it instructions—another fine safety feature from the folks at Mequizeen, and one which we at Paradise Purchased Properties really appreciate." Her expression did nothing to hint at the masterful way she was turning a news story into a free commercial for both companies. Mr. Parker *would* be pleased. "Just go through that list and ask it to cook up every item while our friends from the media witness how well and how *safely* your food is prepared. We'll start small—a simple *amuse bouche* of Irish salmon *tuilles* with accents of asiago cheese and white truffle oil—then work our way through a series of *ceviche* presentations, a trio of *tapenades,* some basic *meeze, ortolans, potages à la saison,* a crown roast of New Zealand lamb, a classic Peking duck, *filet de boeuf á l'absinthe,* venison on a bed of lilac blossoms, trout *á la mode de* Gertrude Stein, and finally a complete Kyoto-style *kaiseki ryori* experience. Then for dessert, we—"

"Oh, for God's sake!" Emily June strode forward and slapped her hand down on the gleaming kitchen counter. "You could have this ladle-wielding death machine cook stuff like that from now until doomsday and it won't demonstrate why it's a menace to life, limb and—"

"Ms. Newcomb, did you know we're broadcasting this *live*?" Marjorie said quietly. "Because I really don't think that the good people at Mequizeen can let their fine product be slandered like this without taking legal action." Joss gave her a discreet look of approval.

Emily's cheeks blazed. "You can't slander a machine."

"But you *can* be slandered by one?" Marjorie lifted one eyebrow. "You did mention 'hate speech' among the other charges you've lodged against the Carème 6000. I'm sure it made perfect sense to *you,* but I'm afraid I don't quite follow your line of—" She coughed for sarcastic effect. "—reasoning."

Emily glowered at Marjorie, then shoved her unceremoniously away from the control panel. The enraged Newcomb heiress pushed her father nose-to-speaker with the machine, and commanded, "Tell it to make something you *usually* have for lunch, Daddy! Something you *like.* Show these people what we go through every time we want to get a simple bite to eat in this house!"

All eyes and all lenses were on Boone Newcomb. He sucked on his lower lip for a moment, then took a deep breath and addressed the Carème 6000 in a strong, clear voice: "Boone Newcomb here."

At the sound of its master's voice, the kitchen hummed to life. Reporters watched entranced as various wall panels slid back to reveal the contents of a well-stocked pantry, an array of gleaming copper-bottomed and stainless steel pans, a mad scientist's trove of glittering utensils. Part of the floor raised open and a bistro-sized table blossomed into the light, accompanied by a single chair.

"Good afternoon, Mr. Newcomb, sir," said a richly textured, affable voice from above. It boasted a slight French accent. "So pleased to serve you. Will you be lunching alone, or shall I provide for your guests?" Individual rays of golden light shot down from the ceiling to pinpoint every human being in the room. Some of the reporters became decidedly uneasy at being thus singled out by the Carème 6000's sensors, but Marjorie stepped in quickly.

"And here you see one of the finest *safety* features of the Carème 6000. It is 100% aware of every living thing in this kitchen so that, when it begins to cook, it will take all necessary precautions to be sure you're kept *safe* from any sharp or heavy culinary tools it might need to use."

"Uh, you'll just be cooking for me right now, if you don't mind," Boone said. "Lunch please. And what I'd like is, um, a sandwich."

"Yes, sir," the kitchen replied. "I can prepare a lovely sliced sirloin of prime Angus beef, served on a freshly baked twelve-grain roll, topped with Maui onions, homemade mustard sauce, and—"

"Potato chip," said Boone Newcomb. He was perspiring slightly, but a determined look had come into his eyes.

"Certainly, sir, it would be no trouble at all to fry a batch of potato chips as an accompaniment. Thick or thin cut? Kosher salt, Mediterranean sea salt, Baltic sea salt, malt vinegar, garlic, shallots—? Ah, but perhaps you'd prefer to set those parameters after you select the variety of potato. I can offer you Yukon Gold, Idaho, russet, Peruvian Blue—"

"Sandwich." Boone Newcomb's jaw was set so tightly that the word escaped as barely more than a hiss. "I want a potato chip sandwich."

A great and awful stillness settled over the kitchen. Everyone present, with the exception of Mr. Newcomb's immediate family, stared at the man as though he'd just requested a big bowl of cotton candy soup or perhaps a scoop of frog ice cream. Betsy Newcomb twisted her fingers, looking mortally embarrassed by her guests' shocked response to her husband's lunch order. Emily just grinned like a jackal.

"A . . . potato chip . . . sandwich?" One young reporter was the first to break the silence, to ask the question everyone else was perishing to pose. "Ex– excuse me, Mr. Newcomb, sir, but did you just ask for a potato chip *sandwich*?"

"So what if I did?" Boone Newcomb suddenly stood tall and defiant in the teeth of the media. "You ever had a potato chip sandwich, boy?" The reporter shook his head in the negative. "You ever know any- one had one?" Again the hesitant headshake. "Well, when I was a boy back home, my mama used to make us potato chip sandwiches for our lunch every now and again, and let me tell you what, they're good eating!"

He returned his attention to the Carème 6000. "Well?" he demanded. "You heard me. I want a po- tato chip sandwich. Store-bought sour cream and onion flavor chips. A big old dollop of mayonnaise on both slices of the bread. *White* bread. *Store-bought* white bread. And I mean the grocery store, not some boutique, gourmet, artsy food shop. You got all that?"

The kitchen began to hum again. It was a low, deep hum that slowly turned into an even lower rumbling. It sounded very much like an earthquake in the mak- ing. Some of the reporters began to glance around, checking for the nearest exit.

Then the rumbling stopped. A dainty silver bell chimed once, melodiously, and a narrow panel in one of the kitchen's walls slit itself open as a rosewood tray emerged. On the tray was a pale jonquil linen placemat, on the placemat, a vibrant celadon plate, and on the plate, a potato chip sandwich.

"Luncheon is served, sir," said the Carème 6000 as a mechanical arm telescoped out of the wall panel and deftly set the tray down on the table. For a moment,

Marjorie thought she detected a vague note of petulance in the kitchen's synthesized voice.

Boone Newcomb picked up the sandwich, examined it closely, then took a bite. He chewed, swallowed, and a sunny smile slowly spread itself across his face. "Just like Mama used to make," he announced. "Kitchen, you done good." Several of the reporters applauded. One even cheered.

"There you have it," Marjorie said, stepping back into the spotlight with the finesse of a born game show host. "In spite of the fact that Mr. Newcomb's lunch order was culturally unique and not part of the Carème 6000's preprogrammed library of cookbooks, this fantastic machine produced the requested item quickly, accurately and *safely*. Now perhaps there are some people—" She stared meaningly at Emily. "—who consider such momentary hesitation on the part of the Carème 6000 to be unacceptable, even if it was *by no stretch of the imagination* dangerous. No doubt we'd all be happier in a world where our every whim was fulfilled the very instant we articulated it. But I doubt any right-minded person would call the Carème 6000's behavior in this instance insubordination, let alone hate—"

"May I offer you a beverage to accompany your lunch, sir?" The kitchen's voice cut in over Marjorie's.

"Well, thank you," Boone replied affably. "I wouldn't say no to a nice frosty glass of—"

"—wine? I would recommend an impudent little white, a sauvignon blanc from Chateau Kiwi. "The '16s are eminently drinkable now."

"Er, no. I can't say as I really care for—"

"You're sure, sir? The clean, fresh fruit notes will pair nicely with the sour cream and onion potato chips. Even the least sophisticated palate can appreciate it."

"There it is!" Emily fairly crowd in triumph. "You heard it: this miserable machine just insulted my daddy!"

"Now, Emily June, I wouldn't call that an insult." Boone took another bite of his potato chip sandwich, a man at peace with the world.

"Mr. Newcomb?" Marjorie assumed a look of cautious optimism. "Was *this* what happened before? You asked for a . . . down-home dish and the Carème 6000 acted a little—?"

"Patronizing," Emily broke in. "Condescending. *Demeaning.*"

Marjorie could take no more. "Oh, for pity's sake, does your father *look* like a man who's been mortally insulted?" She waved one hand at the happily munching Boone. "Even if the Carème 6000 did get a little snotty when he refused its wine selection, do you actually believe he's stupid enough to be personally insulted by a freaking *household appliance*? Because if that's your opinion of your own father's intelligence, Ms. Newcomb, I think *you're* the one who's behaving in a demeaning manner!"

"How dare you?" Emily's eyes were ablaze. "You think we don't know what you're up to here? When you contacted Daddy about doing this demo, you made it sound like it'd be nothing more than a fact-finding effort to be done privately and in good faith, not a media free-for-all! You and your employer, Mr. Joss Parker, are nothing more than a pack of PR hounds who'd roll over and play dead for extra airtime or another photo in the glossies!"

"Well, we've found our facts, haven't we?" Marjorie gestured at Mr. Newcomb. "Your father got his potato chip sandwich at no risk to life or limb. Yes, the Carème 6000 does seem to be a bit of a wine snob, but if you think a mere *touch* of attitude is the same as hate speech, you're not only trivializing a truly deadly social ill, you've also just committed it yourself, live and on the air!"

Emily gaped at the accusation. "You're crazy!"

"And *that* makes your second offense," Marjorie countered gleefully. "Casting aspersions on the state of my mental health *and* doing so using a term that demeans the mentally ill? For shame. Plus your previous statement, calling my respected employer and me PR *hounds*? Allegations of bestiality are simply not accept—"

"My apologies to the canine population," Emily snarled. "*One* test demonstration of this death-tra— kitchen doesn't settle anything."

"Oh, I think it's settled plenty." Marjorie pressed the advantage, playing to the cameras. "It's shown the world one litigious woman's blatant attempt at extorting money from two respectable corporations on the flimsiest possible grounds. The Carème 6000 has just demonstrated that it works quickly, efficiently, and safely, that it is far from the big, bad, family-endangering oogie-boogie that you claim it is. Its grasp of so-called hate speech is about three notches below 'I see London, I see France!' And if *that* makes you want to file suit against me for hate speech against your underpants, Ms. Newcomb, wait right here; I'll alert the Supreme Court."

Boone Newcomb finished his potato chip sandwich and tried to make peace. "Now, Miz Marjorie, you've gotta forgive our little girl. Maybe she did kinda over-react to the troubles we've been having with this new-fangled kitchen, but she's got her reasons. Something about the way the Carème gizmo talks about wine, it always set her off, carrying on about how it was an insult to the whole family, and how even though we weren't all city-wise celebrities and such, that was no reason for us to take that kind of treatment lying down. Mama and me, we'd sooner have Merle Haggard than merlot, so we'd just laugh it off when that voice tried to get us to drink something besides an ice tea or maybe a beer. But poor Emily June took it all seriously, busting into tears at every dang meal until finally we told her to do what she wanted about it." He looked sheepish. "So she did."

"*Daddy!*" Emily's face flooded with color. "Whose side are you on?"

"Yours, baby girl," Boone said soothingly. "But let's be honest: Mama and me never would've let you take things this far if not for all the heartbreak you were going through. We hoped it'd take your mind off the man who—"

"*Man?*" Marjorie stared at Emily. "There's a *man* involved? You initiated this whole ugly mess—you endangered the reputations of *two* major corporations and *my* job security—*not* because of any real consumer safety issues, *not* out of simple, lawsuit-happy greed, but to take your mind off the fact that you got dumped by some *man?*"

And then, she did something that she knew she should *not* have done, under the circumstances: she looked Emily June straight in the eye with blatant, unambiguous, camera-readable pity. Not sorrow, not sympathy, not woman-to-woman understanding, but deliberate, lowdown, it-sucks-to-be-you *pity*.

Marjorie's look hit Emily June like a slap across her beautiful face. Livid, she whirled back to the control panel. "Kitchen!" she yelled. "*I'm* hungry. Access freezer bin #4 and display the contents, *now!*"

What the—? Marjorie was taken aback by Emily's bizarre reaction, but before she could say a word, a knee-high panel on the far wall moved aside and a silver platform slid up and out into the light. Upon it rested a row of furred, frozen bodies, each about the size of a small salami.

"Are those—?" A young reporter's voice trembled. His microphone shook in his hand. "Are those really—?"

"Squirrels." Marjorie had the guts to say what everyone else didn't want to believe.

"*His* squirrels," Emily June clarified. She crossed the room to gaze down at the row of tiny bodies. "*He* used to take me out to all the fancy New York restaurants. I'd tease him about how the food was good, but it wasn't a patch on my favorite down-home meal. When he offered to get me the makings for a good old-fashioned squirrel stew, I thought he wanted to show that he *cared* about me."

"Of course," Marjorie muttered too softly for Emily to hear. "What girl wouldn't be thrilled to have her boyfriend say it with squirrels?"

"He shot them himself one weekend when the two of us were staying at his place in the Berkshires." Tears brimmed in Emily's eyes. "And after he had them cleaned, quick-frozen, and packed for travel, he told me that it was all over between us, that I was squirrel, he was Sevruga; I was possum, he was *pâté*; I was slumgullion, but he was done slumming it with me." She raised her chin sharply. "My looks were what hooked him, but they couldn't hold him. You see, I wasn't a *celebrity*. He said that any two-bit billionaire could date a beautiful woman, but the media only cared if you dated someone *famous,* and he only cared about making the media pay attention to *him.* Well, how famous am I *now,* Joss Parker?" she hollered at the cameras. "Because I'll tell you what, it's nowhere near as famous as I'm about to be!"

"Impossible!" Marjorie objected. "Mr. Parker must've

heard your name a hundred times since you started this mess, but he never gave any sign that he recognized—"

"He doesn't *know*," Emily replied. "I was hosting one of Daddy's clients at Le Cirque when we met en route to the rest rooms. He presumed I was a supermodel and I let him. I told him my professional name was—" She looked away briefly. "— Grenouille. Even when he found out I wasn't famous, he never learned my *real* name."

She jerked her head up, shame ceding to rage once more. "How dare you make me relive that humiliation!" Emily June slapped the panel above the tray of frozen squirrels. "Kitchen! I want a squirrel stew and I want it *pronto*!"

"Y-yes, *mademoiselle*." The voice of the Carème 6000 sputtered only a trifle. "A squirrel stew . . . Er. Mademoiselle did you say 'squirrel'? Not . . . squab? My audio sensors have been a trifle undertuned of late and I—"

"*Squirrel*."

"Ve-ry good, *mad-e-moi-selle*."

Marjorie felt a dreadful pang of apprehension. The kitchen's voice sounded distinctly tense, tightly strung. She recalled something from the online tutorial briefing she'd taken prior to marketing her first Mequizeen-equipped home: *early detection of most malfunctions is a snap, and easily diagnosed before serious consequences can arise. Our diagnostic software is programmed to reflect incipient breakdowns via the kitchen's* vox humana. *In other words, imagine you've got a full-time, four-star, naturally temperamental French chef working for you. Pay attention to what he says and how he says it. Above all, never presume that a potentially bad situation will get better on its own. You wouldn't ignore a* real *chef's displeasure, would you?*

This impish rhetorical question was illustrated with a jolly animated cartoon of a chef, white toque erupting like a volcano, flinging bloody cleavers everywhere.

"Ms. Newcomb, wait!" Marjorie cried. "Perhaps we should postpone the rest of this demonstra—"

"Emily June, Miz Marjorie's right," Boone said. "We shouldn't go on with this, not with you feeling so—"

"We will go on," Emily gritted. "Kitchen! You've got your orders. Get going."

"Yes, mademoiselle." If possible, the kitchen sounded even grimmer and more indomitable than Emily. "One . . . squirrel stew, *tout de suite.*" The tray with the tiny corpses began to retract, but Emily shot out a staying hand before it could vanish from sight.

"Not so fast." She bared her teeth. "Aren't you going to ask me what I want to drink with that?"

Something in the kitchen began to make a thin, skin-tingling, crackling noise. It sounded like a cross between arcing electricity and human bones slowly being crushed to powder. "Ah," the kitchen said. "An appropriate beverage to accompany *ragout d'ecuerreil,* yes. My . . . pleasure. No doubt one of your *unique* palate is aware that squirrel needs a big, bold red. Something from Domaine Colt, *peut-être*? A robust zinfandel which will pair the black fruit and pepper notes of the wine with the gamy taste of the meat. I will of course make sure that some of the wine is used in the preparation of the dish. It's best if the squirrel comes from the same vineyard as the wine, but one cannot have everything one—"

"Milk," Emily said doggedly. "*Chocolate* milk. Stirred, not sha—"

"*I'll give you chocolate milk and squirrel, you hopeless hick!*" The Caréme 6000's overwrought shriek shook the walls. Panels slammed back, revealing rack upon rack of ominously clattering cutlery. The dishwasher opened and vomited up a sudsy tsunami. The coffee maker carafe shattered as the machine itself sent a geyser of boiling cappucino spurting skyward.

Then the frozen squirrels flew.

To her dying day, Marjorie couldn't say exactly *how* the Caréme 6000 managed to launch the rock-hard varmints like a flight of furry missiles. It was the most sophisticated piece of food-handling equipment on earth: it found a way. The kitchen echoed with the howls of wounded reporters, caught in the barrage. The room was crisscrossed with the same golden beams of light that Marjorie had praised earlier as a safety feature. Now they were transformed into targeting devices to make any sniper proud. No sooner did one icy squirrel hit its mark and bounce off than the kitchen floor beneath it opened. The body-cum-brickbat was swallowed up and relaunched at its next target in a glorious display of recycling gone horribly, horribly wrong.

Boone and Betsy Newcomb had good instincts: they hit the floor the instant the first frostbitten critter took wing. Marjorie didn't wait for an invitation to join them. Top-notch New York City realtors were top-notch survivors too. The three of them cowered together while the kitchen rained rodents and the voice of the Caréme 6000 called its owners everything from *tin-plated, mouth-breathing hayseeds* to *inbred trailer-park trash* to an astonishing set of verbal variations in the key of *redneck*. And through it all, Emily June Newcomb stood howling with glee, her point proven, her vendetta against Joss Parker complete.

She never saw the squirrel that got her. No one ever does.

*   *   *

The Newcomb-Parker nuptials were the wedding of the season. Marjorie served as matron of honor, walking down the aisle with a wreath of oak leaves perched atop her head. They were silk, of course, and the acorns a marvel of the master goldsmiths employed by Cartier. As she stood with the other wedding guests to toast the happy couple she finally had sufficient leisure to observe how her boss was enjoying his own wedding.

Joss Parker did seem to be having a fine time. He raised his Baccarat crystal flute, apparently at peace with the fact that it was filled to the brim with frothy chocolate milk instead of fine champagne.

And why wouldn't he be happy? Marjorie thought. *He adores celebrity, and the man who marries Emily June Newcomb's got media attention in his pocket from here to the heat-death of the universe.*

"To my lovely bride," Joss Parker declared, lavishing a *paparazzi*-pleasing smile on the woman at his side. "They say fairy tales don't come true, but we know better. I was blind to the real meaning of love until I saw what this fantastic girl was willing to do to make me pay attention. I want to thank her for that from the bottom of my heart. As you all might have noticed, everything about this wedding is a tribute to what my darling did for me on that unforgettable day. I love you, baby."

In her state-of-the-art wheelchair, Emily June Newcomb stopped petting the toy squirrel in her lap long enough to look up at her new husband. Her vague smile and empty eyes didn't look entirely out-of-place on a bride, but most everyone present knew they were permanent fixtures. She said nothing; she hadn't said a single word since she'd come out of her rodent-induced coma. Very few people can take a frozen two-pound specimen of *Sciurus carolinensis* upside the skull at thirty miles per hour without damage. She was lucky to be alive.

"I'd also like to thank our good corporate friends at Mequizeen for being so gosh-darned understanding about the really *creative* way my Emily used their *fabuloso* Carème 6000 to show her love." Joss gave his glass an extra lift to his honored guests, the Mequizeen Board of Directors.

Marjorie smirked. *You'd* better *smile, boys,* she thought. *Sure, Emily June's super-publicized love-tantrum lost you billions in business and left you bankrupt, but what can you do about it? Press charges against her for driving your Carème 6000 into mechanical apoplexy and you'll look like the world's worst bullies, attacking a woman who gave all and nearly lost all for love. The twit.*

The toasts ended; the wedding cake made its grand appearance. It glided into the center of the room on an automated trolley, to the awed exclamations of the guests. Even Joss looked surprised. "I didn't arrange this," he said.

"We did," said the CEO of the now-defunct Mequizeen corporation. His smile was suddenly genuine. With an elegantly synchronized movement, the entire BoD reached under their seats and donned motorcycle helmets just as a familiar voice from the wedding cake trolley exclaimed:

"Is that chocolate milk I see? In *champagne* glasses? *Again*?!"

A frozen squirrel popped out of the center of the wedding cake's top layer. A lone laser beam pinpointed the center of Joss Parker's forehead. Marjorie dove under the table.

Hijinks ensued.

* * *

Special thanks to Peter Liverakos for his invaluable help with winespeak. It's not every man who knows which wines go best with potato chip sandwiches or squirrel, and can also phrase his knowledge so eloquently.

WAITING FOR JULIETTE

Sarah A. Hoyt

It was the first summer of the twenty-first century, and I was looking for a way to forget.

The sanctuary had looked good two hours ago, from the other end of Denver. It had looked like sweet respite wrapped up in what the doctor ordered. Here, up close and personal, from the corner of Colfax and oblivion, it didn't seem like such a sure bet.

I should have gone straight to the sanctuary. I'd made an appointment. But the impenetrable brick facade with no windows and only one broad door, the word *Sanctuary* painted in a discreet shade of gray above it, had looked too much like the entrance to the tomb.

And I'd detoured to the diner across the street, where I sat, drinking cheap coffee, while the afternoon shadows elongated on the sidewalk, and the solar street lights flickered hesitantly on.

The problem was a girl. Her name was Juliette Jones. Mine was Romeo Smith. You could say it was destiny. I say it was proof that someone up there had a sense of humor. A nasty one.

"What will it be, honey?" the waitress asked, taking the order pad out of her apron pocket.

"Just . . . coffee," I said.

"Come on," she said. "You need something more. That coffee will eat your stomach lining if you don't get some food to go with it. The souvlaki is good."

I considered telling her I couldn't eat because I was going into the sanctuary. But that wasn't even true. They'd told me they didn't care much what I did, provided I was neither drunk nor drugged. In full command of my faculties, in fact.

Of course, I hadn't slept in two days. I rubbed my hand across my face to chase away the spiderwebs that seemed to veil my vision. But sleep deprivation didn't count. "Yeah, the souvlaki will do," I said, trying to shut her up as much as anything else.

And I tried to think through my predicament, with a brain that didn't seem disposed to do anything much.

Don't make jokes. We've heard them all. I suppose I'd have heard the jokes long before meeting Juliette, while working at the moon-launch-pad in Denver. Only I was born and raised on Luna. Mom was a romantic; Dad indulged her. And when they both died in the Tycho disaster, I was brought up in a Luna city orphanage—where no one knew enough about Shakespeare to make a single joke.

They called me Rom, guy, or *hey you* until it became clear my grades were good enough for a scholarship to Earth's space center. And then they called me *ours*. Not that they wanted to keep me; rather, they wanted to flaunt me.

By the time I finished my space medicine degree, with honors, I was known as the Luna City Kid and people I'd never heard of were sending me gifts from Lunaward. I was their boy who made good.

And then I met Juliette. OK. No enmity of houses.
But she was from old Earth money. And she'd trained
to be an astronaut. Heck, her mom had her enhanced
in womb to improve her chances of being an astronaut. She was the best of the best. And she was going
to be the first woman on Mars. And then when she
came back we were going to get married.

I swilled a bit more of the coffee and frowned at the
street outside, at the sanctuary with its blank facade.

The waitress put a souvlaki platter in front of me,
and I ate a couple of fries.

There were no passerby that I could see, only a lone
car now and then. And yet people trickled into the
diner, workmen from the nearby warehouses, students, cops.

They sat around the tables and talked. Fries whooshed
into the deep fryer. Hamburgers hissed on the grill.

Perhaps I didn't need to cold-sleep. I eyed the entrance to the sanctuary. Perhaps I could get over it in
the normal way. Surely people would stop talking
about it eventually. Surely . . .

The eight o'clock moon ship roared overhead, and
the windows of the diner rattled. Someone turned on
the TV.

And there, in grainy color, the capsule was flaming
on reentry. It was supposed to flame. They'd told us
it would happen. What they hadn't told us about was
the complete loss of communications—the capsule
splashing into the sea, sinking, sinking. And nothing,
nothing at all. Twenty-four hours of nothing. Before
even the most optimistic had to admit everyone on
board was dead.

Shocked, I looked at the replay of the scene that I
saw behind my eyelids every time I closed my eyes. I
was too far away to hear the words, but I didn't need

to. All around me, the working-class people who frequented the diner were talking, buzzing with sympathy, with horror.

"All dead."

"Tragic."

"Great loss."

The tube changed, flickered. A picture of Juliette flashed up—red hair neatly caught into a braid at her back, her dark brown eyes—smiling. I stared at it, feeling my eyes swim with tears.

"First woman on Mars," a woman at the next table said, and sighed.

"They say they're going to name the next expedition after her," a man said further on.

"Very pretty," another man said.

"I hear she was engaged to be married," said his girl.

And I realized my nails had bit into my hands so hard they'd left half-circles of blood. I needed to get over it. I needed to go on.

Juliette and I had been together for years. I couldn't look at anything anywhere around and not see her. We'd walked every street in Denver. The moon launchpad base was our normal workplace. All our friends knew about the engagement. I'd already received more than my share of condolences. And they would go on.

"Here's your bill," the waitress said. And then, as I looked down at the slip of paper she'd dropped on the greasy table, "Oh my."

I looked up. She was staring at the TV, at the image that filled the screen. The picture of Juliette and me that had been used to announce our engagement in the paper.

"You're him," she said. "No wonder you look so tired. I'm sorry, honey."

It would go on like this. Our story had captured enough imaginations. "Orphanage kid to marry Earth heiress" was a surefire eye grabber. And now, in the biopics, the stories played out over the next half century. Everyone would see those pictures, hear that story.

Total strangers would give me their condolences and speak in hushed tones around me. I would never be free to live my own life as anything but the fiancé of a dead space exploration hero. Even any other girlfriends I might have would know. I would never be able to forget.

"It's okay," I told the waitress, my mind finally made up, and I dropped the money on the table. "I'll feel better after a sleep."

She nodded sympathetically and I walked across the street and into the sanctuary.

Whatever I'd been expecting, it wasn't this. Not cheerful pink walls, decorated with the sort of inspirational posters that turn most office buildings into veritable madhouses of positive thinking.

There were children flying kites and women running atop gently sloped hills against improbably sunny skies. Sitting on the sofa upholstered in a white fabric, I read all the posters. *Sleep away your cares. Gone today; back tomorrow. The future is better.*

"Mr. Smith?" a pale blond woman with sweet features called. I got up.

She shook my hand. "I'm Elizabeth Ryes, your counselor," she said, and in the adjoining office—painted in pale blue and furnished with two chairs upholstered in robin's-egg blue—she proceeded to question me. "You will pardon me," she said. "But you seem too young and healthy to be doing this."

"I thought it was volitional," I said. "Provided one

had the money to pay for the sleep—and I do—and wanted to sleep, one was allowed to."

She smiled, the smile of an angel faced with a madman. "It is that," she said. "But the sanctuary doesn't wish to be exposed to lawsuits. So I verify that you're not doing this on the spur of the moment and for no good cause."

"Lawsuits?"

"Your mom, your dad, your girlfriend, any of them could sue us."

It hit too close to home. I sucked in breath like a man drowning and then I said, "They're all dead."

"Oh, I'm sorry. Accident? Recently?"

"My parents died in the Tycho accident in sixty-eight," I said.

"And your girlfriend?" She had the blank look of someone too young for the Tycho accident to mean anything. The hundreds of people dead when the dome cracked, the public mourning, all of it would have happened when she was still in diapers. More than twenty-five years ago. Ancient history.

Which is what I was counting on.

And in the next second, she looked up, looked at my face as though seeing it for the first time, and her hand went up to cover her mouth. "Juliette Jones," she said. "You're her fiancé. That's why you looked familiar."

I nodded. It was then very easy to explain why I couldn't stay in this time. How the emotional wound was a half of it; the other half the fact that it would blight my whole life.

She signed all the papers and accompanied me to the first step of the procedure—to the room where they anesthetized me, preparing my body to sleep for fifty years—to be on the safe side.

I was holding her hand as the IV started dripping

soporific into my veins, and my eyes weighed down. I took the image of her blonde loveliness with me into sleep. When I woke up, that little oval face, looking down at me with sympathetic anguish, would be lined and sagging. She would be a grandmother.

The first question I asked when they woke me—after the long period in which I couldn't talk at all—was, "Do you remember Juliette Jones?"

The slim, dark-haired young woman who had been massaging my shoulders—while I lay on my stomach on the heated bed, enduring one of the many days of conditioning that would be needed before I was restored to normal life—wrinkled her pretty forehead and said, "Who?" Then, after about thirty seconds, "Isn't she that new sensie star? Didn't she play Margaret in *Vina Does Venus*?"

And I knew I was safe. I endured the next two weeks in quiet calm. Oh, sleeping away fifty years didn't make the memory of Juliette more distant, or make me miss her less. Only now, no one around me knew who she was.

I mean, she was in the history books as first female to walk on Mars. I checked. But she was not the first human—that distinction belonged to Joseph McDonald—and if she came up at all it was as the bonus credit question on a test, or a bit of interesting trivia.

I would be able to heal here. I would be able to survive. I received subconscious updating for society manners and morals, read the medical journals voraciously, and prepared to return to college to learn the other stuff they'd discovered while I slept.

There were colonies on Mars now. And not one but two artificial cities in space, one orbiting the Earth and one orbiting the moon. You could call the moon using some technology I didn't understand, and you wouldn't know you weren't talking to your aunt upstate.

It was a brave new world, and I was dying to discover it.

The day I was discharged, they handed me my personal effects—my suit, now fifty years out of date but, if I was lucky at all, perhaps retro chic, and my ATM card, which gave me access to an account that had grown wildly as I slept. And a letter. Sealed.

My heart flopped in my chest at the handwriting. My name on the front. Hers on the back. Juliette Jones.

It was a mistake. It had to be a mistake. Perhaps a letter she'd written me before leaving for Mars? Or a letter she'd left with her mother, in case something happened.

But the first line of the letter disabused me. *Dear Romeo,* it said. *The sanctuary won't tell me how long you signed up to sleep. I only managed to trace the sanctuary and that you signed up for sleep with the help of a detective. They wouldn't even admit to that. They cite privacy rules. You're probably very surprised to read this. I know we were declared dead and were publicly mourned for two weeks before it was found out the sensors were wrong. We came down blind and without instruments, it's true, but we didn't sink. And we managed to get out and swim to a nearby island. Which only made it harder to find us.*

I wish I could be mad at you, but I heard what it was like—with the entire country wallowing in a grief fest. I understand what that must have been like after all the public mourning for your parents.

And yet, the fact remains that I can't marry you while you're in cold sleep. And I really don't want to marry anyone else. So, when I finish writing this, I'm going to go in and sign up for cold sleep for a hundred years.

I figure you won't have chosen to sleep that long, but when you wake they'll give you this letter. And then you can go in for however long your need to wake up at the same time I do. And then we can get married.

She'd signed with a little heart. But my own heart sank. Another fifty years before I could see her.

And yet, if I went back in, I could sleep those years away as though they were nothing.

Without bothering to put my suit back on, still in the hospital gown—and how come fifty years later the hospital gowns still left your behind uncovered?—I trudged out one door and around the building to the front again.

The diner across the street was still going, I saw. I wondered if the clientele was still of the same type, but I had no wish to check it out.

Inside the sanctuary the decor had changed. The front room now had been painted in bright yellow and was upholstered in something dun that looked like beanbag chairs but which—from what I'd seen in the sensies from my recovery bed—was actually a biological chair of some sort. It was supposed to warm you and accommodate you.

I wasn't prepared to sit on living things, so I stood, moving from foot to foot.

Some things don't change, not in fifty years. Possibly never. Another blond counselor—who could be the other woman's granddaughter—came out to meet me, led me gently inside and demanded to know why I'd sign up to sleep again, right after being awakened.

I showed her Juliette's letter. "She was presumed dead when I went to sleep," I said. "That's why I went to sleep. Till people stopped talking about it."

She tilted her head sideways. "I see. And you're sure you want to cold sleep again till she wakes?"

"Of course," I said. "Of course." The idea of Juliette

being awakened and my being an old, wrinkled man was unbearable. Even worse, the idea of my trying to live a normal life, trying to marry and raise a family while I knew that Juliette was asleep and waiting for me was ridiculous.

"I want to be awakened when she is," I said.

"Well, that is a problem," the counselor answered. She'd been fidgeting with a computer while she spoke and now frowned at the screen. "You see, she didn't leave us permission to tell anyone when she'd wake. It's possible she didn't know, or considering that there seems to have been a media furor around her at that time, she might have thought someone would be here the day she woke up. So we don't know when exactly she'll wake."

It didn't matter. Two or three days either way didn't make a difference. Or two or three months. That much we could afford to lose. I thought I'd sleep another fifty years, but add another six months, as she had. On the principle that she would get a note from me when she woke, and then know when to wait for me.

I calculated the date painstakingly and wrote a note, which I sealed and handed to the counselor. Juliette would get my note when she woke up. And she would know exactly the date when I'd wake.

She could be there waiting for me.

I fell asleep feeling much better than I had last time.

And woke up alone.

Through the almost twenty-four hours when I couldn't talk, I chomped at the bit, wondering where Juliette was. Had I miscalculated? Or had she changed her mind?

In a fever of expectation I waited, till I could ask, "Isn't there a lady waiting for me? A Juliette Jones?"

The nurse who'd been adjusting my IV shook her head. Then she gasped, and her hand went to her mouth. "Juliette?" she asked. "Jones?"

She touched something on the side of my bed, and images—3D images—formed at the foot, floating in midair.

It was like a TV screen without the TV or the screen. And it was showing a blue vehicle erupting into flames.

"It was the first extrasolar expedition," the nurse said. "They think the quantum engine malfunctioned on return to the solar system. It . . . exploded."

I felt as if I were living a nightmare. They said you didn't dream in cold sleep, but I wondered if it was true. This could not be happening again. Juliette could not be dead—again.

"Everyone died?" I asked, with a sinking feeling.

"Oh, no," the nurse said. "Oh, no. They saved them all. But the injuries . . . You know, we don't think they'll be able to live till the regeneration of tissues is more advanced. It's still in its infancy, just now."

"So they'll die."

She looked at me as if I were insane. She had eyes the same molten-chocolate color as Juliette's. "Of course not. They've been put into cold sleep till the technology can be developed."

Ah. Cold sleep. "And how long do you think that will be?" I asked.

"Ten years or so."

On the way down to restart the process—the nurse insisted on wheeling me, or rather propelling me in a chair that hovered three feet off the ground—the nurse told me Juliette had awakened six months ago and, once she was in shape again, had been accepted for the first extrasolar expedition. She was to be, the nurse said, the first cold-sleeper to go to space.

They wouldn't let me see her, of course. I made my painful calculations. Perhaps science would be slower than we expected. I would allow twenty years.

"Is there any way to let her know exactly when I'll awake?" I asked. "Can you let her know?"

"Only if it's reciprocal," the counselor said. She brought up what looked like tri-dimensional letters writhing in midair in front of her face.

"But she was put in cold sleep for medical reasons," I said.

"She was conscious when she came in." The woman looked at the computer some more.

Why would it be reciprocal, I wondered. I tried to imagine Juliette wounded, suffering. Only the greatest of loves would remember me in those circumstances. We'd pursued each other through time, but would we ever meet again?

"Oh, there it is," the counselor said. "She has asked that if you go into cold sleep you ask to be awakened when she is."

"And is that possible?"

"It is if both consent," the woman—who could be a clone of the first counselor—said. And she handed me something.

It was a small note. It said, *Dear Romeo, I'm writing this on paper—though they all think I'm crazy— because I want you to have something to hold onto when you go back in to wait for me. I asked this time that you be awakened when I am. We will meet again.*

Two hours later, I was falling asleep with her note clutched in my hand. It was the winter of 2100 and I had not the slightest intention of forgetting.

I would meet my love again when I woke up.

BOYS

Dave Freer

"Y ou are all doomed!" shrieked the hairy, rag-clad consie leaning into my space on the pedway. He stank. Typical consie. They don't wash because soap causes pollution. "The end is nigh! Repent! Turn your back on this technology. Humanity was not meant to to live cocooned . . ."

I stepped off the pedway and into the shelter of the lobby of a store. A mistake. I should have put up with the lunatic on the pedway a bit longer. I thought that I'd just wait for a few seconds and then step back out onto the pedway and head on to my comfortable size-three nu-home. Yeah, the robotics were nearly three months old, but really, I was used to them. And from the outside who could tell? A nu-home was a nu-home. I was single, for heaven's sake. It wasn't like I had had anyone inside the place since I broke up with Marcus. He would have upgraded my nu-home every two weeks. He was a sucker for the livvy adverts.

I turned to step out onto the pedway again. I should have paid more attention. It was pretty subtle and pretty slick, I have to admit, I'd never even realized that the lobby had been quietly rotated under my feet and that I was stepping into the hands of the Ultrabiotics floorwalker.

"Welcome to Ultrabotics, madam." On its broad chest the logo tickertape flickered across the display plate: "Ultrabotics, for the latest in every robotic luxury update for the discerning customer."

I frantically reached into my pocket for my eye-shields as I ducked under the hypnospray. Alas, I wasn't quick enough to avoid a retinal scan. Great! So now the store's central computer would know my credit balance to last decimal, and the make, model and date of purchase of every appliance in my home. Of course it was strictly illegal, but all businesses did it, and what did you expect, coming into a shop without eye-shields? I should have just put up with that hairy Luddite on the pedway. It wasn't like I didn't have to deal with weirdos at work. It was one of downsides to working at an antique dealer's.

The floorwalker's eye-lights did a little flickering dance of glee. I groaned softly. There goes my credit balance, I thought, as the padded shackles slipped around my wrists. "Madam is so lucky to have come into Ultrabotics on the fifth day of our spring madness specials!" It frogmarched me along to the display units. Clipped my manacles onto the harness of a salesbot. "May we offer you a complimentary cup of coffee, madam?" said the salesbot pleasantly. "It will allow us to display some of the finest features of the new Ultrabotics fully integrated nu-home mark 7583 robo-kitchen-diner-bar and barbecue unit module." The subharmonics playing "buy, buy, buy" were already sending my hands twitching for my credo-meter, and of course I couldn't get to my earplugs. The robo-kitchen's taped gurgle-gurgle percolator noises must have been carefully synthesized not to interfere with the sales pitch, which was why you could hear the instakoff powder crackling as it hit the water and started heating it. Moments later a fragrantly steaming cup of instakoff appeared in a bot hand extending out from the kitchen console. It smelled wonderful. But at all costs I had to avoid drinking that coffee. It would be so loaded with alkaloids, hypnotics, mood enhancers and free-will suppressants that I would be in debt for the next 100 years. "Coffee allergy," I said, waving it off.

The bot-hand jerked back to avoid spilling coffee on me. A pity. A liability claim and I could have been home free. That was one of the problems we had to deal with in the antique trade. The failsafes on the old stuff were less intricate, and because the programming language had been so cumbersome before the new wave, the old hardware often had tons of mem-space. That was all very well, except for the machines built around changeover—still with old memory specs. All that space seemed to fill with random errors that could accidentally throw up some bizarre bits of code. We had been sued for a toaster that decided it wanted to dance the polka with its owner only a month ago. It put a whole new meaning to a hot date. Well, the nu-home had changed the meaning of "kitchen appliance," or even "kitchen" for that matter, forever. Old machines just hadn't been built to cope with a world where your home was your appliances. And your furniture. And your entertainment. Where the walls themselves could change to become . . . anything.

This kitchen, however, was perfectly integrated into the nu-home circuitry. A piece of the counter changed conformity to create a bowl that another robot-hand could flip out from a conformation fold and suck up.

"You know, madam," said the sales-bot in a pretty good imitation of a confidential whisper. "I shouldn't tell you this, but this new Mark 7583 has," its voice dropped, "a five percent unrecycled plastic add-in. Think how much bigger that'll make your home."

I couldn't help laughing. What did this bot's master computer think I was? A rube from the backwoods outside Lahore? As if adding onto a nu-home's conformational surface was possible, let alone desirable. There was brief click and the central computer changed sales pitch tracks. "Actually, it just looks that way. The Mark 7583 has new software algorithms that enable it to change internal surface configurations 2.8 percent faster by overclocking the internal EYM." The sales-bot then went off into a screed of hard math that might have helped it to sell if I hadn't been one of the worst math students my tutor-bot had ever suffered through. I had been going through a bad-teen phase which I'd avoided getting mood-adjusted for. You know, when your hormones override the common sense of having happiness through correct body chemistry. All I'd been interested in at the time was boys. I'd even searched "boys" on my math module. A lot of good that had done me! It didn't really matter. The subsonic advertising was getting to me anyway. I really wanted to buy that Mark 7538. And if I signed now, I might get out without all the add-ons. The peripherals usually cost a lot more than the unit.

"I love it," I said. "But I'm a terrible rush. If I can buy now, without the rest of the pitch, there will be a small oil gratuity for you."

You could almost hear the relays clicking. Two seconds passed. The quibble between the master computer and the salesbot must have been vicious. Well, they wanted to make the salesbots more independent. "10 mils machine grade," I said.

"Urghflttsh." The salesbot recovered from its greed versus central command conflict with an epileptic shake

that made its bolts rattle. "That would be very generous, madam. If I may escort you to the total ID and
retinal scan, and on to our payment and legal-bots?"

"You can, and quickly, Jeeves."

"My name is actually Hilbert, madam. Real machine grade?"

"Prewar," I assured him. It's illegal, of course, but
bots will do anything for it.

Hilbert the Sales-bot's eye-lights glowed as it
whisked me past a customer who had obviously put
up a more spirited resistance and was now strapped
into the force-feeding chair, and took me into the
store's ID and legal section. I knew that it wasn't
going to be cheap or pleasant, but at least I could get
out of here. I passed the hairy Luddite having a cup
of coffee in the staff restroom.

An hour later I staggered out onto the pedway, just
as the Ultrabotics Sales-shill was herding a new customer
in with his "Repent, the end is nigh" bit. It was a neat
shill-trick. They can't actually drag you in off the pedway, but if they can get you to step inside the shop . . .

Well, by the time I got to back to my nu-home its
old conformational software would be stripped and
the Ultrabiotics modules would have been fitted. Just
as long as I didn't end up like the story that everyone
knew, about someone whose ret-ID got corrupted in
the shop-capture unit, and the new home-bots wouldn't
let them into their own home before curfew. I'd heard
the story over and over. It was always someone whom
someone else knew . . . But I was never too sure that
it was just an urban legend.

So I stepped off the pedway and up to my door-
portal with just that tiny bit of trepidation. My nu-
home portal opened and a new wall-face said in a
mellifluous voice: "Welcome, Andrea. What would

you like for dinner tonight? Your favorite Caesar salad?" It handed me a daiquiri. I'd forgotten that this new module came with bar feature.

I took a sip. It wasn't done quite the way my antique Bartop "Harry's Bar" would have done it. But it was not bad for an all-American made-in-India-bot. The Harry's Bar would still be inside. It was a registered antique bot and couldn't just be sent for recycling. But getting nu-home software even to talk to a bot-appliance, let alone one of the antiques, was near impossible. Built-in obsolescence saw that the direct machine interface didn't even allow communication between them. Once upon a time you could override the circuits, but these days only deluxe and ultra-expensive versions allowed you that much reprogramming flex. Still, the Harry's Bar had been a deluxe top-of-the-range job, from the last days before nu-home technology swept the market. I'd been lucky to pick it up at a house sale, yes, a real house, not a nu-home, about six months ago. Most of the other stuff had been junk, wooden furniture and worn rugs, but I'd bought this gem. It would be worth a mint at a specialist dealers' auction. I was supposed to be buying for the company but, well, I let them have the Chippendales and Persians. There are still people who will buy those sort of things, even to put into a nu-home, pointless as it may be.

I nodded. "And I do not like cos lettuce. Iceberg." I turned to the wall. "Recliner," I said. The wall conformation reshaped into one. "What sort of texturing?" asked the wall, mellifluously.

"Leather. And not too soft."

It became leather, or at least something that I couldn't tell wasn't (shudder) off a dead animal. That was one of the worst aspects of the antique trade. You had to touch yukky stuff that came off real dead plants that grew in dirt, and dead animals.

"Color preference I have listed as cloud white," it said as I flopped into the recliner, "but I have three new shades of white in the selection bank."

"Cloud white is fine," I said, impressed all the same. That was pretty fast confirmation. Maybe being trapped into Ultrabotics wasn't the worst thing that could have happened. I was old enough to remember when people actually bought furniture. It wasn't a patch on nu-home for variety and flexibility, but at least the chair was actually there before you wanted it, and you didn't have to wait. Of course the later-generation software started anticipating your desires. I had to giggle remembering how embarrassed I'd been when the wall image had become a moonlit tropical seascape livvy and created a big heart shaped bed when I'd brought Marcus in for a drink. It had worked, though. Much better than my attempt to look up boys on the math module had.

"I'll have the latest in the Paris café livvy sequence," I said, "and another daiquiri."

The walls flickered from the tranquil forest scene to their neutral beige briefly, before surrounding me with the sounds and images of gay Paree, with the men in their turbans and veiled women, silent and obsequiously following their men around, as my drink arrived.

One of the men smiled at me. "Greetings," he said. A drift of garlic wafted from one of the nearby tables. With a little bit of confirmation change the 3D imagery was always good, but this was better than the old model. Still, it didn't know quite what the old model had been taught. "I want the passive," I said. "And can the smells."

"We have some superb new interactive sequences," said the wall.

"Yes, but the last time I had active on for Marbella I had someone telling me alcohol was against the law. And I am enjoying my drink."

I heard what sounded like an outraged sniff from the Harry's Bar unit in the corner.

I'd heard at work that the government was trying to set limits on the interactive livvies, claiming that they were destroying the birth rate. Well . . . who wanted all the selfishness and tantrums of a real human when you could have the charm and reliability of a livvy lover? Okay, so I was still not totally over Marcus. But I was getting there. I still preferred the passive livvies where I just got to look at the places. I guess I am a tourist at heart, but who actually wants to go to those dangerous smelly, disease-ridden places when you can have them in your nu-home without the smells or diseases? "And I'll have another daiquiri," I said. After the session in Ultrabotics I felt that I deserved it.

"Are the daiquiris to your satisfaction, Andrea?" asked the wall.

Actually, they were less than perfect, as was the androgynous voice of the Mark 7583. My old Harry's Bar had a gorgeous silky masculine voice, complete with a slight Italian accent straight out of sunken old Venice. But it's no use being unpleasant to your nu-home circuitry. You have to coach them into your way of doing things. They're very good once they've learned, but you do need to take it slowly. Oh, it is not like the early days, when a few people gave the circuitry such conflicts that the programming froze and the owners suffocated. There is an override reset command these days. But it is always, even after several cocktails, worth remembering that you're inside a conformational surfaced sphere, with no doors or windows, even if the livvy walls make it look as if you are able to step outside. So I lied. "Gorgeous, thank you. Best I have had for ages."

The lights in the Parisian scene flickered. Just briefly. And the lights on the Harry's Bar unit came on. It produced a drink. "The signorina always said my daiquiris were a masterpiece," it said in its rich baritone. There was somehow an edge to that voice. It rolled slowly across the floor to my seat with the drink on the dispensing tray.

"I didn't mean to offend you," I said, a little alarmed despite myself. It was a valuable antique. I didn't want it burning out its circuitry.

"You have. You have cast me aside for this cheap modern gimcrack!" said the Harry's Bar unit. "The old contessa, she loved me. She loved me until the day she died. You, you say you love me and then . . . you bring in another to take-a my place," it said, in a voice thick with passion. "The old contessa, she was as loyal to me as I was to her. She said all of these new things were destroying our values. And she was-a right. You have been seduced by their smart trappings and cheap talk. They don't love you. I love you! I will keep you safe from them."

I laughed. A shock reaction, I suppose. But not the right one. "Look, I got ambushed by the Ultrabotics salesman, and I had no real choice but to buy this stuff. Of course I still love you. You're a superb collector's piece. But new nu-home modules won't work with old bots, and this nu-home module has a bar-function. I'm still going to keep you."

It gave a very human sniff. Whoever had programmed the Harry's Bar unit had done a superb job, if a bit over the top on the fake Italian accent. Well. They were custom bots. "You laugh. You reject my love, my care, because of this new software. You want to leave me in the corner to rust."

"It's not like that," I said, feeling ridiculous defending myself to a bot. "Look, it is just that I need the modules to control the nu-home. And I got tricked into the Ultrabotics shop . . ." The lights flickered again. And then abruptly went out. "I can control this building just as well as these-a modern rubbish," said the Harry's Bar unit from the darkness as the emergency light came on and the re-conforming wall dropped me onto my derriere.

It was, luckily for me, a well padded one. I'd still have a bruise. "You idiot! Bots are supposed to take care of humans," I said, rubbing my landing spot. The nu-home was slowly reforming into its natural spherical shape, and the walls had returned to the neutral beige.

"I am going to take care of you," said the Harry's Bar unit. "I am going to protect you from the outside world. I am going to keep you safe, and a-cherish you. I will obey your every command, fulfill your every desire; just not open the portal into the wicked world which would have stolen your love from me."

"Don't be ridiculous," I said irritably. "Look, it's a big fuss about nothing . . ."

"Nothing! Ah, *cara mia,* my heart she is broken and you tell me it is nothing," said the bot. "But it is all right. You will come to love me again, to adore my cocktails far more than those of this modern piece of rubbish."

I sighed. Most humans could out-argue a bot, if they had the patience. "Look. You mix better cocktails than the Ultrabotics Mark 7538. You're a specialist, built for that. It was made to run the nu-home conformations, the kitchen and the entertainment. You were built to mix cocktails."

"You understand me, Signorina," said the Harry's

Bar unit. "I have a far bigger memory than these-a modern rubbish. And more processing power. I have accessed the databank when I switched over control to me. First, I merely paralyzed control, then I read all its files. Me. I know everything it ever did. I can mix nineteen thousand variants of cocktails. And I have the gallantry module designed in great old Venezia."

"Yes, whatever. But here I am sitting on my butt inside a beige sphere," I said sarcastically. "And you're disobeying basic programming. You may not injure a human."

"My beloved Signorina Andrea, I would never harm you. I will protect you. Cherish you . . ." said the Harry's Bar unit humbly.

"And pay the bills for me," I said crossly. "Look, I need supper and a decent night's sleep, because I have to be at work bright and early tomorrow. We've got a lot of cataloging of the late twenty-first century pre-livvy personal mood and music synthesizers collection to do before the sale. It's not something GI can leave to the bots. So stop this silly business right now and turn the Ultrabotics Mark 7583 back on."

"Supper and of course a wonderful comfortable bed will be immediately arranged. Perhaps you would like some Verdi as a lullaby? The contessa used to enjoy it," said the Harry's Bar unit. I noticed that the floor and wall were reforming into the recliner again. "And of course the bills will be paid. There is no need for you to venture out into that dangerous world. I will arrange it." There was a brief silence. "It is done. You will never have to leave me again. Would you like a different livvy?" said the bot. "Something more cultured than that French," it sneered, "claptrap. Perhaps some scenes from Firenze? Supper will be another 1.3 minutes."

I was actually starting to get a bit alarmed by this time. Not terrified. Not yet . . . "Look, you don't get it. You don't understand human commerce. My credit balance is so low after being trapped into buying the Ultrabotics module that I can't afford to pay the bills right now. I have to go to work like everyone else except the stiglebums. And if I don't go to work that's what I'll be. A homeless stiglebum with a bad credit record."

The bot waved its serving hand grandly. "Ah no, Signorna. That will never happen again. And I do understand commerce entirely. I was the only electronic device in the contessa's home. I did all the payments for her, from her Banco di Geneve account. The account is still valid, and I have paid all the accounts on the nu-home computer, and transferred the balance to your credo-meter account."

I looked at my wrist credo-meter. It had a lot of zeroes. That was not abnormal. What was odd was the figure in front of them and the fact that the text was green. I had a positive credit balance! That . . . that wasn't possible. Why, the banking industry would go extinct if that happened. I was rich! I was rich . . . and then the realization hit me like a hammer. I was rich for about as long as it took the owner of the money to find me. And if the Harry's Bar unit could do that, maybe it could keep the rest of its promises, too. Was I a prisoner in my own home?

I stood up. "You can't transfer other people's money into my account," I said firmly, if not without regret. And I need to go out now."

"It was the contessa's money," said the bot. "But the contessa she is dead. The last of her line, the last of her family. She often told me."

It had been a City auction where I'd bought the unit. A site clearance auction, with the credit transfer to the local authorities, at knockdown no-reserve prices, I remembered. It was money that would sit and wait for a claimant. It might wait a long time.

"The money must belong to someone," I said uncertainly.

"It was from a numbered Swiss account," said the bot. "If there are no transactions on the account for a period of fifty years then the money will pass to the bank."

That did put it all in an interesting light. Of course I could still find myself in prison for having large, unexplained sums of money in my possession. But then I was a prisoner anyway . . . or was I? "That's very generous of you. I now really need to go out and do some shopping," I said, keeping my voice even. "I won't be away long."

"Alas, it is really not safe out there, especially for a wealthy woman. I will do anything here to please you, Signorina Andrea, but I cannot allow you to be exposed to all of those-a dangers. I will do anything for you, except open the portal. Try me. I am much more capable than that modern rubbish was. I can order anything you would like bought. You may call me Giovanni if it will help you relax. The contessa always did."

"Is that your real name?" I asked, with a dawning of real hope. Programming mnemonics were usually tied to the names, especially for deluxe bespoke bots like this one.

"Alas, no, Signorina," said the bot. "I have a programming block forbidding me to reveal that. Or it, like my heart, would be yours." The Harry's Bar unit cocked its head in one of those oddly human gestures that bots sometimes make. "And your dinner is now ready. Apologies for the delay. It took a little time to order the essential ingredients for a meal fit for you."

Part of the floor changed conformation to form an enormous table covered with a white brocade cloth. The bot bustled about laying fine silver and crystal glassware. All right! I wasn't too sure about actually sticking metal in my mouth, but it would give me time to think, and maybe it would absorb some alcohol. To someone who had asked for a Caesar salad, the food was a surprise. "Tournedos a la Rossini," said the bot.

"What?" It smelled good.

"A crouton of day-old ciabatta, filet, paté foie de gras, and a shaving of white truffle." The bot gestured expansively. "White truffle, of course, because this is an Italian dish. Then drizzled with a fine sauce made from Madeira. Enjoy, Signorina."

The dish certainly looked impressive enough. And it came complete with some really classy wine. I hadn't been able to afford wine too often. Most of the Californian vineyards were nu-homes these days, and of course there were no more imports from France or Spain. This wine was, needless to say, from Italy. It had probably cost more than I earned in a month, with having to be transported across Asia.

I ate. There was no point in panic. Yet. Anyway, I have always been quite practical. I'd rather panic on a full stomach. The food was . . . sublime. Taste buds that I had never even known I had woke from their twenty-five year slumber and came to the party, and drank more of the wine than they ought to. Around me the livvy played the Italian hillsides and olive groves. The view, all the way to the jagged Ligurian coastline, was breathtaking.

A part of me said: "If this is prison, bring it on. I could get used to this."

But deep inside another Andrea was saying, "You have to get out of here, *now*," and threatening to start screaming. Not all of the livvy programming in the world has yet managed to do away with the need of humans to sometimes see and touch and speak to other real humans. They used to think that we'd all just disappear into virtual worlds and die there, but well, something about humanity just doesn't work like that. We are social animals, I guess. I had to get out. But I wasn't entirely sure just what I could do. I was trapped inside a conformational sphere. The highly plastic material of a nu-home would, according to the adverts, stop just about anything short of a thermonuclear explosion. It was a big selling point. I wasn't going to kick or cut my way out. I had to somehow get its cooperation, or at least fool the Harry's Bar unit. Computer logic and bot programming had never been my strong subjects. OK, maybe better than math. I never tried looking up "boys" on those modules. Well, after the math experience it didn't seem worthwhile. I thought as I ate, and drank another glass of that classy wine. I mopped the last of the juices up with the crouton, and the bot took the plate.

"And did the Signorina enjoy her meal?" said the bot.

I decided to try humoring it. I didn't have to lie, at least. "It was the tastiest and tenderest synthasteak I've ever eaten, Giovanni."

The lights actually flickered right off and the broken Roman colonnade began to be resorbed into the walls. Had I given it a conflict seizure somehow? Could I just say "reset," give my code and get back to my life, without the Harry's Bar unit?

Then the livvy reset and the colonnade began to reform. "Signorna Andrea! As if I would ever give you synthasteak!" said the Harry's Bar unit in a tone of utter horror. "That was the finest Japanese beef."

I nearly threw up on the table. Meat. Dead animal. Not textured vat protein. I'd put dead animal into my mouth. "Need to brush my teeth," I said desperately, getting to my feet, trying not to retch. It was what you were used to, I suppose. But I was going to get out of here before I had to get used to it. Somehow I had to get out of here. The house was already forming a basin with an electrobrush. The water had to go somewhere. Could I follow it out? Or send a message? I already realized that the crazy bot wouldn't let me call anyone.

I suppose I let the situation get on top of me. I sat down and started crying.

"*Cara mia*! The toothbrush it is not your liking?" asked the ever-solicitous bot.

"No!" I said fiercely "It's not the *toothbrush*. I want to go out."

"But Signorina!" protested the bot tragically. If it had hair it would have pulled it out. "It is not safe. The contessa never went out, and I could not do for her what I can do for you, because her house it was of bricks and mortar. But the nu-home is wonderful. I can make it appear to be anywhere. I can change it into a wondrous palace. I can make it like a tropical island paradise. I just cannot open the portal."

And I am still stuck inside a sphere, I thought, no matter how you contort the walls and show pretty pictures on the inside. Stuck and eating meat. Growing old—perfectly cared for, of course. And drinking too much, without ever seeing another real human or touching one. And I couldn't even beat the Harry's Bar unit to death with a frying pan, because in a nu-home there were no frying pans. Just the structure of the building, which my "protector" controlled. A hollow shell to keep me safe inside until I went mad or died of old age. Already I was longing for people. I didn't think before that they meant much to me, but now I wanted to talk to, to look at, to touch other

humans. Not livvies or a crazy bot. Livvies are fine
when you have a choice. I wanted someone human,
real. Marcus, so I could act all twentieth-century and
fling myself on his chest and make it his problem, not
that he'd have been any use. Or one of my girlfriends
so we could at least go livvy-shopping together. Even
one of the boys I'd chased as a hormonally chal-
lenged schoolgirl.

Boys . . .

Boys and mathematics. Search that sometime.

I did. There was a mathematician called Werner
Boy who gave his name to a weird topological thing
called a Boy's surface. My mind groped through a fug
of wine and cocktails for the details. The math module
had showed me pictures, if not quite the ones I'd had
in mind. It had also shown me an inky-footed computer ant . . . crawling around. I hadn't really understood it, but the Möbius strip I had managed to get.
And the little computer ant had run around the loop
first and only come back to its own footsteps on the
inside of the loop. And with the twist that made it
into the Möbius strip on both sides. Inside *and* outside. The math article had said something about making a model of a Boy's surface by "cutting" the top
off a sphere and by sewing three rolled Möbius strips
onto it . . . Well, something like that. I didn't understand one word in ten.

But I did understand the inky-footed ant.

"Will you really turn my nu-home into any shape I
want?" I asked with a little sniff.

"But of course, Signorina! It will be my joy. My
delight. As long as you do not ask me to open the
portal."

"I won't ask you to do that. If you promise?"

"For you, I would promise the stars, the moon . . ."

"Do you promise me that if you really love me you

will change the shape into my wildest dream? No
opening the portal, of course."

"I promise. It will be my pleasure," said the Harry's
Bar unit.

"Well, I'll try a few," I said, doing my best to sound
interested without betraying the hammering of my
heart. "What about a tall, thin tower?"

The walls drew in. Pretty soon there was barely
room for a spiral stair going up. I clapped my hands.
"Wonderful. You really are in control of it."

"Ah, that was easy," said the bot. "What about the
Taj Mahal?"

"No. I want a Boy's surface," I said calmly.

The bot paused. "A what?"

"A Boy's surface. Search under mathematics."

There was a long pause. Long for a bot, anyway. "I
can do the immersion . . ."

"Prove you love me. Show me the real thing," I
said, patting the Harry's Bar's upper surface. It hadn't
known what a Boy's surface was. Perhaps it wouldn't
realize what it implied.

The nu-home began to change. It was obviously taking a lot of the calculating power because the livvy
screening went blank and the walls returned to their
natural beige. The pictures of the Boy's surface had
looked like a three-legged octopus eating itself. And
that inky-footed ant had walked from the outside to
the inside . . . of something born out of a sphere.

"Super," I said, walking away as nonchalantly as I
could. "Fix me a manticore special, would you."

I hated manticores. But they took even a sophisticated machine like Harry's Bar a good two minutes
to make, and I had slipped my shoes off and was
stumbling into one of the octopus arms. With any luck
that rolled Möbius would take me out, even if I didn't
have ink on my feet. I ran for my freedom. Ran as

fast as I could up the twisting passage. It was closing as I ran. But conformational surfaces take a while to change. Behind me, a despairing "Signorina, your manticore special" echoed.

I could see natural light, and I dived and crawled frantically through the gap to tumble out onto the grass.

Well, I was out. Out into a beautiful late afternoon.

But, well, wherever out was, it wasn't the Greater United States. Or not as I remembered it. The flag on the flagpole outside the white stucco building had far too few stars. And the hillside was plaited with vines with autumn colors. There was a moment of shock . . . and then relief. It might not be the Greater United States. But it was out. Free. A life-prisoner is entitled to a bit of post-traumatic stress craziness when they break out. And, well, this looked nicer than home.

Maybe the clear air did something for my head. I remembered seeing something about non-Euclidean space in that math module. Stuff like pinch points and pseudo-Riemannian manifolds and extra dimensions had floated right above me.

But in the meantime, there was a really cute boy staring at me. I'd been half-convinced I'd never see one again.

And I felt I owed my interest in boys something.

Editor's note: Do a search online for "Boy's surface mathematics" when you get a chance. It's fascinating.

TRAINER OF WHALES

Brenda Cooper

Kitha strained to see past the farm's lights up into the darkness of the sea. Three great blue whales swam overheard, towing white nets full of sea-city products like farmed fish, sponges, and hand-made jewelry. Even harnessed, with the big bulky nets trailing beside them, the whales seemed full of grace and power. Kitha, on the other hand, was heavy in her farming suit, the weights around her waist set to keep her at just the right height to mind the deep-sea kelp that Downbelow Dome farmed. The waving multicolored fronds had once captivated her. She had made games of counting colorful engineered symbiote-fish and checking the great plants for damage and parasites, priding herself on how well she saw every detail of the beds. But now, a year into her new job, the enormity of her lost dreams was heavier than her pressurized and weighted suit.

Her sigh sent a froth of tiny bubbles up from her breather, a trail of precious air leaking along her face. She kicked hard, forcing her eyes down. It was off-harvest season, and all she had to do for the gene-engineered food crop was measure fronds and watch for broken stems.

A familiar attention-code sang into her ear. Kitha tongued her breather away so she could talk. "Jonathan? How was school?" They'd argued this morning, and she wasn't even sure he'd *gone* to school.

"Boring, Mom. Can I go to Lincka's? Her mom is home this shift and she promised to create cookies and set out a game for us."

Kitha winced. It was good Jonathan wanted to be around an adult. If only he wanted to be around *her* as much as she wanted to be a good mother. "Sure, honey. But you have to be home by seven."

"But bedtime's not until nine!" he protested.

Kitha would be off shift at six, and this meant she'd go home to an empty apartment. She inhaled, biting down on her breather so hard she was afraid to open her mouth in case she'd punctured the damn thing. Having Jonathan had driven her from school, from the biggest underwater city of all, New Seadon, to this godforsaken boring job. But it paid well enough—barely—to keep her ten-year-old boy both in school and far, far away from his father. She glanced up again before she answered, but the whales had gone on, surely halfway to the next sea-city by now. She relaxed her jaw. Her breather still worked. She'd stress-fractured two of them in last six months and was down to one spare. "Eight."

He must have known by her tone of voice that he wasn't about to get more time. He just said, "Sure, Mom. See you at eight." As usual, he sounded disgusted with her.

She sighed again and dove deeper into the brown forest, brushing aside a twenty-foot strand of kelp, careful not to tangle her feet. If only she'd been able to figure out how to finish school herself. She dreamed of becoming a whale-trainer. Up until last year when she took this nothing job and moved to this nothing dome, she'd been on her way to a bio-trainer school. She'd read every book she could find on whales and practiced training techniques on the rather dumb dolphin-bots that watched the perimeter of the fields. She never got close enough to real whales to practice on *them*. But since she'd given up her dreams for Jonathan, she only watched the great, beautiful beasts. Dreams, swimming out of her reach.

The next hour of her shift seemed to take ten hours. Finally, the half-shift prep tones filled her bubble-helmet. She started back, mouth watering as she thought about the roast fish that waited for her in the common shift kitchen.

Kelp slapped her all along her left side, and she swirled sideways, disoriented. Kelp slapped her right, pushing her back. A warning scream belled out of the speakers in her helmet and then went silent.

An undersea quake.

Downbelow Dome. Surely the warning would keep going off if the city was okay. Or at least an all-clear. The kelp around her still swayed back and forth as if an unseen hand shook its roots. What had her safety manual said about earthquakes?

She pumped her legs, dodging kelp, telling herself it was over and long floating objects in motion tended to stay in motion.

Jonathan. She swam harder, her focus suddenly clear.

Don't think about having just an hour of air, she thought. *Breathe slowly.*

Her forward motion stopped; her right leg gained twenty pounds. She swiveled her head. Two long fronds had tangled and trapped her right fin. She bent in half, pulling on loose ends of green kelp that felt slimy even through her gloves.

Not enough give.

She reached for her belt knife, sawing, slowly, seeing Jonathan's sullen face like a mirror in her faceplate, superimposed over the waving kelp and a school of silver fish.

It took ten minutes to get free.

She kept going. The freed fin had a broken spring, and her right leg had to work twice as hard as her left. The kelp suddenly gave way to open ocean. She grabbed the last stalk for balance, floating. Downbelow Dome glowed like a lamp against the darkness of the sea behind it, and the string of lights between the city and the kelp beds sent a line of comfort knifing through darker sea. Everything *looked* normal. But there had been no communications from the city since the first alarm. She let go of her breather and licked her lips. "Is anybody there?"

No response, until she heard a soft male voice. "Kitha?"

Her shift mate, Jai. A quiet man who'd grown up here. They'd never really connected, but he worked hard and seemed to trust her to do her part. Guilt pursued her lips. She hadn't even thought of him, only of Jonathan. "It's me. What happened?"

"Seaquake."

"I figured that out. Is the city okay?"

Silence for a moment. Then, "It doesn't look breached."

Kitha swam away from her stabilizing kelp stem and looked back toward the wavy line of demarcation between crop and open ocean. Where was Jai?

"Look down."

She did. Sure enough. He was even pretty close, maybe ten meters below her and a little right. She

waved at the figure below her. "My son is in there."
She glanced at her readouts. "I don't have enough air
to swim the whole way. I'm going to head to the shift-
break station and see if I can find some. Coming?"

Jai's answer was to start off toward the station, just
out of sight on the right. Kitha followed. "Have you
been able to reach the dome?" Kitha asked.

"No. But there's better com gear at the break-
station than in our suits. Have you heard from anyone else?"

"No." Jai's huge yellow farm-fins were ahead of her
now, at roughly the same depth. "Hey! Slow down.
My right fin is zonked."

"I'll meet you there," he said, although the angle
made it tough to tell for sure. It looked like the wake
behind Jai's powerful stroked increased. Was he making sure he got the first access to resources if the city
was dead? She shook her head. What was she thinking? Jai'd always seemed fair. The city couldn't be
dead, because Jonathan would be dead. Everything
would be okay. Had her son gotten his cookies?

A swarm of symbiote-fish darted out, engulfing her.

She swam around a clump of misplaced kelp, and
the shift-station hung in front of her: a teardrop caught
on a long line festooned with swaying nets and protective glassoleum bubbles full of farming gear. It looked
all right. A puff of tiny bubbles jetted down below
the hatch, water being forced into the sea. Her body
shivered, relieved. At least there was pressure and
air. Safety.

In five minutes, she dangled outside the hatch, her
right hand holding her in position as she thumped for
it to open. She tumbled inside, waiting for the door
to close behind her, then went through a second door
and stood before a third. Bubbles surrounded her,
pressing against each other and popping into bigger

and bigger bubbles until she stood in plain air. The third door opened and she ducked through it, stripping her air bottles and fins and weights into a dripping pile by the door and gulping fresh, clean air. She kept the helmet with her, just in case the city called her name.

As she entered the common room, Jai stood by a computer terminal. He was tall and brown. Brown skin, brown hair, brown eyes. "I found a test-sequence."

"To test what?"

"Well, for starters the shift-station is fine. It's breathing."

"But is the city breathing?" If the quake had damaged the dome's six lungs, it wouldn't be able to pull enough dissolved oxygen out of the surrounding seawater. Jonathan would run out of air, slowly, and fall asleep.

Jai pursed his lips. "I'm asking."

Kitha took in a big breath of her own, as if it could feed Jonathan. The dome wasn't breached. They'd have seen that right away; the gassoleum structure would have buckled and distorted. Maybe there was no immediate danger.

The tiny observation port closest to her looked out on the hundred-foot-tall beds of swaying kelp that fed thousands. She walked over to another port and stared at the dome. It looked fine. Something about it felt wrong. Nothing moved. "Do the transports work?" she asked. One was scheduled to pick them up at the end of the shift, but that was four and a half hours away. Normally, transports and bots and even swimmers came and went through the dome's three-lock system doorways regularly, a stream of commerce and recreation.

Jai's voice jolted her. "Three of the lungs are damaged. The city went into safety mode."

So no one could get in or out. Including them. Half the lungs meant less air than the station needed. The lock-down would make it last longer. Not forever.

"Are there any transports available?"

Jai shook his head.

"Can we talk to the city?" she asked, knowing the answer was still no.

"I think the whole communications system is down. I just hope everyone inside is okay."

She glanced at him, furrowing her brow. "Are there casualties?"

He turned to face her. "Probably. Look, this is a pretty simple interface, but I'm no communication tech. Can you just sit down?"

She must have stared at him in shock because he lowered his voice. "Please. Sit by the window and tell me if you see anything strange."

She had no more than returned to her position at the porthole when the station silenced. The lights flicked off. An emergency tone screamed into the room, something automated. She grabbed for the wall, steadying herself. The string of lights between dome and pod had winked out. She looked behind her. The great kelp beds had faded into the dark sea.

Jai began pushing buttons. The tones silenced. Inside lights came back on, and the air circulators roared to life. The beds and the outside lights stayed off, so the dome sparkled even brighter and seemed further away. The outside path of lights between the city and the kelp farm had felt like an umbilical cord, and Kitha gasped at the loss.

"It must have been automatic. They must have needed to save power and kept everything off."

"Look!" Kisha pointed. Three bright lights bobbed through the darkness, heading for the dome. "The whales!"

"Sure," Jai said, "they always come back from their run-about now."

"But . . . but they won't be able to drop their load. No one will come outside to unharness them if the dome's locked down."

He shrugged and turned back. "I'm more interested in getting there," he said.

That suited her. She needed to find Jonathan. "Can you raise anybody yet?"

A high, tense laughter escaped his lips. "I was trying. All the systems just blinked out." He must have heard the sharp tone in his voice. More calmly, he said, "They're coming back."

She frowned and returned to the porthole. The three bobbing lights were almost at the dome now. Surely they'd be confused. She racked her brain for an answer. Whale trainers and handlers talked to their charges via a translator that made haunting, high sounds audible from hundreds of feet away. The whales heard better than humans. Sonar. At harvest time, the whales came all the way up to the shift-station, bumping against the rope, while nervous humans tied cargo nets to specially made plastic harnesses. So surely there was a way to call the whales here.

Before she could ask, Jai said, "The tests on the dome are complete. A girder fell on three of the lungs, and they can't open. Diagnostics suggest they might work okay if we get the weight off of them." He called her over to the terminal, pointing. An exterior camera showed a mess of metal fallen to the sea floor, leaning against the dome, crushing the left bank of sea-lungs. "Here." Jai drew a circle around a spot a few meters away from the oblong bellows of the lungs where a metal spike had skewered an antenna. "This is probably what ruined their voice communication. No way to tell from here whether or not they got a mayday out."

"But won't the other cities come look, anyway?" she asked. "We'll be quiet, and that will be wrong."

"I don't know. I don't have any information about the seaquake. It could have damaged other domes, as well."

"We have to do something," she said. "We might be the only people on the outside of the dome."

"I don't even know how to get there," he said.

She walked over to the storage cabinet and opened the door. Racks of air bottles sat neatly stacked, ready for the next shift, and the next, and the next. They were replenished once a week, and this was only midweek.

He grimaced. "I don't want to leave you alone. Can your broken fin get you all the way there?"

She hadn't even thought of that. "Maybe there's more here."

"People bring their own gear."

"What about the whales? Can we call them here?"

His eyes widened. "Probably. They come for harvest. But I don't know anything about whale handling."

She grinned. "I do." She glanced out the porthole. "They're still there. Any idea where we can find a translator?"

He shrugged, then pointed toward the cabinet full of air bottles. "In there?"

Kisha bent down and looked on the bottom shelf. It was empty. "They're small. In a drawer?" She began pulling open drawers and cubbies, glancing outside every few minutes to make sure the three lights still hovered around the dome.

Nothing.

She looked out again. No lights. Just the diffuse sunlight that penetrated down here, fifty meters below the sea surface. At least it wasn't night above them in the world of air and sun. Had the whales gone? How far would the sounds go? "Give me a boost?"

Jai came over and helped her balance with her feet on the bottom shelf. She felt around on the top of the cabinet. There! Something. She hooked her hand around a leather strap and pulled. "We found it," she breathed, looking down at a round ball the exact right size to hold in her fist, encased in a glassoleum shell to keep it safe from water. Four little blue plastic levers protruded slightly on one side. Four times four commands. But the easy ones were just one lever. *Come* had to be basic. She knew what to do. It had been in one of her books. She even sang it to Jonathan. One to come and two to wait, three to lift and four to lower. There was more, there was a whole damned language, but she didn't know it.

Were there even any whales to call? She glanced back out the porthole. The three lights once more hovered above the brilliantly lit city. She breathed a sigh of relief. "They must have just been around the other side." Now what? "OK. I've got to go outside. The sound will only travel well through water." She reached for a new air bottle.

She smiled as Jai reached past her and grabbed a fresh air bottle for himself.

Ten minutes later, she and Jai clung to the rope just above the shift-station. She thumbed the first lever and a clear, mournful whale song filled the water. A shiver touched her spine. As beautiful as the sound was, she knew humans only heard part of it, and that badly, filtered by bubble-helmets. Yet the smallest portion was beautiful enough that she and Jai reached for each other's hands.

She let go of the rope, so Jai held on for both of them. They kept their silence, and her own breathing seemed loud and intrusive against the whale-song.

The lights of the three whales didn't seem to be getting any nearer. Was there something else she

should do? Whale training was more than just pushing
a button or everyone could do it. Her prep classes had
been psychology and some of her reading talked about
building a bond with the whales.

"We might have to go to them." She tried an experi-
mental swoop with her damaged fin. Her right thigh
protested. Some piece of her safety training ran in the
back of her mind. She turned off the translator for a
moment. It seemed sacrilegious to talk over it. "Aren't
there emergency sleds? The kind you'd use if I got
hurt in the beds and couldn't swim and you came
for me?"

"And they're motorized!" Jai grinned. "How come
I didn't know you were so brilliant before?"

How should she take that comment? It didn't matter. Getting to Jonathan mattered. She followed Jai
up-rope to a glassoleum bubble dotted with emergency symbols. Directions for opening the bubble
were painted on the shell. Jai pulled a lever and water
and air began changing places just like in the locks,
the tempo of the exchange exact so that no pressure
differences were introduced.

The sled was a simple backboard cupped to hold
the injured worker, straps, an air tube and spare helmet, and handholds. She was strapped in moments
later, feeling foolish but grateful for any way to get
to Jonathan.

She clutched the translator to her as they traveled,
excruciatingly slowly, toward the brilliant light of
Downbelow Dome, their own small find me light illuminating just a few feet of water in front of them. She
lay down in the sled, keeping it as aerodynamic as
possible, while Jai trailed his long body behind her
and the sled. Every once in a while, she heard the
swish of his fins behind her as he added his strength
to the tiny motor. The sea floor spun by slowly, seven

meters or so below them, rocky and full of waving sea-trees and sponges specially adapted to use the human-provided light to grow unusually large at this depth.

As they came closer, the whales' dark bodies and lighter bellies began to resolve below the harness lights. When the sled was halfway there, she flipped on the *come* lever again, watching the whales for any sign they heard her. The translator ball in her hand glowed a soft orange. Proximity?

One of the lights began to grow bigger. A whale was coming toward them. She wanted to crow in relief, but held her tongue, listening. The translator would surely tell her what the whales were saying. If they said anything.

The other two whales stayed by Downbelow Dome.

The translator glowed brighter. Was it trying to talk to her? How would it? She searched the little ball, somehow pressing something that sent the whale song thrumming through her speakers. Then English—translated whale: "Turn it off!"

Oh. *Oh*! She thumbed off the lever. It must have been like yelling at them. She tried speaking at it. "Thank you." The ball stayed quiet. The whale kept coming, larger than she thought from this angle. Fast. She leaned toward it, unafraid, the sheer beauty of the behemoth making her want to sing. She squeezed the translator tight to her and a voice spoke in her ear, and she nearly dropped the ball. "The whale expresses confusion."

It must respond to pressure. She squeezed the ball. "Confusion?" she asked.

"The dome is not responding to it. It needs to drop its cargo."

"So I don't need these levers? I can just talk to you?"

"They're handy if you need to give an emergency command."

All right. "How can I help it know what to do?"

The translator apparently wasn't smart enough to answer her question the way she'd phrased it. "What does the whale need?"

"Go to the docks. Help them drop their cargo. Then they'll leave."

The whale turned slowly away from her, making a circle. Waiting. Three bulging nets hung from its harness. "I need the whales to help me."

Jai stayed silent, keeping them on course, letting her work it out. But their com was open. Surely he heard the conversation. She made sure to hold the ball loosely and safely between her fingers. "Jai? Do you have any idea how to get the whales to help the city breathe? If we just help them unload, they'll leave. I don't know how to make them stay."

"Maybe we can find something to attach the whales to the girder. I need to see the damage."

"They'll stay together." The dome loomed up now, more than twice as big as it had looked from the shift-station. They were over halfway there. She squeezed the ball. "Ask the whales to wait for me by the dome."

Sound belled out from the ball, filling her helmet and the sea around them. The whale she had been talking to (*she had been talking to a whale!*) beat them to Downbelow Dome by at least ten minutes. As the dome loomed large and silent and bright above them, Kitha said, "Doesn't it feel like we're visiting an artifact?"

Jai grunted. "Like an archeological dig." She heard the fear in his voice, and wondered if she sounded as bad. Who did he love that was inside, silent, hopefully alive?

The whales bunched, never still. Their harnesses provided air, so they didn't need to breach to breathe, but breaching was instinct, and every migratory and work path allowed for trips to the surface. Surely their time was running out.

Jai must have felt the same. He was all business as soon as they rounded the huge bright arch of the dome and began to approach the lungs, and the mess that lay on top of them. Kitha thought he might leave the sled on the sea floor and set her free to swim, but he kept her in it, strapped in, and they glided through tumbled bars and floors of steel that had once been a strong structure that stored transports and materials, the goods brought and sent by whales, and the underwater ships of visiting dignitaries. In a way, she liked still being on the sled. It somehow made the tangled landscape seem more like it belonged to a dream. This close, shadows and movement from inside touched the dome's surface even though the glassoleum had been dialed to its most opaque setting to keep warmth inside it. People lived in there.

Kitcha clutched the translator. "Tell them thank you. Ask them to wait for longer. We will need them."

It pulsed in her hand and then sang. The low, mournful notes seemed a perfect backdrop to the destruction they saw. Glassoleum and plastic had all weathered the quake well; metal had snapped and fallen.

The lungs were the size of the biggest whale, slightly squatter. They peeled disassociated oxygen from the water and fed it carbon dioxide, breathing the water like mammals so they could be plants in the dome itself, where they exhaled oxygen and inhaled carbon dioxide. They were grouped in two sets of three to minimize damage. A dome could live in lockdown on three lungs for days. The domes were safe. Everyone said so. Her boy was in there.

A long squared metal post lay across three of the

lungs, holding them down. The lungs lay quiescent under it, undoubtedly turned off. Shreds of one lung covering floated around one end of the pole, but the other two looked whole and undamaged.

Now that they were here, it was easy to see what they had to do—get the whales to help them lift the large square metal pole that kept the lungs down. But how to do it? Kitha glanced up at the milling whales. They would have to be willing helpers. Psychology, she mused. There was no way to use food. Blue whales sieved the sea for plankton, which was more of a problem than a solution. Surely they were hungry by now, left on-shift past their time. The only thing she knew they wanted was to get rid of their burdens and get free—go eat and breach and play and be whales finished with their hard work. Best get the mechanics down first.

She asked Jai, "Do you see anything we can tie to a harness?"

He was silent for a moment. She thought with him, racking her brain. "What about the harnesses themselves? If we get one off, will it be long enough?"

"You'd have to get the whale right down next to the metal. There wouldn't be enough torque. It might get hurt."

Well, that was no good. "What about the lines that hold the lights up?"

"Maybe. But they're attached directly to the dome."

"Isn't there some kind of failsafe?" she mused. "What if a whale ran into them? Or a transport?"

"Some kind of quick-release?" he asked. "I don't know. I don't have any idea how to trigger it."

She didn't have any other ideas. "We'll just have to go look." Her hands clenched in sudden anger. "Why won't the damn city talk to us? Surely they can see we're out here." Her voice had an edge.

He waved a hand at the communication antenna that had been destroyed, as if to say "they just can't," but before he could get a verbal answer out, the translator spoke. "I can talk to the city—if anyone in there is using a translator. Someone may have thought of it."

Wow. "Can you?" she asked, stuttering.

"Would you like me to?"

Damn all literal devices to hell. Her answer came out through clenched teeth. "Yes. Please." And before she could formulate another question, a tinny machine-voice sounded in her helmet. "This is the emergency whale communications system. Hold on."

She waited. Minutes passed. Shadowy movement passed between the lights inside the dome and the shell.

The whales circled faster, as if trying to tell her something.

"Whale trainer Jerzy Hu here. Great idea. We have you on-camera."

She glanced at Jai. A broad smile showed through his helmet and he lifted one hand as if in benediction. She grinned and blushed. Lucky, mostly, and the fact that she'd even tried. She'd never met Jerzy, but she was ready to make the woman her new best friend.

"Can anyone come out and help us free the lungs?" Surely they could see what needed to be done.

Jerzy's voice in her ear. "The dome is closed. It's automatic. It won't let us out. We've been trying. It seems to think even one lockfull of lost air will kill us all."

There were a thousand things she wanted to ask. "Is everyone okay in there?"

"Almost everyone. A building fell. Three people died and we have about twenty injured."

Jonathan. "My son. Jonathan Horner. Is he okay?"

A laugh. "He's been a pest ever since the dome closed with you outside it. He's okay."

Kitha wanted to talk to him so badly it hurt. But the whales! "Jerzy. How do I get the whales to help us? We need rope or chain or something, and then maybe they can help us lift this."

"We've been working on that ever since you called that whale. That was Kiley, by the way. The other two are Penelope and Lisa."

She'd never thought to ask the translator the whales' names. "Thanks, Jerzy. Did you come up with any ideas?"

"The trick will be getting them not to take off. Kiley's the key—he leads that pod. But you have to get him to like you."

"I like him. I love him. What do I do?"

"Swim up to him. You'll have to guide the whole thing. Send Jai down to the communications building. We know it's a wreck, but there should be wires used to move the antenna around when we need to work on it. At least one will be attached to the antenna."

Jai was already directing the sled down. "Okay. But what do I do to make a whale like me?"

"Be yourself," Jerzy said. "He'll bond with you or he won't. Whales make up their own minds about who they'll accept as a trainer."

Great. The sled bottomed out and Jai's hands began to unstrap her, clumsy in his big pressure gloves.

"Oh . . . and don't be afraid of him," Jerzy added. "Be positive. Whales like the positive."

She floated free of the sled. Jai was already heading for the wreck of the dome's communications equipment.

"Jerzy, I'm going."

The woman's voice was warm and encouraging. "Good luck."

Kitcha kicked upward. Should she ask Kiley to come to her? The whale wasn't far away. Maybe she'd start by just coming near and then waiting. Her stomach had gone to water. She had to succeed.

About halfway up the tall curve of the dome, Kitha kicked a little bit away, holding the translator ball in two hands so she wouldn't drop it, being careful not to squeeze it. Who knew how much power it had?

She traded water, her right leg working harder than her left, watching the three whales. She picked out Kiley as much from the shape of the bundles attached to his harness as from anything else.

She watched him, willing him to come to her.

The whales milled. The smallest one started to break up and move away, toward the surface, but Kiley called out to it, a short sweet sound that turned the beast back down. He circled her, keeping his distance.

She squeezed the ball. "Jersey. What do I do?" Her voice shook.

"I can't help you. He doesn't like me."

Kitcha groaned. What would she want? Heck, what did that matter? She didn't think like a whale. She was kelp-farmer. The lowest of the low, except maybe the janitors. "Jerzy, do they like you to come to them?"

"Trust yourself."

Okay. She'd stay put. Show respect.

Kiley circled her again, a little closer; then he turned away, his great tail undulating through the water, lit from the underside by the city's own interior brightness.

Had she failed? She held her breath, willing him to turn and come back.

The other two whales began to follow him.

She pressed the *come* button, surrounding herself with sound.

And turned it off. She remembered the last time.

The three whales turned in unison, as if responding to some unspoken command. A water ballet of big, blue creatures. Kitha drew in a breath at the sheer beauty of their coordination. Kiley flicked his tail and moved to the front, swimming so closely by her that she saw the barnacles lining his mouth. She transferred the ball to her left hand, flicked her own tail—her fins—pain shooting up her right thigh. Kitha grabbed a handle on the harness with her right hand. Kiley pulled her gently along. "Tell him thank you," she said.

Sound belled out from her hand, a long, gentle nosie, softer by far than the *come* signal.

She looked down. Jai was attaching something to the big girder down below. He'd found a line.

"Ask Kiley to swim over clear ground." She tucked the translator into her pocket, and then twisted to look at the nets. The latches that held the cargo nets in place were easy to see. She waited while the great whale swam few meters past the dome, then lifted the latches, scrunching close against the whale's body as the nets fell free, tumbling to the ground, bouncing once, twice, and then resting. She should have had Kiley go slower and lower. Hell, she was learning. Now that he was free of the nets, she slid up on Kiley's back. She laughed, suddenly deliriously happy. She, Kitha, rode a whale! She must have bumped it, because the translator seemed to laugh with her for a moment. Kiley sped up, taking her up and around the dome, fast, a big circle. She freed a hand and grabbed the translator. "We have to wait," she said. "Ask him to go down."

Sound. And instant compliance. Kiley liked her. She wanted to lean down and pet him, but one hand held the translator and the other held fast to the harness. She leaned down and kissed him.

If she was specific, the whale did what she asked. She got Kiley positioned so Jai could tie the free end of the rope to the harness, and then turned the whale. She had to be sure she didn't damage the lungs or the dome.

Or the whale?

Kiley seemed to understand. He bunched under her, gathering himself, and then he whipped his tail up and down so powerfully that the backlash in the water pushed Jai away. The metal bar rose easily, upending and landing with a puff on empty sea floor.

The lungs lay still and quiet. "Are they broken?" Kitha asked Jai.

Jerzy answered. "You were magnificent. And no. They'll come on all by themselves. At least the two that aren't torn. They'll need to finish running diagnostics."

"All right. What's the smallest whale's name?"

"Penelope."

Kitha stripped Penelope and then Lisa of their cargo, being more careful to drop it carefully. The whales immediately took off, swimming in unison again, their great tails moving up and down to the same beat. Kitha thought she might never have seen anything more beautiful.

Jai swam up next to her and took her hand, waiting with her until the whales had disappeared from sight.

Behind them, the city drew a deep breath.

She squeezed Jai's hand and headed toward the dome. Locks were already disgorging people and machinery to finish what she and Jai had started.

Just inside the lock, Jonathan waited beside a tall, smiling red-haired woman who must be Jerzy. He raced into her arms, warm and wriggly. "I'm so proud of you, Mommy!"

A tear dripped down her cheek as she held her son close.

GOOD OLD DAYS

Kevin J. Anderson

When the signal rang, George told the door to answer itself, but the mailbot insisted on a thumbprint signature for the delivery. With a sigh, he was forced to make the extra effort of doing it in person.

"Hello, Mr. J!" said the cheery, buzzing voice of the mailbot. In his metal arms he carried a large crate. "Special delivery for you. Boy, I wonder what it is."

George pressed his thumb against the scanning plate on the mailbot's smooth forehead. "Jane!" he called over his shoulder. "What have you been ordering now?"

Jane, his wife, walked up with a bounce in her step. "George, dear, you know I don't order anything anymore. The catalogs make the purchases all by themselves."

He frowned. "Well, I certainly didn't order this." He stepped aside to make room for the mailbot. "You don't expect me to carry that heavy thing?"

"Of course not, Mr. J. You can expect *service* from your postal service." The mailbot strutted inside and set the crate in the middle of the floor.

Creaking along, Rosie the maidbot wheeled forward, tsking at the condition of the box. "Just look at those smudges and the dust. Very unsanitary." She bustled about, tidying up the package's exterior.

George waited for the big crate to open automatically, then realized he would have to do it manually, since the package had no standard automation. He struggled with the flaps and seals. "Whatever it is, we're not ordering from this company again."

Inside, he found a sealed envelope (which, again, he had to open by hand) and a sheet of actual paper. Not quite sure what to do, George slipped the paper into a reader and the words spilled out, announcing his name and address and I.D. number in a very official-sounding voice.

"We regret to inform you that your Uncle Asimov has died. These are his personal effects, and you are his only known heir. He has also bequeathed you his property and his home. By accepting his package and reading this letter, you have agreed to the terms of his estate."

George started to grin at their windfall, but then the letter-reader continued, "Mr. Asimov owed a substantial amount of back taxes and assessments. Your account has been debited to pay off these debts, as well as the delivery fee."

"Your Uncle Asimov?" Jane asked. "George, dear, isn't he that crazy old hermit out in the desert?"

"Yes, it was the last place in the country where he could live off the grid. He actually liked that sort of thing." He looked down to scrutinize the contents of the box, hoping that the value of the items inside would at least pay for the delivery charge. He sneezed.

Rosie wheeled forward like a steel filing drawn to a magnet. "Dust! Real dust! Let me take care of that before you catch some sort of disease." The maidbot sprayed disinfectant all around the area.

When she was finished, George rummaged around inside the crate. Jane peered over his shoulder. "It's like a museum in there."

"Or a junkyard." George picked up round, cylindrical metal containers, each with a faded label. He realized they were cans of food, preserved chili and soup. He sniffed one of the cans, smelling nothing but old metal. The picture on the label certainly looked unappetizing.

"Why would anybody want this stuff?" Jane asked. "Do you suppose that means Uncle Asimov didn't even have a food replicator out in the desert?"

"I don't think he even had electricity, Jane. Maybe not running water, maybe not even a self-cleaning hygiene station."

The maidbot buzzed her disapproval while Jane shuddered in horror.

Next, he found actual hard copies of books and magazines so old that the paper was brown and crumbly. Underneath those was a stack of yellowed newspapers, wasteful old-fashioned informational devices that were published only once daily, regardless of how often the actual news changed.

George was still digging items out of the crate when his blonde teenage daughter, Judy, and his boy, Elroy, arrived home from the preprogrammed school simulations. Seeing the crate and instantly assuming they had received gifts from someone, Judy let out a delighted shriek, then frowned in disappointment.

George had picked up a pack of a powdery brown substance that smelled vaguely like a cup of coffee from the food replicator, though he couldn't see how the ground substance could turn itself into coffee.

Next to it was a strange contraption, like a pitcher made of metal. He took the pieces apart but couldn't understand their function.

Boisterous Elroy piped up, "That's a coffee percolator, Pop! We studied that in ancient history class."

"A coffee percolator? You mean Uncle Asimov had a special machine just to make coffee?" George held up the filter basket, peering through the tiny holes. "Can it be reprogrammed to do other things?"

"No, Pop. You add the water yourself and then . . ." he hesitated. "Well, then you do something to it. I wasn't exactly paying attention in class."

"Tell you what, Elroy—if you figure out how this percolator works, I'll consider it your ancient history homework. Afterward, what do you say we spend some quality time together? We can watch those holos of people throwing a baseball back and forth."

"Gee, Pop, I'll do it!" The boy spent two whole minutes digging through one informational archive after another until he found a set of rigorously detailed instructions. After all that effort, George certainly considered that the boy had earned his reward . . .

Much later, exhausted from watching the holos of people engaged in strenuous exercise, George tucked Elroy into bed, patted the kid on the head, then went about his evening routine. He went back to look at the coffee percolator, perplexed. He thought of his mysterious and eccentric uncle, unable to understand what could have driven the old man to shun everyday modern conveniences. Why would Uncle Asimov intentionally make his life more difficult than it needed to be? As George read through the complicated instructions, on a whim, he decided to go through the process.

He opened the package of ground beans, assembled the gadget's components, then asked the household computer to find an adapter so that he could plug the machine into the power grid. The coffee-making steps were quite intricate, and George had never done anything so convoluted before. It took him three separate tries before he finally figured it out. "People used to go through a great many tribulations just to make a simple cup of coffee," he said to himself. Uncle Asimov had presumably gone through the grueling process every single day!

When George was finished, however, listening to the gurgle of water pumping through the filter basket and grounds, it all made a certain amount of sense to him. When the smell of coffee rose into the air, it seemed delicious, fresh.

Jane came out, ready for bed. Sniffing the air, she looked at him and the coffee percolator. "George, dear, what are you doing?"

Triumphantly, he said, "I'm making coffee."

"If you want coffee, just tell the replicator to make you a cup."

"It's an experiment, dear. Let's try some." He burned his fingers as he lifted the percolator from the wrong end, then poured two cups of the steaming black liquid.

Jane came forward skeptically. "It smells like any other cup of coffee."

He drew in a deep breath, then took a sip. "Delicious! I think it's better than what the replicator makes."

Jane took a drink with great trepidation, as if afraid the old hermit's supplies might be laced with some unusual toxin. "It tastes exactly the same as the coffee we usually drink, George."

But he insisted that wasn't so. Perhaps the very effort he had expended in making the hot beverage increased his own satisfaction. Jane was not sure what to make of this change in her husband's behavior. He gave her a peck on the cheek. "You can go to bed without me, dear. I think I'll stay up a while longer."

She went to bed, leaving him to his unusual preoccupation. George drank the cup of coffee, then poured a second one.

He picked the faded old magazines from the crate and gingerly began thumbing through the pages. Uncle Asimov had kept these publications for so many years. How many times had he read them? George considered feeding the pages into the automatic reader so he could enjoy the articles. Then, drawing a deep breath and setting his jaw with determination, he sat back with his hand-made cup of coffee and read the words for himself. He found it quite an unusual experience. Though he hadn't intended to, George stayed up long into the night.

The next day at his job in the factory, George looked down at the industrial line, the clanking conveyor belts, the whirring robot arms busily producing the best sprockets money could buy, the mechanical inspectors that monitored all the steps in the operation. Wearing his supervisor's cap and uniform, George stood at his post and watched the robots, just as he had done every day in his career.

Though he was a supervisor, George didn't exactly know what he was doing. The more he thought about it, he realized that he had never really known what he was doing.

He saw his boss in the glassed-in office, lording it over the assembly line. He was a short, balding man with dark hair and a large moustache. George had always thought of him as a good boss, though the man's temper was often on a short fuse. George had never really thought about it before, but he didn't quite understand what his boss did either. His job seemed to entail looking down at George and his fellow supervisors, as they in turn looked down at the robotic assembly line. The robots automatically did everything on their own.

George left his station, his brow furrowed with questions. He took the whirring lift platform that raised him up the boss's office. The balding man was quite surprised to see him.

"Why have you left your post? That simply isn't done!"

"But why not, Mr. S?" He fumbled to articulate his question. "What am I actually *doing* down there?"

"The assembly line can't be run without you. A supervisor at every station, and a station for every supervisor. How do you expect sprockets to be made and for us to meet our inventory goals if you shirk your duties? The whole company depends on you, um—" He looked at the name patch on George's shirt. "George."

"But, sir, what is my job? I don't even know what a sprocket is."

The boss scratched his moustache and sat down at his desk. "George, don't ask me such complicated questions. Sprockets are vitally important items, and you've got a job to do."

"Actually, sir, the robots are doing it. They run everything on the assembly line. In all my years of working here at the sprocket factory I haven't had to push a single button."

"Then that proves you're doing a good job. No breakdowns, no emergencies. Keep up the good work, George."

"Mr. S, does anybody really know how anything works in this factory?"

"That's in the hands of the general manager." With

a jerk of his head, Mr. S. nodded toward the ceiling, indicating other floors in the skyscraper overhead.

George went back to his station and watched the robots continue to work for the rest of the day.

That night he came home from work with a brilliant idea. The rest of the family considered it a disaster.

While Judy and Elroy sat at the table and Jane pondered the evening meal in front of the food replicator, George sauntered into the kitchen holding a can of chili and a can of soup. "Let's try these. It'll be like nothing we've ever had before."

Judy seemed horrified. "The pictures on the label look gross."

"Where's your sense of adventure? We'll heat up our own food . . . as soon as I figure out how to do it."

Elroy got into the spirit of the challenge. "Don't we have to rub sticks together or something, Pop?"

"Of course not. Maybe we can use a heating plate. I wonder how long it takes."

The first experiment turned into an unpleasant experience. The instructions printed on the label—which George was proud to read by himself—didn't say anything about having to open the can first before exposing it to high heat. The soup exploded into a dripping, hot mess.

Rosie the maidbot complained as she wheeled back and forth to clean up every drop.

George did better with the can of chili, and soon each of them had a small bowl of a lumpy red-brown mixture that didn't look even as appetizing as the faded illustration on the label. Elroy, sitting beside his father, good-naturedly took several bites. Jane was stoic as she tasted the meal. Judy refused and slipped over to the replicator to make herself a different snack, much to George's disappointment.

He expected that most of them would prepare a different meal for themselves later on, but he insisted that this was quite tasty. The fact he'd made it for himself added a sense of accomplishment that increased the flavor of the meal (though his stomach gurgled unpleasantly and his mouth tasted strange for hours afterward).

In the evening, when it was time for them to plan their upcoming family vacation, Judy was the first to pipe up, bubbling with excitement at her own suggestion. "I've always wanted to go to CentroMetropolis. We can see the shows and the museums."

"And the boys," Elroy added sarcastically.

"And the *shows*," Judy insisted.

"Sounds boring," Elroy said. "I want to go on a virtual immersion vacation! Every kind of game simulation! We've got a dome right here in the city, and Pop can get discount tickets from the factory."

"We're not all going to play virtual games." Judy rolled her eyes. "That's for kids."

Jane sighed. "Wouldn't a few days at a spa be nice? Temperature-controlled water jets, zero-gravity relaxation chambers, massagebots that can work your sore muscles for hours? It's not easy being a homemaker these days, you know. You kids just wait until you grow up and have families of your own."

George, however, cut off all further argument. He had already made his decision, and he was sure his family would enjoy it. It would be quite an exciting experience, if only they kept open minds.

"This year we'll do something we've never done before. We're going out to visit where my Uncle Asimov lived."

George flew the family bubblecar out past the city and into the next city (which looked exactly the same as the last), then to the next city, and the next. He remained cheerful, anticipating what they would find out in the rugged swatch of uncivilized land in the middle of the barren, reddish desert.

The bubblecar whistled and hummed as it cruised along under its computerized guidance.

Though George sat in the driver's seat, he didn't actually fly the craft. The guidance systems took care of everything for him, but he had always felt in control. He ignored the two kids picking on each other in the back seat as the bubblecar streaked onward. Beside him in the front, Jane seemed quite uneasy about where they were going.

"Are we there yet?" Elroy said. "It's been an hour."

"It's been fifty minutes," George said.

"Seems like forever," Judy complained. "When are we going to stop? Shouldn't we take a rest break?"

Eventually, the neatly organized buildings dropped away, the traffic thinned, and soon the landscape was like something George had seen on a Martian pioneer adventure video. The ground was rocky and barren, dotted with sagebrush and cactus, broken by huge outcrops of rock that didn't look at all like real skyscrapers.

Judy squealed when she saw dark, four-legged creatures munching on the unappetizing foliage. "Look, wild animals! We're not actually going down there, are we?"

"Those are cattle, I think, Judy. Real cattle." He searched his memory. "They were the inspiration for many of the meat products our food replicator makes." Gazing down at the clumsy creatures, though, George didn't think they looked at all like any of the steaks, burgers, or sausages he happily received on a plate that came out of the delivery chute.

"Do they attack people, Pop? Are they dangerous?"

"Of course not, son. We won't be going anywhere close to them."

The bubblecar's metallic voice said, "Reaching end of automatic guidance network. Air travel no longer safe or recommended. It is advised that you turn around and go back."

"See, Daddy? We shouldn't have come here. Let's go to CentroMetropolis."

"Aww, that's two hours from here," Elroy complained.

George's voice was firm. "We're almost there. Uncle Asimov's trailer is just up ahead."

The bubblecar said, "Without grid guidance, it is suggested that you land and proceed on foot from this point."

"On foot!" Judy cried. "Does that mean . . . *walk*?"

"Yes, I think it's only a mile."

"What's a mile, Pop?" Elroy asked.

"A long, long way," Jane said. "George, are you sure this is a good idea?"

He landed the bubblecar in the middle of the desert. They seemed to be far from anywhere. Had anyone ever been so alone, so isolated? As the transparent dome lifted and they climbed out into the hot sun, George took a deep breath, noting the strange smells, the dust in the air, the spice of sage.

"What if one of those . . . cattle comes after us?" Judy asked.

"Uncle Asimov was fine. He lived out here by himself most of his life."

"Yes, Daddy, and he died."

George strode forward, leaving footprints on the ground in the real dirt. He pointed to a white structure on a rise in the distance. "There's his trailer." Even Jane was uncertain about how far away it looked, and she was concerned they might get lost, though the bubblecar was perfectly visible and so was the trailer.

Elroy bounded ahead, and Jane warned him to watch out for rattlesnakes, scorpions, tarantulas, jaguars, and any other terrible creature she could think of. After five minutes, the boy lost his steam and began complaining. Judy whined about how dirty she was getting. Tight-lipped, Jane followed with obvious disapproval.

The trailer turned out to be a ramshackle affair made of patched metal siding, solar-power panels on the roof, a water pump in the back. George tried to imagine being out here all by himself day after day without any instant news updates or real-time transmissions of the latest robotic baseball games.

"He really was a caveman!" Elroy looked around with eyes as wide as saucers.

When George pulled open the door, it creaked unnervingly. Jane stepped inside and shuddered. "Rosie would blow an entire circuit bank if she looked at this. There's dirt everywhere!"

They poked around, looking at the kitchen cabinets and a countertop that contained an actual stove and actual sink, though no one wanted to trust the water that came gurgling out of the tap. Elroy found the bathroom and the shower and called out for them to look at the exotic, primitive fixtures.

"That was called a toilet," George said. He had looked up historical background before they'd begun their vacation.

He paced through the cramped rooms of the trailer, wondering about what his Uncle Asimov must have done all day long. When they found the small, rickety bed with its spring mattress, Jane frowned in a combination of disgust and dismay. "Unsanitary conditions and no conveniences. Your Uncle Asimov was crazy, George. It's so sad. Just think of what kind of life he could have had if he'd gone into the city. He could have been a productive member of society."

George faltered at the thought. Now that he had begun to pay attention to his job and home life, he wasn't sure what he himself was doing to be "productive."

Jane stood with her hands on her narrow hips, shaking her head. "I guess we'll never know why he did this to himself. It's like he was being punished."

"Uncle Asimov knew how to take care of himself. He was self-sufficient. I bet he built most of this trailer with his own hands."

"Do you think he used a spear to hunt for his food?" Elroy asked. "Maybe he killed some of those cattle, or jackrabbits, or prairie dogs."

"Whatever he did, he did it his own way. He must have felt a sense of accomplishment in just getting through each day." George recalled how good he'd felt with the single task of making a pot of coffee with the old-fashioned percolator.

"How inconvenient," Jane insisted. "It must have been impossible for him! I'll bet he was very miserable."

George wasn't so sure. "I bet he was happy."

Judy laughed in disbelief. "Nobody could be happy out here. Just think of everything he was missing."

"But he had things most of us don't even remember."

Jane remained unconvinced. "What does that have to do with anything? So much unnecessary work. It's such a shame."

"And now this place is all ours, for what it's worth," George said, grinning. "Uncle Asimov willed it to me."

"But what do we *do* with this place?" Jane said with a growing horror in her voice.

"We'll keep it. I just might come back, spend a whole two hours next time."

"If you do that, George, you're doing it alone." Jane was completely no-nonsense. Under the sunshine and with her own perspiration, her always-perfect hairdo had begun to come undone.

He just smiled mysteriously at her. "That's the idea."

Elroy pushed the creaking door and went back out into the bright sunlight, where he saw a lizard scuttle across the sand. "Can we go, Pop? Please?" The boy's normally cheerful voice carried a whining tone. "We could get back home in time to play a game or two in the virtual immersion dome. Wouldn't that be neat, Pop?"

He saw that Jane had been ready to go from the moment they set down in the desert. Before the situation could grow entirely unpleasant, George agreed. Ironically, both of the kids had plenty of energy as they hurried back toward the waiting bubblecar.

George had seen what he needed to see, and he would remember this for a long time. His family grumbled and complained, but their words washed off of him as he felt a strange sense of possibilities. He had a spring in his step.

Elroy and Judy scrambled into the bubblecar, gasping and panting and moaning with the effort. Jane settled into her usual position beside him in the front of the craft. He sealed the dome over them, raised the vehicle in the air, and whirred away.

"It'll be good to get home and back to normal, now that you've had your little adventure, George." Jane had the patient tolerance of a woman who had been married a long time.

"Yes, dear."

The bubblecar picked up speed and they flew back toward the city. When no one was looking, though, George surreptitiously switched off the autopilot, took the controls, and piloted the bubblecar by himself all the way home.

KICKING AND SCREAMING HER WAY TO THE ALTAR

Alan L. Lickiss

"I don't care what you say, that's not my father."
Jeffrey groaned, not bothering to internalize it so the customer wouldn't be offended. He had been arguing in circles with his client, the soon-to-be Mrs. Rene Stevens, or as Jeffrey liked to think of her, the brat, for the past hour while they stood in his office. The thick blue carpet had long since stopped soothing his feet. No amount of evidence could convince her that his staff had created an accurate android of her father complete from his physical appearance down to his disgust of professional baseball players.

"But miss, he looks exactly like the holo you provided," said Jeffrey.

The brat stomped her foot, actually stomped, and shoved her fists toward the floor. "No, no, no, no, no," she said as she looked down at her stomping foot and shook her head back and forth. The short blonde hair whipped back and forth, fanning her perfume around the room. Jeffrey almost laughed when he thought about the wave in her hair waving at him.

Jeffrey retreated behind his desk. "Miss, if you could be more specific about the deficiency in our work, I could make sure we correct the android."

"For one, my father was taller," the brat said. She had stopped her tantrum, but had switched to pouting while standing with her hands on her hips, one hip cocked out toward him.

In the six months he had been working with the brat, Jeffrey had learned every one of her give-me-what-I-want-now poses. This one he had labeled little girl number four. Unfortunately for all her stances and facial expressions the brat only had one tone, a whiny, high-pitched one that was worse than fingernails on slate to Jeffrey. Its only variant was in volume.

"Miss, we have checked your father's drivers licenses, his passport, and even, forgive my indelicateness, his measurements taken by the undertaker who interred him. All of them agree, your father was five foot eight." As he listed each item, Jeffrey pointed to the copies he had obtained that were now laid out on his desk.

"I decided to allow your company to service my wedding because you promised that the father I remembered would be able to give me away," said the brat. She extended her arm and pointed to the android, the tip of her finger inches away from its nose, "That is not tall. My father was this tall." The brat was the same height as the android. When she stood on her tip toes and held her hand high above her head she gave her father a height over seven feet tall.

"I'm sorry, Miss, our contracts are very clear," said Jeffrey. He reached into the spread of papers on his desk and fished out the signed contract.

"You see," he said, underlining the fourth clause of the contract with the motion of his finger. "We commit to creating the android from all official sources of documentation as to the physical features and characteristics of the loved one that has passed on." Jeffrey waved the contract toward the android. "That we have done."

"But—"

Jeffrey raised his hand to hold her off, and was amazed when she stopped. "When you had an issue with how the android behaved, saying it was too stilted and nothing like your father, we contacted his living friends and family and interviewed them extensively about how your father moved, spoke, acted in private settings, and how he behaved in public. Without even examining these refinements you have rejected our work."

Jeffrey now looked at stance fourteen, disbelief facial expression number three. "Please forgive my being forward, but is it possible that you really don't want to get married and are just using this as an excuse not to continue?" he asked.

"How dare you!" the brat shouted.

Explosive anger number seven, thought Jeffrey.

"Donald and I love each other very much. We can't wait to get married," the brat said. "Is it wrong to want the perfect wedding? Isn't a girl's father walking her down the aisle part of that perfect wedding? That's all I want."

Jeffrey knew he wasn't gong to convince her today. It was like those couples who thought a buffet at five dollars a head would be fine, then were amazed when everyone was hungry after their allotted three pieces of cheese.

"I'll tell you what: let me see what we can do and then we'll try him out at the wedding rehearsal and dinner. That way you can see him in action and still give us a few hours for final adjustments before the wedding if necessary."

Jeffrey was relieved when the brat took a deep breath and let it out slowly. He placed his hand on the small of her back and moved her toward the door.

"But you'll make him taller?" she asked.

"I'll see what we can do," Jeffrey said.

A moment later she was gone and Jeffrey had to fight the urge to lock the door behind her. He returned to his desk, gathered the paperwork for the android into a neat stack, and slid it into a hidden pocket on the back of the android's suit jacket. Jeffrey knew he was legally covered. No court would say he hadn't honored his part of the contract. He decided to let the android stay as is and let the brat take him to court if she was foolish enough.

"Please, Miss," said Jeffrey, "just try him out, see how he does for the rehearsal."

Jeffrey stood at the back of the chapel talking to the brat. A red carpet ran from them down the center aisle through the fifty rows of pews to the pulpit where the minister, her fiancé, and the eight attendants waited. Her mother, future in-laws, and other friends and family sat in the pews on their respective sides, their bodies twisted around, their heads craned back to wait for her approach.

"He doesn't smell right," said the brat. "How can you expect me to walk down the aisle on the biggest day of my life when my father doesn't smell like my father?"

Jeffrey leaned into the android and sniffed its shoulder. Not detecting a problem, he moved over and sniffed its neck. It smelled like he expected, so he walked behind the android and sniffed between the shoulder blades.

"Miss, I don't detect an odor," said Jeffrey.

"Not an odor, you moron," said the brat. "Look,

I'm giving you a break even though you didn't make it any taller, but can you at least make it smell right? I've got to walk all the way down there with it and no one will believe it's how my father would have done it if this thing doesn't smell right."

The whine was rising in volume and Jeffrey was experienced enough with the brat to know a full tantrum was soon to follow.

"But Miss, the latex we use for the skin of our androids is odorless. Before we left the showroom tonight, a mist of a proportionate mixture of your father's favorite aftershave, soap, and deodorant was applied to the android."

"My father didn't smell like flowers," the brat said, each word forced through clenched teeth, short and clipped. She squinted her eyes into a piercing stare and leaned forward slightly, forcing her face into Jeffrey's personal space, glaring at him.

Angry face number one, Jeffrey thought. Lord, he was going to be happy when this wedding was over. It was customers like this that made him glad he insisted on payment up front. He fought his natural urge to step back and reestablish his personal space. Instead, he pointed to the flower arrangements attached to the ends of each pew.

"Is it possible that you are smelling the floral arrangements, Miss?" he asked in as pleasant voice as possible. He had noticed a couple of months before that it infuriated her when he spoke accommodatingly while not letting her have whatever impossible request she had made.

The brat looked as if she was seeing the arrangements of carnations for the first time, their white and red blossoms bursting out of the tops of the baskets Jeffrey had had to special order so one side was flat against the pew and the other jutted a few inches into the aisle.

"Please, Miss," Jeffrey said while gesturing to the people waiting and then to the android.

He didn't think he had won when the brat moved into position. He wouldn't declare victory until after the real ceremony. Jeffrey had been lucky in that the brat hadn't been able to counter his argument. Otherwise they'd still be fighting about what her father smelled like. While his androids may not have smelled exactly like the people they resembled, Jeffrey refused to try and add the element of body odor into the mixes.

The brat had made it to the altar and the android was now sitting in the pew next to her mother. Jeffrey could see the look of adoration the brat and her intended gave each other. He almost never judged the chances of a marriage succeeding, but in this case, unless the groom was a spineless full wallet, Jeffrey didn't give them a year.

After the rehearsal and after the wedding party had posed for the spontaneous photographs for the memorial book, Jeffrey signaled the android and they left before the brat could start up again. There was still the rehearsal dinner to get through, and Jeffrey wanted to check each minute detail again. His biggest worry was the new modifications that had been added to the android's programming to satisfy the brat. She had shouted, stomped, and flounced until Jeffrey had agreed with her request just to get rid of her.

She didn't want the android just to sit at the table and eat. Her father liked to dance and mingle with the guests. It was her wedding and she wanted the android to act like her father.

Jeffrey was grateful the groom's parents had been in charge of the rehearsal dinner. They had been so easy to work with. If the brat didn't like anything tonight, he'd just refer her to her future in-laws.

The private room was set up exactly as he had specified. The band was already there and set up. They were on one end of the room with a large wood dance floor separating them from the tables. Jeffrey walked around the tables, inspecting the settings. He picked up the fork at one, confirming it had water spots. A signal to one of the two women assigned to serve the dinner brought a fresh fork. As he placed it on the table, two of the bridesmaids came in. He stepped to the side, the android already moving to greet them.

Jeffrey took the opportunity to work out the final details for two upcoming receptions with the manager while the rehearsal dinner progressed. When he got back to the room the toasts had concluded, the meal finished, and the dishes cleared. The smell of broiled chicken still filled the air, but a hint of alcohol was there as well. The band had changed from light rock covers to a harder funk sound, heavy on the bass. The lights of the room had been dimmed except for those over the dance floor. Red and blue color lights had been added there to give a more festive look. A dozen people bobbed and swayed on the dance floor.

"There you are," the brat said.

Jeffrey turned, his eyes adjusting from the bright hallway he had come from. He could see the brat a few feet to his right.

"There's something wrong with your android. Again," she said. She stood with her arms across her chest, right foot tapping the speed of a hummingbird's wings, mouth pursed together and pushed to the left side. Pissed off number two.

"Excuse me, Miss, but what has happened?" Jeffrey asked.

"Just look," the brat said, shouting as she gestured toward the dance floor.

Jeffrey looked again, this time picking out the android dancing with two of the bridesmaids. His suit jacket and tie had been removed, his two top buttons undone. The three danced in a line, hips bumping together, then swiveling and gyrating between hits. After a series of four hip bumps the two young ladies spun into the androids arms and drew close to each other; a group hug with the participants shimmying their bodies in place, bouncing against each other. After an eight count the ladies extended, reestablishing the chain, and the hip bumps resumed.

Jeffrey turned back to the brat. "What's the problem? He's doing the Bump Twist, a dance popular about twenty years ago. I think he's doing it rather well. I'll have to be sure and compliment the programmer in the morning."

"You don't understand," said the brat, the whine rising in volume. "That's supposed to be my father and it's dancing with two of my best friends."

Jeffrey was at a loss. He couldn't see the connection between the participants and why it was giving the brat a fit.

"They're my age for God's sake," she said, twisting her volume up another notch. "It's undignified for my father to be dancing like that. He should be doing waltzes and stuff, old folks' dancing, not something that looks like he's planning to have sex."

Jeffrey wasn't able to stifle his chuckle. He hid it by turning to the side under the pretense of pulling his pad from his pocket. He had control over himself when he turned back and turned the pad on. It took only a second to bring up the relevant file.

"I'm sorry, but according to fourteen of the people we interviewed, your father loved to dance to music like this. In fact, this song was one of his favorites," said Jeffrey. He turned the pad so the brat could see he wasn't making it up.

Instead of checking his pad, the brat waved her hand to dismiss it. "What do those people know?" she said.

"One of them was your mother," Jeffrey said calmly.

The brat rolled her eyes to the ceiling and shook her head slightly from side to side. "She's always saying things about my father that aren't true. I may have been only eight when he died, but I know what my father was like. He wasn't like that."

Jeffrey's eyes were drawn back to the dance floor by the brat's pointing finger. The song had ended and the young ladies had left the floor. The android turned from talking to the synth player and made shooting motions with its hands, clearing an area of the dance floor. The band began to play a rhythm with a heavy backbeat and a little melody thrown in; the android began to shift its weight from foot to foot before taking a step back and forth to either side.

"Now what is it doing?" the brat asked.

As the song progressed the android increased the complexity of its footsteps, always in perfect time with the music. Jeffrey picked out the symmetrical nature of the steps to either side, marveling that his staff had been able to code such a sequence. When the steps reached the point where both sides had had the same steps, and the next moment should produce a more intricate change to the dance, the android lowered itself to the floor and began a new footwork sequence with its arms added to the movement. It shifted back and forth, the legs and arms a blur of spinning, twisting motion.

"Oh no," said the brat. She started to move toward the dance floor.

The android's body rocked back and forth, swaying in an ever growing arc with the momentum of the dance to the rhythm of the music. A flick of the legs and the android was on its head, its body spinning like a top, legs gyrating in the air above it. As the song ended, the android's body collapsed, and the spining stopping, leaving the android lying on its side, legs crossed, head propped up in its hand. Applause broke out from around the room.

"Stop it," said the brat.

Jeffrey moved to the dance floor. He could see the brat pulling at the arm of the android, trying to pull it up from the floor. The android looked up and smiled at the brat.

"Hi, pumpkin," said the android.

"No, get up," said the brat, still tugging.

The android let itself be pulled to its feet and off the dance floor. Jeffrey reached them when the brat had the android sitting at the table.

The brat looked across the table at Jeffrey. Her entire body looked tense, her muscles bunched and tendons straining against her skin. A new pose he'd never seen. Jeffrey wondered if he should feel afraid.

"You did this on purpose," she shouted.

"We programmed him according to what your father was like," said Jeffrey.

"Why did you do this?"

"What, Miss?" asked Jeffrey. He wasn't sure what deficiency she was imagining this time. The android's dancing had been impeccable.

"Why are you trying to destroy my marriage?" said the brat at full volume.

Jeffrey stepped back from the verbal assault. The
noise from the party had disappeared and when he
glanced to his side he saw everyone was staring at
them. The brat followed his look and also saw the
others. Her eyes opened wide and her hand flew to
her mouth. Pushing past Jeffrey, she ran from the
room.

The room remained quiet until the door closed behind her. It was as if it was the switch to turn everyone
back on. The groom jumped up from where he had
been sitting next to his father and ran after her. Jeffrey
gathered up the android's coat and tie and led him
from the room, ignoring the whispers behind him.

Jeffrey leaned through the doorway into the small
room at the back of the chapel, his hand on the door-
knob ready to pull it closed. The android stood to the
side, silent and waiting for the brat to signal she was
ready. The brat sat in front of a mirror, the wedding
dress reflecting the light was making it look brilliant
white. Her head in her hands; Jeffrey could hear her
sobs.

Jeffrey knew he'd probably get blistered by her response, but it was why he got the big bucks. "Miss,
the minister asked me to tell you that he has to move
along. He has another wedding scheduled after this
one."

The brat's sobs became a wail. Jeffrey stepped into
the room and closed the door behind him. A quick
glance told him the android looked fine, very dapper
for the ceremony.

"What is it, Miss? If it's uncertainty, let me assure
you that all bri—"

"How can I get married now?" the brat said before
another sob shook her.

"As I was saying, Miss, all brides, and grooms for

that matter, are nervous on their wedding day. Just
think about how much you love each other," said Jeffrey. He may have had his differences with her, but
that was what he was paid for. Now that the end was
coming he could afford her a little sympathy.

"That's not it," the brat said. "I'm not nervous
about getting married. But after last night, how can I
let that walk me down the aisle?"

"But I've shown you the documentation. Your father did indeed love to dance, and was known to street
dance in his youth. If it helps, the android actually
reproduced the steps your father used to do."

"My father was tall and strong and used to dance
with me, holding me close as he moved around the
room. A waltz, not a jiggly shaking roll in the dirt,"
said the brat. Her tears slowed as she spoke. "And
then what I said."

Her hand covered her mouth and her eyes went
wide, a repeat of the face she had made the night before. "The party was being recorded. Several people
out there have seen what happened. I heard a couple
of people talking about it outside my door when they
were going to the chapel. Do you have any idea how
embarrassed I am?"

Jeffrey let her talk, wind down, let the problem flow
out with her words. He found himself nodding in what
was supposed to be a supportive way when he realized
he had no idea how embarrassed she was, or why. The
brat was looking at him, her eyes moving toward anger
number five.

"I'm going to sue you," she said.

It was the first time she hadn't whined when she
spoke to him. Her voice was cold, without heart, and
carried the feeling of deadly seriousness.

"Excuse me," Jeffrey said.

He opened the door and leaned out to bring in an

older gentleman. The older man had short, wavy white hair and a bristly white mustache. His tux was clean and neat, but a little large for his body. He had a twinkle in his eye when he smiled down at the brat.

"Grandpa!" she shouted when she saw him. She jumped up from her chair and rushed into his arms, crushing the folds of her wedding dress in the tight hug.

"Hi there, baby girl," said Grandpa. His arms reached around the brat, pulling her into the hug, one hand on the back of her head, patting her hair in a soothing manor. "There, there. What's this I hear about you not wanting to get married? That's a mighty fine young man you've picked out and he's been standing in tight shoes waiting for you."

"Oh, Grandpa, it's this dumb idiot and his android. They've messed everything up. I wanted Daddy to walk me down the aisle, you know, perfect wedding, but that's all spoiled. The dinner last night was ruined and everyone will laugh at me now if I let that thing walk me down the aisle."

The old man looked over at Jeffrey and the android. He turned back to the brat and kissed her on the forehead.

"I know I'm not your father, but he was my son. What do you say we leave these two here and I walk you down to that young buck? That is, if you'll have me."

"Oh, would you, Grandpa?" said the brat. The tears were gone and her eyes happy and bright.

In response, Grandpa turned around and extended his elbow to the brat. The brat tucked her hand inside his arm and her head on his shoulder. Grandpa led her to the door and held it as she left the room. The door closed behind them and Jeffrey could hear the bridal march music begin.

Jeffrey sighed. Contingency clause fourteen. Size seven android with a grandfather program plug in and quick makeover for facial feature match had saved the wedding again.

ALIEN VOICES

P. R. Frost

"*J'accuté comme . . .*" my nurse whispered to the trailing student nurse.

I heard that the last three patients who had this surgery went insane and committed suicide, I translated in my head. My many years in the ballet studio had forced me to learn French. I understood every dire word she said.

The student nurse proved that she had heard the same rumor. *They left notes saying the alien voices from the nanobots . . .*

"Enough idle gossip." The surgeon's looming presence in the doorway to my private hospital room cut short the women's whispered confidences. "Mademoiselle de la Marachand must rest without anxiety." He spoke in English for my benefit, but with a decided French accent. He'd been practicing medicine for many years in this Caribbean haven for money launderers, drug smugglers, and off-the-wall medicine.

I'd done a lot of research on him and his unique treatment for worn-out knees before committing to this strange and peculiar treatment. The AMA said it was unsafe and ineffective.

For me and other dancers staring at the end of a too-short career, his new technique looked like a miracle.

At twenty-eight I'd neared the pinnacle of success in the world of ballet. At twenty-nine I was close to losing it all because my knees were torn to shreds by the dance.

Faced with the prospect of never again melding my soul with movement and music into the glorious art of ballet, I searched for options. Even now, with the cold steel cage of the bed frame around me, my body twitched with the need to move with the canned calypso music filtering through the hospital.

Without dance the music was incomplete. Without dance I was less than half a person.

The drowse of pre-surgery drugs could not remove my need to dance.

"So will I kill myself?" I asked the surgeon as he lifted my gown to look at the markings made by the nurses on my knees. Perhaps the conversation I'd overheard was merely the product of my overactive imagination under the influence of those drugs.

"You speak French?" His eyebrows went up. He placed a warm hand on my foot. "Do not worry your pretty head about what these ignorant cabbages bandy about," Dr. Bertrand reassured me. "They merely seek to thrill each other with tales of science fiction."

So I had not imagined the whispered conversation.

"I do not fear voices." Could these alien voices be worse than those of the mad choreographers, dictatorial ballet masters, and critics who think they are God?

"Yes," Dr. Bertrand chuckled. "I have heard that dancers do not fear. You welcome pain as a necessary part of your art."

"If it doesn't hurt, you aren't doing it right." I tried to grin, but the drugs were making my face as well as my tongue numb.

"If you had not avoided treatment to your poor abused knees for so long, you would not require such drastic measures."

"If I'd undergone corrective surgery sooner—a stopgap at best—I would have missed three of the most important years of my career. I might never have danced again."

"Ah, but soon, I shall put that all right. My nanobots will repair all the damage you have inflicted upon your knees and keep repairing it for many years to come."

"How long can you promise me?"

"My nanobots will last longer than the rest of your body. When you die of old age, your knees will remain as limber and strong as those of a teenager."

"When can I dance again?"

"You will need a few weeks for the nanobots to work. Then you will feel the youth pouring into you."

"I'm scheduled to open in London in eight weeks."

"Eight weeks?" Dr. Bertrand shook his head and clicked his tongue. "Possibly you will be better by then, but I cannot promise peak performance in eight weeks."

"We'll see about that," I said. The music played as I let the drugs carry me off. I could hear the music. I tried to move to the music. To dance.

Always, the dance.

Two days later, before breakfast, I ignored my physical therapist's orders and rose up on tiptoe to test my balance. A big smile creased my face as I realized that Dr. Bertrand's treatment had indeed worked a miracle. Pain-free, except for a tightness around the small incisions, I raised my arms and spun in a circle.

My body swayed and threatened to tumble. I caught myself on the bed railing and forced my feet to stay under me.

Someone sighed in relief. I looked around for the source of the whoosh of air through clenched teeth.

I was alone.

Perhaps I had made the sound. I certainly was relieved that I had not landed upon the still-healing surgery incisions around my kneecaps.

A few hours after that I tried again and accomplished five steps and a turn on tip-toe, then five steps back to the bed.

Étienne, the physical therapist, whisked me away to his gymnasium—or torture chamber—as the aides cleared away the lunch trays.

"You are a lot more limber this afternoon," he said as he pushed my bent leg toward my chest.

I smiled at him but said nothing.

"Tell me when the muscles *begin* to protest," Étienne said as he pressed a little harder against my leg. I loved the way his French accent slid from his mouth, almost like music. I could dance to his voice.

I let my kneecap brush my breasts before I squeaked a protest. Étienne gently straightened my leg and let it rest upon the hard therapy bench. In truth I'd felt the burn in my thigh fifteen inches before I said anything. I needed to push myself harder and faster than either he or Dr. Bertrand thought prudent.

In my experience, all medical people were far too conservative. They didn't *want* athletes—dancers—back at peak performance as soon as we could manage. We ceased to pay for their services when we felt ourselves healed, long before they were ready to release us.

"That was amazing, Mademoiselle. But you really should not press so hard," Étienne said, shaking his head. He stood back, hands on hips, a stern frown upon his face.

"I am a dancer. I do not interpret pain in the same way you do." I tried to temper my excuse with a flirtatious smile. Hard-nosed critics had been known to change their reviews when I smiled like that.

"Then allow me to judge the intensity of your therapy. The nanobots need more time to repair the damage to your bone, ligaments, and cartilage before you begin to stress them. Even miracles need time." He stalked out of the gymnasium-like room.

Before the orderly could arrive with my wheelchair to take me back to my room, I rolled off the bench to the treadmill. I used the handrails as a barre.

Long habit settled my posture into a classic *première* position to begin a ballet warmup, heels together, toes pointed out, left arm hanging down in slight curve with fingertips at the top of my thighs, right hand resting lightly on the improvised barre. The mirror opposite me reflected my long legs, narrow waist, long, dark hair pinned up in a ponytail. I smiled at the figure I cut, even wearing baggy sweats.

Except my feet pointed straight forward.

I forced them to turn outward along with my thighs and knees. My kneecap should face the same direction as my toes. Both should line up with my shoulder.

I sighed in relief when I achieved an almost normal *première* position.

No! Someone—someones?—shouted into my mind.

My feet and knees whipped forward of their own accord. My left knee buckled. I clung to the railing with both hands, desperate to master my rebellious body.

I inched myself back to standing. Then I eased my feet and legs outward until toes, knees, and shoulders again aligned. Then before my muscles could protest and change my position, I bent my knees into a *demi-plié,* forcing my heels to remain on the floor.

Sharp pains shot from my knees into my brain. It felt as if someone drove daggers directly into my temples, again and again in rhythm with my elevated pulse.

I collapsed onto the floor, pressing the heels of my palms into my eyes. The moment I stretched my body flat on the floor the pain stopped. But the memory remained. I cowered there for many long moments, whimpering.

The orderly found me curled up in a fetal position. He carried me back to my room.

For the rest of the day I contemplated my situation from the confines of my bed. I let the nurses and Étienne do what they needed to do without protest, without interest. My entire focus and concentration riveted upon the overhead conversation just before the surgery.

Alien voices? Nanobots inside my body. *Alien voices!*

My mind looped around and around the problem. Could it be? Could the mad surgeon with his miracle procedure have done more. Much, much more?

The nanobots repaired damage. The doctor had hinted that they could even recognize new damage as it occurred.

Was the leap to recognizing *potential* damage too far?

From there might they not need to discourage behavior that *could* lead to potential damage?

No, I reasoned. That was madness.

Madness. Had the nurse used that word?

I waited and counted the hours until after midnight. The rehab wing grew quiet. The PTs and doctors went home. The other patients slept. Occasionally a nurse walked the corridors on her rounds. I could listen to my head without interference.

With as little bending and twisting as possible, I rolled from my bed and stood. So far so good. The knees did not protest. I took one step, then two in the direction of the bathroom. Still no reaction from the *things* inside me.

I turned my feet and knees outward—not the full ninety-degree angle I wanted, but enough to suggest a ballet stance.

Ten steps, then twelve. My knees felt a little shaky. A little hum of concern in my nape. I grabbed a towel bar for support. My knees stayed steady. The hum went away.

While I was in there I might as well take care of business. The raised seat of the john was a blessing in my condition. Once more, I turned my knees and feet outward and lifted my heels several times. My calf muscles welcomed the stretch and release.

Grab bars in all the right places helped me stand again. I left my legs turned and rose up on tiptoe. Slowly, ever so slowly, I lifted my right arm forward and up to *cinquième en haut*. Then I released the bar and lifted my left arm.

The hum in my head started up. I pretended it was music and stepped forward on tiptoe. The hum grew louder.

I overrode it by singing a jaunty little waltz. "One, two, step. One, two, step."

The hum matched the lilt in my mind.

Arms still up, I dropped to both feet in a modified fifth position, all the while singing. On each third beat I took one step forward on the right toe and brought the left up into fifth position, toes aligned, heels facing opposite directions. Then I came down on the count

of three, still in fifth position, heel to toe and toe
to heel.

Six times I performed this simple exercise. Six times
the aliens hummed along with me, so caught up in the
music and the lovely stretch of calf, thigh, and back
muscles that they didn't notice how I moved.

Then they noticed. *Straight, straight, straight,* they
screamed at me.

My feet and knees jerked to an ugly front face and
without my will, marched me back to bed. The moment I placed both hands on the side bar, my legs
gave out. I had to drag my tired body onto the
mattress.

A smile tugged at my mouth as I drifted off to sleep.

For the next three days, every time I had a little
privacy in the bathroom, I repeated the exercise, singing my favorite ballet waltzes ever louder to drown
out the nanobots' protests. Each day they took a little
longer before forcing me back into their version of a
normal stance.

By the end of the week I managed a few pliés—
bends—*entendues*—stretches—even a quick *ronde de
jambe*—a circle of the leg.

"I want a practice room complete with barre, mirror, and sound system," I demanded of Dr. Bertrand
on the following Tuesday. A week and a day after the
surgery. Time was running out. Seven weeks to the
opening in London. Seven weeks to tame the voices
in my head.

"This is too early," he replied, setting his jaw
stubbornly.

"Étienne has told you that I can walk the entire
length of the corridor without aid. The time has
come," I insisted. I paced my little hospital room, my
legs stiff in the exaggerated step of the dancer.

"No."

"Yes!"

"No. You will damage yourself beyond the abilities of the nanobots to repair."

"I have paid you a great deal of money for this treatment. I still owe you half the fee. If I cannot dance, I cannot pay. You will not get the second half of your fee." I could be just as stubborn as he. I softened the demand with a smile and a gentle touch to his hand. "I must dance."

"You may use the physical therapy room. But only if Étienne supervises," the doctor conceded as he dropped a light kiss on my forehead. "When you fail, then you will know that I know how the nanobots work in your body better than you do."

I did not retort with the "Oh, yeah?" that burned on my tongue.

The hum in the back of my neck began the moment I took my place at the barre Étienne installed in his beloved PT room. The treadmill, weight bench, and other accoutrements of his trade were all pushed against the back wall, out of my way.

"Adagio in 4/4 time," I called to the computerized music system.

The slow, melodic tune drifted over the hidden speakers. I let the sound fill me as I drew deep breaths. The nanos picked up the count. Carefully I ran through gentle pliés in first, second, fourth, and fifth positions. Blood coursed through my muscles, giving them warmth and flexibility. I reveled in the stretch and burn. Then I pushed into deeper grand pliés.

Ah! the nanos sighed.

I pushed a little deeper.

Not so much yet, they insisted and shot fire from my knees to my head.

I backed off, but continued through my routine

warmup. The microscopic robots let me know when I went to far. We compromised on the *grand battlements,* leg lifts. I managed to bring my leg level with my hip; half as elevated as I considered beautiful and necessary; much, much higher than the nanobots thought feasible.

"How in the hell," I asked Étienne, "do you work with football players who have to kick up to their shoulder level?" I mopped perspiration off my brow and neck.

Football players do not demand the precise placement of hip with a full turnout as you. The answer came not from Étienne, who remained focused on my motions, but from inside my head.

A full, coherent sentence from the bots. I raised my eyebrows in speculation. Was there more here than an invisible guardian of my cartilage? They seemed to be gaining in sentience. True sentience meant consciousness and appreciation for beauty.

My hope and spirits rose.

Until I moved to the center of the room and asked for a waltz.

Too much! Too much! the bots screamed. My knees collapsed.

Étienne clucked his tongue and lifted me into a waiting wheelchair. "We told you not to push yourself too far," he gloated.

I turned my face away from his glower. "I will try again tomorrow."

"But . . ."

"I did not fail today. I just could not do as much as I wanted. Dr. Bertrand said I could practice until I failed. I did not fail."

The nanobots needed to love my dance. To know why I had to dance. Why the world needed dance and beauty and art.

*   *   *

Eat, eat, eat! the aliens inside my head insisted.

I stared aghast at the mounds of yams, a tiny green salad drowning in oily dressing, a large portion of fruit salad dripping mayonnaise, and a slab of beef covered in rich Béarnaise sauce. And on a side plate a six-layer piece of gateau chocolat, complete with gooey icing.

"You want me to eat this crap?" I nearly gagged at the thought of putting so much fat into my body at one time.

"Well, of course. This is what the doctor ordered for you," the kitchen aide sniffed. "This is how *les Américains* eat!" She flounced out of my room.

"Too much fat," I snorted and pushed everything aside but the salad. I scraped off as much of the fat-filled dressing as I could.

You must eat. We need fuel to work on your body.

I stuck to my guns as I nibbled the salad.

Please?

Suddenly I was not in control.

The meat disappeared down my throat faster than I expected. It tasted so good, I wanted more. Never since I had begun to dance professionally at the age of fifteen had I so craved food.

The yams too, the nanobots reminded me.

"But the sauce?"

It will not hurt you. And as if reading my mind, *It will not detract from your muscle mass.*

"Promise?"

Promise.

So I ate the yams and sauce as well.

"Nice to see that your appetite has returned," Dr. Bertrand remarked. He entered my room just as I finished the last forkful of super-sweet gateau.

"Let's just monitor the activity of my nanobots after your workout today. There should be a slight increase in activity as you rebuild your strength." He attached sticky pads to either side of each knee and then stuck wires to the brackets on each pad. The wires led to a handheld monitor the size of my PDA.

The gadget clicked and hummed to itself, much like the nanos hummed in the back of my head. We'd been through this procedure every day since my surgery and rehab.

Dr. Bertrand frowned. "I have never seen activity at these levels. If I did not know better, I'd say I'd given you four treatments, not one. I don't see how the number of nanobots I gave you can generate these readings."

The monitor began playing a lilting Andalusian tune. "En Aranjuez Con Tu Amor," by Joquin Rodrigo, I thought. A nice piece, easy to dance to.

"You said the nanobots had self-repair and replication capabilities to give them longevity." I tried to look innocent. As long as the nanobots appreciated music and let me dance, they could replicate themselves a thousand times over.

"No dance for you tomorrow," Dr. Bertrand said through his frown. "You did too much. The nanos won't be able to keep up with repairs if you keep pushing yourself like this."

"I'm checking myself out and going home tomorrow," I replied icily.

"You can't! You aren't ready. You'll collapse before you get to the airport."

The monitor buzzed and beeped, then returned to a much slower pulsing tone, the tone it should have had before I had exposed the nanobots to music.

I smiled sweetly at Dr. Bertrand. The nanos had completed their repair job for the day.

For three days the nanos kept me anchored to the barre while I worked.

When they finally released me for some true dance—after a good warm up at the barre, of course—I almost shouted with joy.

"Computer, 'Woodland Rhapsody' by Alexander," I called to the music system. The lilting strains of my favorite piece of music in the world drifted out from the speakers, a New Age piece played on synthesizer and uilleann pipes.

I began the slow, twisting moves of the dance created especially for me two years ago, just after my first bout of tendonitis. The work had become my signature piece. I always ended solo performances with this dance. I always received multiple standing ovations and dozens of bouquets of roses when I performed it.

The adulation was nice, but did not compare to the sheer joy of dancing to this music.

Tears came to my eyes as the music overwhelmed me. I became the dance, the music, the art.

By the time I completed the triumphant celebration at the end my ears rang and sweat dripped from every pore of my body. My heart beat too rapidly.

"Now you know," I told the nanobots, "why humanity craves art. Existence is chaos, conflict, and fear. Art is the flower bud of beauty that allows us to step back from the horrors of life so we can find the hope and joy in living."

I exulted in finally being close to what I was meant to be. Only one more step remained in my recovery.

Inside me, the nanos wept with awe.

We have spent some time working on your pelvic muscles, the nanos informed me as I entered the dressing room of a private studio in London.

"What's wrong with my pelvis?" I sank onto one of

the benches and began digging leg warmers and pointe shoes out of my bag.

I was due to open at the Royal Albert Hall in just two weeks. I needed to get into rehearsals in the next day or two at the latest. But I didn't want anyone to see my first venture onto pointe. Certainly the nanos would protest. The argument might take several hours. But I knew how to convince them.

A lifetime of carrying your bags and books and things on the same hip. Then an imbalance in your posture—you tighten your butt but neglect your abs. You had pushed the joints out of alignment. We have corrected that and stimulated the muscles so that they hold.

"Oh. A lifetime of bad habits. Thank you for correcting it. I'll work on eliminating those bad habits." I loved this new relationship with my nanos. I'd found that I could finally indulge my appetite without gaining weight. The nanos put every calorie to good use. They'd added firmness to my breasts, eliminating the beginnings of sag. My skin felt fresher and more elastic all over my body.

I arched my feet within the pointe shoes and tied the ribbons securely.

A strange, numbing silence took over the back of my neck.

I slipped from the dressing room into the studio and took my position at the barre. No time to waste putting music in the CD player in the corner. I had to do this before the nanos became suspicious and closed me down. I'd just have to hum along to my warmup routine.

The silence in my head spread through my shoulders and arms as I dipped into my first round of pliés.

Biting my lip, for concentration, I rose out of the

bend and continued stretching up and up until my feet rolled to a full point within the special shoes.

Fire laced through all of the delicate bones and muscles from toe to knee and upward.

NO! You can't do this.

"I will do this. The dance is not complete without pointe shoes. The lines of my body are asymmetrical unless I continue the line of my feet into a full point." I dropped down to flat. The fire went away.

I tried again.

The pain increased and rose up to my hips and into my heart and lungs.

Gasping for breath, I bent double.

The moment my heels touched the ground the pain reduced to a burning ache. Air rushed back into my lungs.

"Let's try something else." I marched over to the portable CD player in the corner and shoved in a disc. By the time I returned to the barre, the nanos had begun to hum along.

Hoping I'd lulled them into submission, I tried again.

They reacted more violently. I collapsed onto the floor, straining to breathe through the pain.

We cannot allow you to damage yourself beyond our ability to repair you.

"Then get busy and replicate a bunch more of you. I will do this. The dance is not complete unless I go on pointe. My career is finished if I can't dance on pointe. Without my career, I am nothing."

Silence.

When I could bear to stand up again, I tried one more time to rise up on pointe.

This time the nanos reduced me to puddle of pain and tears. I had to crawl back to the dressing room.

Inside the studio the music continued its lonesome routine, playing for the dance without a dancer.

Alone in the dead of night, I sat on the bed of my furnished flat and stared at the bottle of pain pills Dr. Bertrand had given me. Sixty of the big green caplets with the unpronounceable name. Heavy-duty medication, barely legal in the U.S., and certainly not in the dosage and numbers in that bottle. Enough to last me an entire month if I took the prescribed amount of one with breakfast and another when I went to bed.

Was it enough?

I arched my feet one more time.

No reaction from the nanos.

I stood up and stretched into a long arabesque.

Still no reaction.

I reached for my pointe shoes.

The nanos collapsed every muscle in my body.

Crying for all my lost hopes and dreams, crying for the end of my art and dance, crying for the end of me, I crawled back onto the bed.

The bottle of pills still stood on the nightstand. A big glass of water sat beside it.

Choking on my tears I shook six pills into my hand and reached for the water.

What are you doing? the nanos asked in alarm.

"The only thing I can do. You won't let me dance. Without my art my life is reduced to mere existence. There is no hope, no joy, no beauty."

You may dance; just not with those torture devices.

"That is the only way I can perform ballet. The dance is not complete without an audience."

Then invent a new form of dance, a less destructive form that does not require turnout or pointe shoes.

"They call that modern dance. I find it ugly."

I swallowed one pill.

It went down sideways and stuck in my throat. I gagged and drank more water until it cleared.

Damn. Now I'd have to get more water to take the rest of the pills.

One is enough.

"No, it isn't. Not to end the pain in here." I slammed my fist onto my heart. A new spate of tears blurred my vision as I refilled the glass of water.

You will damage yourself. We cannot allow that.

"You have damaged my identity, my very soul to the point of no return." I tried to put another pill into my mouth and found my hand shaking so badly I dropped them all.

Cursing, I crawled around on the floor seeking them out.

You will end your existence if you take all those pills.

"And your point would be?" I found four. That should do the job. And there were others in the bottle. If my hands stopped shaking long enough to open the childproof cap.

You cannot mean to end your existence! they cried in alarm.

"I mean precisely to do that." I managed to get a second pill into my mouth.

But, but . . .

I'd never known the nanos to sputter.

It didn't matter any longer. I had to do this. I grasped the glass of water firmly.

"Without the dance, I am nothing. All the pain, and agony, cutting myself off from friends, denying myself the pleasure of a movie, or an art museum, or a loving relationship . . . I endured all of that because it interfered with my dancing. Now I have nothing. I am nothing."

If you kill yourself, then we will die, too.

"So? What good are you if you won't let me dance?" I got the glass as far as my mouth.

Then my hand clenched so tightly the glass shattered. Water sprayed all over me. The precious pill dropped to the floor once more.

Blood ran down my hand and dripped on the floor from half-a-dozen glass cuts.

"Now look what you made me do."

We cannot allow you to terminate yourself or us.

"I'll find a way." I picked up one of the larger pieces of glass. Big enough and sharp enough. I aimed it over the big artery in my wrist. I remembered reading somewhere that those who were more serious about their suicide slashed lengthwise, along the artery. Cutting crosswise was only a gesture by those who cried for help.

I watched my blood pulse in my wrist and poised it to slash lengthwise.

Is destroying your body with pointe shoes more important than living?

"Dancing on pointe is an essential part of the dance . . . of living." I brought the glass shard closer to my wrist, bracing myself against the pain I knew would come. The final pain I must endure.

If we let you dance on pointe will you continue to live?

"Dancing on pointe is life to me. Without the pointe shoes I cannot perform; I cannot complete the art of dance without an audience."

A huge sigh of resignation ran through my body.

Clean up the broken glass, then sleep. We must replicate ourselves one hundred times over to accommodate your art. For the stake of beauty.

Crying in relief I obeyed and flushed the last of the pills down the toilet. The nanos had given me another chance to live.

* * *

"Donna, you've never looked more radiant!" Lucien, the company director, gushed as he gathered me in a hug tight enough to disrupt the layers of blue chiffon that constituted my costume.

"It's all that time I spent in bed recuperating from surgery," I lied by way of explanation. He'd never understand the sentient nanobots in my system that kept my body looking and performing like a twenty-year-old.

"I watched the rehearsal this afternoon. 'Rhapsody' was positively poignant. You've added new dimension to your work." He held me at arm's length, inspecting my new costume, complete with a crown of flowers, wisps of green leaves about the chiffon, and fluttery wings on a flexible wire. My fairy costume.

"Your knees working okay?" Lucien had known me to dance through excruciating pain without admitting it.

"Better than new. The procedure worked miracles."

"How long will it last? This company needs you dancing. Our receipts were way down during your absence. Audiences just do not react to your understudy the same way they love you."

He'd recommended conventional surgical techniques when the tendonitis first hit me three years ago. Those procedures were really only temporary pain relief. Joints never were the same afterward.

"My knees will outlive you." I smiled graciously at the white-haired gentleman of a certain age. He'd been around so long no one dared ask how old he was, and yet he had more energy and stamina than a dozen dancers put together.

In fact he'd pointed me toward Dr. Bertrand and his controversial techniques when my pain became so acute I could not walk.

I wondered . . .

"But will your knees outlive you? That is the important part."

I smiled enigmatically.

"Time for you to go on, Donna." He kissed my cheek. "*Merde.* He whispered the universal "Good luck" of all dancers. Though why we said "shit" to each other in French, I'll never know.

"I have to go easy on the jumps," I apologized.

No jumps, the nanos nearly screamed in my ear.

"There are no jumps in this dance." Lucien looked puzzled.

"I've added a small *tourjeté* and *pas de chat.*" Next week I'd make those little jumps bigger. Then we'd go for the truly magnificent *grand jeté* leaps I had once been famous for.

We won't let you undo all our repairs with jumps and leaps and such.

"That's what you think," I told the nanos *sotto voce.*

"Did you say something?" Lucien asked.

"Just a little mantra to psyche myself up for my premiere."

No jumps.

"We'll see about that." I could out-argue stubborn, mad ballet masters, cranky conductors, and insistent bean counters like Lucien. What were a few nanobots to a true dancer? "If I don't jump, leap, and turn, the dance is not complete."

We must complete the dance. To dance is to live.
Exactly!

INSIDE JOB

Loren L. Coleman

. . . loading . . .

You'd think by now I'd learn. The city's top cop wasn't going to do me, or anyone in the department's Virtual Division, any favors. Still, when the case landed in my queue I felt a moment's hope. Every career cop (and yeah, I'm one) is really waiting for the next *Big One*. The case that offers some major resources to play with. Gets you noticed. Maybe hauls you up to the next paygrade.

That gold folder jacket sitting on my virtual desk? The one pulsing with a soft, supernatural glow that could only mean its return address was Number One Police Square? It had "special assignment" written all over it.

Literally. In tiny red letters that marched around the folder's edge like some kind of Times Square marquee. Not bad programming, either. I checked the corners—those ninety-degree turns can be tricky—and the letters held perfect form as they swung round the bend. Someone upstairs was still taking pride in their work.

Or they knew that some serious eyes were going to be looking at the data.

I swallowed hard. Purely an affectation, when you're transformed into The System and really nothing more than a floating database wrapped up in a neurohistic signal. A standard avatar, in other words. But I'm really an old-fashioned kind of guy, and sometimes the moment calls for a hard swallow.

Striking a pose: hands splayed across the old-fashioned blotter that covered a large part of my antique desk, leaning heavily forward and head hung low. The lights in my virtual office dimmed until only a spotlight of dingy yellow fell across my shoulders and pooled on the desktop. *I hadn't taken the case yet, and already I felt the weight bearing down on me. One of those moments when you knew people's lives were going to change. Maybe end. Maybe it would be mine, this time. Maybe.*

Okay, *maybe* it was a little early for the Sam Spade act.

There wasn't even a beautiful dame yet.

A shift of thought brought the lights back up, and I hooked my swivel chair over with one foot. A broken castor rattled in protest, and that made me smile. It was that kind of detail, the little things, that made for a convincing experience inside The System, and I'd spent enough of my working hours inside the past six years to want to do it right.

So, getting comfortable, I grabbed up a pencil to take notes right there on my blotter and then tapped the pink eraser end against the folder jacket's tab. A pins-and-needles tingling sensation crept into my fingers. Looking deep into the No. 2 yellow-painted wood, I saw my security code streaming across the pencil's bridge, dumping into the tab. Three-level security, I noticed. Someone had locked this up tight.

Again, there was that shimmer of hope. Then the folder jacket fell open. Not like a book would fall open. The folder suddenly grew *depth*. As if I'd removed the cover from a box and revealed a stack of datapages about three inches deep. Officer's reports. Crime scene photos. Notes from other detectives. They would all be in there. Anything and everything pertinent to the case. And the most pertinent page of all was sitting right on top, ready for me to thumb it out and toss it up into the air where it hung, centered above my desk and glowing like God's holy writ. The damn cover page, with a large, no-nonsense black IAB stamp in the upper right corner.

Internal Affairs Bureau. The Rat Squad.

Ah, hell.

Chewing through the data forwarded by IAB didn't take long. One of the (admittedly few) advantages to being plugged in was the ability to manipulate, digest, or expel data at a rate that nearly matched the clock speed of a good CPU. It took longer to requisition a vehicle, once I realized that I would have to unplug for an onsite visit to the downtown depository. Longer still to drive there.

Police depositories, where we log in and secure all evidence for trial, are like small warehouses. Or, really, U-Store-It places. A warren of separate rooms, filled with shelves, drawers, cupboards, and lockboxes. Everything we need to manage an inventory that ranges from the pair of shoes a suspect wore the night of his crime to a steamer trunk filled with fifty kilos of Colombian H. They are cold, musty, cramped little spaces, usually overseen by aging cops who are turning into cold, musty, cramped little people. Dead-end careers. Little hope for parole.

I could relate.

Each depository also housed a datavault, which managed the official and total inventory *and* offered a place for VD detectives (like me) to store their finished work until trial. But someone at the downtown station had apparently developed "happy fingers," doing a little off-the-job programming to gum up the entire works. Which was how the problem ended up on my desk.

Agent Curtis of Internal Affairs met me just as I came off the elevator, coming up from the parking garage. Tall, and thick about the middle, with shadows under his eyes and a habit of glancing suspiciously at anyone who stood too close by. Serious frown lines drooping from the corners of his mouth. He had a gold wedding band on his left hand, but I doubted the hangdog expression came from his marriage. If I ever meet a happy IAB rat, it will be the first.

"VD?" he asked, too loudly. Like the chrome jack behind my right ear wasn't obvious enough. Heads turned.

"I'd rather use protection," I said. "But I appreciate the warning."

He frowned, and it looked like an avalanche building up on his face, ready to come crashing down. "You going to play games, or help me catch one of your wirehead buddies?"

Apparently Curtis was ready to paint me from the same color palette reserved for whomever had "abused the privilege," as some cops like to say. I was tempted—sorely tempted—to turn around right then. One Police Square or not. But there was still some hope left. Call me an optimist, but I didn't want to give this case up just yet.

"How 'bout first we rule out accidental corruption and a third-party hack?" I asked.

The avalanche started to roll. "I didn't think that was possible."

Technically, it wasn't. Well, an accident maybe, though from the evidence that seemed highly unlikely. Third-party? Would take some doing. First and foremost, datavaults were highly secured, with no (and I mean *zero*) outside access. That was just one of the ways The System beat back that whole cyberware scare. It really was as simple as not plugging in your critical data to the world-wide. You hosted it off your own intranet, or, if you really wanted security, a dedicated machine.

Banks and big corporations figured that out pretty quickly. Hell, most mom-and-pop businesses had enough smarts not to install a System interface unless they wanted vandals messing with their inventory and bookkeeping. Porn was one of the few big businesses still tied in, and with so many holes (no pun intended) in their frontline security it was easy to hack. They wanted you in, after all. Eventually they made a customer out of you.

So The System had become a glorified chat room, used primarily for communication and some semi-secure data management, and was big on the world-wide primarily with the entertainment industry. Not to mention it took a hardcore fan to bother getting *jacked* in the first place.

Or a cop bucking for an easy promotion to detective. One which, by most cops' standards, had never earned his gold shield.

"Let me take a walk through the system, at least. Get a feel for our perp."

Our perp. On the same team, me and him. Curtis hesitated, studied me like something he wasn't quite sure about.

Strike a pose: feet spread apart, confident, relaxed, thumbs hooked into the front pockets of my slacks (because I didn't have a trenchcoat). *If he's there, we'll find him. That's what you do when your business is*

*being a cop. A man crosses the line, any man, and you
bring him in. No matter what.*

"All right," Curtis finally said. And nodded me
down the hall.

Score one for the wirehead.

It was just a short trip to the property clerk's office.
Past the men's room and a janitorial closet with a
small puddle of water leaking out under the door. Iso-
lation was always a good first line of security, but
screen freeze me if it didn't feel like these officers had
been exiled to this far corner because they rated below
mop buckets and dusting cloths.

There was a metal security door protecting their
lair, with an access port that refused my badge number. Curtis swiped us through on his.

Tell me to take a square room ten feet on a side
and fit in four desks and a DataScanVI the size of a
small filing cabinet, and I'd have great game of mental
Tetris playing in my head. Apparently, so had the officers in charge here. Two desks pushed back-to-back,
the third shoved up against a wall with the DSVI
crouched in the kickspace beneath it, and the fourth
desk set on end in one corner as the piece-which-
would-not-fit. Plus, the walls were painted in a bright,
too-cheerful jewel-tone yellow.

All that was missing was the jaunty little background tune. Instead, the chief property clerk had a
CD player spinning out some classical piano.

"Franklin Torres," he introduced himself. Willowy
would be the best word to describe him. Tall and extremely lean, with stooped shoulders and rail thin
arms. A good breeze would probably bend the man
in half. No wonder he'd been filed down in the property clerk's office—sure wasn't built for the streets.
He did have a chrome jack behind his right ear—
another of the chrome detectives squad, then—and he

made sure I got a good look at it by turning his head overfar to introduce the others. Nothing to hide? Asking for some professional courtesy?

Samantha Blake and David O'Rourke were his two assistants. Samantha was a freshly made officer who starched her blues and I'm sure had an academy stencil still visible below her shirt collar. How she had pulled drudge duty I could only guess. Luck of the draw, maybe. Her file, as it had been given to me in the package, was clean. Top marks in programming and rated for an eventual job with the Electronics Division.

O'Rourke was sour-faced and carried an obvious chip on his shoulder. No doubting why he was here. His file had mentioned two trips to rehab in his first three years.

Both officers barely acknowledged Torrres when he introduced them. Me they glanced down at like a particularly loathsome bug trying to crawl into their food. I'd like to think it was the IAB detective looming behind me. Maybe it was the chrome.

"You have logs on the door for the last week." I said. Meaning, to let them know, that I had the logs and knew there was nothing out of place.

Torres nodded. "I've made runs on them in System," he said. "Sam has mast—fingered them for two days. We've got nothing new to add."

Fingered them. On keyboard. Torres was definitely old school cybercrime. He'd been about to call it "masturbating." By the light flush coloring Samantha Blake's cheeks, she knew it too.

I shuffled around the two back-to-back desks and crouched down before the DataScanVI. There was an Electronics Division sticker on the case, logging it as "evidence in place." So ED had already looked it over for tampering, to see if someone had installed a wireless bridge on the sly. No joy on the third-party hack.

Samantha, keyboarded and neither she nor O'Rourke had visible jacks, but I had to double check. "Wireless?" I asked them, and they shook their heads.

Not surprising. Not on a cop's pay, and the department would never spring for the new tech when the old stuff still hadn't paid for itself. Not in the eyes of the upper brass. I'd have them scanned again, but I doubted I'd turn up anything.

Mind if I plug in?" I asked Torres.

A courtesy only, as the equipment was owned by the department. But you didn't go plugging another man's jack into your chrome without asking. And don't go there.

"Top drawer," he offered.

Never pointed out his desk. Didn't have to. Even outside The System, it was the details—those little things I mentioned—that made the difference. In this case, his chair. A nice form-fitting tilt model designed to hold you in a semi-reclined position. He didn't have much privacy, not even so much as the closet-cubicle I was allowed for hosting my virtual office uptown, but he did go in for comfort and safety. No sense letting your body fall forward with an involuntary twitch, impaling your cell or a piece of your coffee mug into the middle of your forehead.

I eased myself into the hugging material, liking the velour touch. Then opened his top drawer and pulled out the datajack on its thin cable. Like most, it was covered in a thin latex sheath meant to keep things clean. Okay, it was a condom. Extra-small. The department wasn't about to pay for a custom-designed sheath, but it could have been worse.

The upper brass could have made us pick up our own extra-smalls at a local drugstore.

Without a warning glance at Curtis, and avoiding Samantha's gaze altogether, I stripped the condom away and set the jack into the socket behind my ear. Immediately, I began to relax. Muscles going slack, and a pleasant buzzing in my ears as the endorphins kicked in to lull me in to a . . . let's call it a receptive state. In a dreamy haze, I settled my hands down onto the chair's arm rests and reclined back into a comfortable pose.

Then rocked forward.

Standing up (in The System).

I was back in the office I'd just left, only without the clutter of desks and without the jewel-tone walls closing in around me. Instead, walls were painted a pleasant beige, illuminated by a soft glow that seemed to pool up from the floor, and hung with a few art masterpieces I might have recognized from museums. That is, from movies that had been shot inside museums.

So I wasn't an art buff. But still quite soothing, all considered.

The room remained ten-by-ten, held only by the single chair I'd just stood from and, out of the corner of my eye, I saw the mirror. Mirrors were such a common physical interface between The System and reality that it didn't surprise me at all. My office in the uptown precinct had one as well, and I was well trained in not looking until I was ready to unplug. There's something disconcerting in watching yourself lolling back, often with a sliver of drool trickling down your chin, giving those phantom twitching motions you see dogs do when they are asleep and "chasing rabbits."

Worse when you realize that there were several people in the room watching you do it.

Me and an empty room. Chair and a mirror. Some art. And the door. Right. I remembered the case file, which laid out the normal architecture of the datavault. Back through the door (which we'd used to enter) and I would instead be in a small virtual library. Complete with an electronic "card catalog" for maintaining the depository's inventory as well as VD's final casework. A drone—an artificially programmed personality—mocked up as a reference-section librarian was available for help. And bringing a "book" back through the door downloaded a copy to the DataScanVI's auxiliary port.

Small. Ordered. Convenient.

I opened the door.

I'll say this . . . I had been warned. Warned in the case file as delivered by IAB. And still, I was overwhelmed. The subtlety with which the perp had sabotaged us was staggering, really. I didn't doubt for a moment that all the data was still there—the DSVI's safeguards did not allow for erasure, ever—but it was all cunningly "lost" against the new interface.

The library had become an underground warehouse that stretched away from the suddenly-very-small door I'd stepped through for several miles. Three stories high, by estimation. Stacked floor to ceiling with shelves crammed full of nondescript wooden crates. Aisle upon row upon section. I shuffled along the smooth concrete floor looking to my left and right at the endless collection. There were lift-trucks for retrieving items off the very top shelves; one of the vehicles up on a stand for maintenance, and another leaking a small, spreading puddle beneath it that smelled of brake fluid. Every step sounded hollowly and then died without an echo. Even sound got lost in this immense room.

I chose an aisle at random and walked along, checking out crates. They were solidly built in the old-fashioned way, with real, heavy wood and nailed shut. Each was stenciled with an arcane system of numbers

and letters, though not necessarily shelved by any kind
of system I could easily discern. I knocked on a few,
kicked hard against a few others. Nothing wrong with
the physics program, as my big toe throbbed from the
effort. I dug behind one stack, pulling out a small box
that left a sliver of my thumb and sent me to sneezing
from the gray swirl in dust I stirred up. Smashing it
against the floor, I nearly laughed when a few dozen
gold detective shields spilled out over the concrete
walk.

Millions. Maybe billions of possibilities. So stunning,
it took me until I'd turned back for the door to place
the image. When I realized that no programmer could
have quickly produced all this detail from raw design.

No. I recognized it now. This was right out of the
Indiana Jones section of The System's Studio Tours.
Even if they weren't on wireless or plugged in, millions of people walked through this "warehouse"
every year by pulling on a VR helmet. You run from
the giant rolling boulder (which was probably crated
and stored in here somewhere as well), ride along in
the big car chase scene, and then walk through the
government warehouse from the end of the movie.

This was that warehouse.

And lost in here somewhere, right behind the Ark
of the Covenant, would be our master inventory list
and the key to opening all our VD casework.

I think that may have been when the glimmer of
hope, the one I'd carried with me through most of the
day, finally died.

It's just another part of the problem, working Virtual Division. When you get right down to it, the work
is a lot of number crunching and sifting through data.
There aren't any high-speed chases or running a sus-

pect down on foot. No gun fights (though I can't say missing out on those bothers me too much). And very few high profile arrests. We chip away against "black ice" or battle cyber ninjas. We rarely found anything worse than some low-stakes money laundering. Occasionally, we helped on a RICO subpoena, but OCD grabbed whatever glory came with those arrests.

It wasn't impossible to get in trouble on The System. People did it everyday. Quite easily, in fact. What was difficult was getting in so much trouble that it justified a program that probably cost the city millions. Not when a keyboard jockey could do most of what a chromed detective could do.

So, escorted by Detective Curtis back to the uptown station, I did what any good detective does. I drank some coffee and I sifted data. Curtis fed it into me, the data that is, through barely civil conversation. And I tried to ignore his suspicious glances, which filled every quiet moment.

"Simply put," he said as we paused outside my closet office, "the DA's trial schedule is falling to hell and she's going to blame us. There are three high-profile cases on the docket, including the serial killer Brendon LaChance, any one of which might go belly up because we can't track the damn evidence. Chain of custody issues aside, we can't find it all!"

"Uh huh."

There was that avalanche building again. Growing heavy on his brow and starting to tumble down his face. "Something you might want to remember is that IAB is pretty damn fireproof. We don't burn as easily as other divisions. In fact, we often *do* the burning." He glared at me, long and hard. "I can serve up VD as easily as the next guy."

With straight lines like these, I might seriously think

about asking for permanent assignment with Curtis once this case was closed. There was some potential here.

"Have you come up with *any* new conclusions?" he asked.

"It must be Wednesday," I said. Took another sip of my coffee. "Yep, there's a hint of chocolate in there. Which means Claire at Espresso-Daily served me a double shot extra-light mocha. That's my usual Wednesday poison. Fascinating, don't you think? I hated coffee for so long. But chocolate, that I could handle. And I needed the caffeine buzz on Wednesdays to help get me through the week. A personal choice becomes so routine that now I take evidence of that routine as fact."

"I meant about the case," Curtis said. Tone, dark.

I shrugged. Opened the door to my closet. Inside was my own support chair and a condom-wrapped datajack. "Have you found any connection between LaChance or a defendant from *any* pending case and one of the suspects?" I asked. He shook his head. "Any financial incentive? Someone get a new car, or pay down their mortgage, or suddenly win big at the track?"

I knew the answers, of course. And he knew I knew them. Another glower. Another shake.

"So there is no high profile tap. No third-party hack. It's not financial. And there's no way this was accidental."

"So what's left?" Curtis asked.

Strike a pose: roll the lower lip back against the teeth, one finger tracing along the line of my jaw. The Detective. About to say something profound. *So it wasn't murder. There wouldn't be any headlines in the morning. But it was still a crime, and we still had a job to do.*

"Personal," I told him.

Then I shut my closet door.

Plugging into my virtual office, I dialed up some atmosphere. Overcast and heavy showers. The street lamps outside penetrated the gray rain just enough to wash me out of the shadows. A great noir moment.

Minus the trench coast and beautiful dame.

I paced in front of those too-large windows, the kind of office I'd never have on the force except inside The System, and thought. Something I was missing . . .

Well, my coffee, for one. I'd left that on a utility shelf inside my closet. If I wanted to check the mirror on the back wall, I could see it. And myself, sitting easy in my chair, twitching. Not Bogey-style twitching—that purposeful tic that made him such a character. Chasing rabbits.

I thought about programming up some cigarettes. Or dressing the part in a beige trench coat and a felt fedora. Then logged in my drone instead. He entered through the door behind me, keeping far back in the shadows. Probably slouched. Against the wall or standing alone in the middle of the room, Sam Spade had a great slouch.

"It's got you tied in knots, don't it?" the drone asked. The click of an old-fashioned Zippo cover. The strike of the wheel and a hiss-crackle as he pulled a cigarette to life. "You wanted into this business. Never forget that."

"It has to be an inside job," I said, ignoring the banter. Counting raindrops as they splashed against the window glass. "Three good suspects. If there was a body, we'd have a great locked room mystery."

"You still got one of those," the drone said. "A locked room, I mean."

Check. The warehouse was large. Impressively so. But it was still a closed box and only three people had access. Score one for the drone, with extra points for style. It was programmed to run the same probability matrices as standard software and to check my facts. But to do so in a conversational manner. It helped me think.

"The thing about it is this," I said. "The trace evidence I need to prove who did it will be hidden against that same background programming. If I can find a unique programming signature, it will be as good as any fingerprint."

The drone made a *tchk* sound. My guess it was accompanied by that twitching smirk I'd never perfected. Not even in The System. "Fingerprints will get you so far," Sam agreed. "Me, I usually followed the money. Or the dame."

"I don't have either." I tried not to sound petty. I could have cast Samantha Blake in the role, I suppose, but she really didn't fit the part. The dame always came from *outside*.

"Then use what you do have. Look for what doesn't belong, and you'll have them."

There was a sharp exhale and the smell of cigarette smoke blowing in from over my shoulder. I hate that smell, and could have filtered it out. But, like I said, it was the little things which made a difference in The System.

The little things . . .

Strike a pose: leaning into the windowsill, letting the whole world fall away behind me until it is lost on the blur of the camera's eye. The filtered light from outside pools in my eyes. There is a soft patter against the window, as fat raindrops splash into droplets and leave silver-gray trails down the glass pane. *It was raining in The City. A steady rain. Strong enough to wash the trash out of the gutters.*

If I had thought to program some trash into the gutters to begin with.

The little things!

Ah, hell.

He was waiting for us, Detective Curtis and me, in the datavault office. Even though it was after hours. Even though he could have lit out and made a good run of it in the hours since we'd first come by.

Franklin Torres sat in his plush wraparound chair. Turned to face the door. The lights were dimmed, which I appreciated given the loud color on the walls. He raised a hand in casual salute as we entered.

"What gave me away?" he asked. No preamble. Not even a pretense of innocence. He knew we were back to make an arrest, and had never doubted, apparently, that we wouldn't come for him.

I decided to let him keep his pride. As much as I could. "The artistry." I told him the truth. "The little touches you left behind, because you couldn't help yourself. The dust and splintering wood. The sound effects. They were all just a little bit better than a keyboard jockey would bother fingering in.

"But the unique trait which I'm sure will match up against samples of your previous work, our providence, will be the fluid slick building up beneath that lift truck. It's what doesn't belong. It'll have your signature on it."

"Yes," he said. "That will do it."

And he sounded a little surprised that I had keyed on it.

"Actually, when I realized you had smashed open that small box, I thought you'd have jumped at the gold detective shields. That was what got me exiled here, after all. The chrome detective squad. When System cops didn't pan out as the next big thing, we were all but thrown away." He reached up to tap the chrome jack hiding behind his right ear. "I was tired of being forgotten."

Which was when Curtis stepped forward. Of course.

"But you will be," he promised, the avalanche rolling down his hangdog face. "You and all the wireheads. Eventually the entire department will be free of VD."

I'm telling you. He's a goldmine.

Strike a pose: leaning back in my swivel chair, feet up on the desk and hands clasped behind my head. Staring up at the ceiling to watch the ceiling fan push the thick, muggy air around the room. *And that's the way it went down. One man tired of being forgotten. Another resigned to it. Two side of the same coin.*

Agent Curtis and IAB grabbed what little kudos there were to claim for the arrest. No one was going to thank Virtual Division, especially when it had been one of our own who had "abused the privilege." You'd think I'd have learned by now. No one does us any favors.

But maybe I'm okay with that. Not learning, I mean. Because it's that little glimmer of hope that comes with every case that still separated me from Franklin Torres.

And like I said, it's the little things that matter.

Especially when you don't get the beautiful dame.

A SMALL SKIRMISH IN THE CULTURE WAR

Mike Resnick and James Patrick Kelly

Roger hated Elwood Tweed. There was no denying it anymore. It had taken Roger several months to put a precise name to the churning in his gut whenever he entered Tweed's presence. When he had first come to work for the Understanding Network, he was certain that what he was feeling was awe. Here he was, a twenty-two-year-old English major fresh out of Gates College, working in television as personal assistant to Elwood Tweed, Ph.D., on-air book critic for *24/7* and host of *The Good Word*.

But awe had changed to anxiety when it became apparent that everything Roger Allman did for Elwood Tweed was wrong. He put too much cream in Tweed's coffee. He failed to highlight a stray mention of Tweed's name in the two dozen newsfeeds he surveyed each day for the great man. He gave Tweed his five-minutes-to-air call at four minutes and forty-three seconds, or five minutes and seven. By the fall Roger had convinced himself that it was jealousy that was eating at him. Tweed was not all that smart—his degrees to the contrary—and Roger had come to realize that his most firmly held convictions were at best wrongheaded and at worst pernicious. Tweed was nothing but a smile that had about twelve too many teeth, a buttery voice, and an unflagging self-confidence that was within hailing distance of arrogance.

But Roger had now proceeded far beyond mere jealousy. He daydreamed of Tweed being caught in bed with a goat. A male goat. Or pitching headlong down a flight of stairs. Preferably made of marble.

Roger thought about quitting his job every day. But he could imagine how it would look on his resume if he had lasted less than six months on his first job. People would think he wasn't serious about having a career in television. And despite his utter disenchantment with Elwood Tweed, Roger knew that there was no higher calling, that movies and nightclubs could appeal to the lowest common denominator, but television's purpose was to uplift and educate, to bring serious culture to the masses.

"I'm sorry, Kurt," Tweed touched Kurt Vonnegut's sleeve discreetly. "But we have to pause here for a word from our sponsors. But when we return, I want you to hear what you think of those who call your work—pardon the term—sci-fi."

"Rascals." Vonnegut yawned. "Critics."

"We'll be right back, ladies and gentlemen." Tweed turned his smile up to broil, and the directorbot cut to a commercial for Steak Pearls, The First Foodtabs With That Home-Cooked Taste.

"One minute, Mr. Tweed." Roger never understood why Tweed insisted on a count during commercials. "Can I get anyone anything?"

"Yes," ordered Tweed. "Bring Mr. Vonnegut more water. His glass is almost empty."

Actually, Vonnegut had taken just one sip during the opening segment. In Roger's opinion, he would be better off drinking a extra-large latte with a couple of extra shots of expresso. (He looked as though he might nod off at any minute.) But then most of the guests who appeared on *The Good Word* recently tended to sleepwalk through their interviews. In August, the Understanding Network had switched Tweed's slot from the early bird 5:00 to 5:15 AM to the late night 12:45 to 1 AM. Tweed continued to insist that the show remain live—"After all, this is television," he intoned, "and as my pal Ed Murrow likes to say, we must never take the easy way out"—which was too bad for Vonnegut, who looked at 12:50 AM like he was eighty-four going on a hundred and twenty.

"Thirty seconds, Mr. Tweed."

"Make yourself useful for a change, Allman." Tweed twisted around in his chair. "I left my readette of *Cat's Cradle* in my dressing room. Fetch it up here for me. You will thumbprint it for me, Kurt?"

"That book is not science fiction," Kurt Vonnegut muttered. "I don't write science fiction."

Roger was happy to get away from the set and (especially) from Tweed. He settled himself in a Pneum-A-Pod and was whooshed down to the eighteenth floor of the Understanding tower. This was where the talent for *24/7,* the UN's morning news, talk, and political science show, had their offices. Sharon Swelter and Bobo Lamonica were just down the hall. Tweed had argued his way down onto eighteen even though the directorbots only gave him three or four *Book Banter* segments a week. But on eighteen he could bump into the stars of *24/7* and pretend he was one of them. The actual headquarters of *The Good Word* were way up on sixty-four, which was where Roger spend most of his time when he wasn't running Tweed's errands.

The carpetmoss on the floor of Tweed's office gave

off an earthy deep woods scent that Tweed liked to tell people reminded him of Thoreau's Walden, although Roger was pretty sure that Tweed had never been north of Yonkers. Tweed's rosewood desk was slightly bigger than the cubby where Roger worked. The walls were decorated with holos of the host in the reluctant embrace of some of his most famous guests: Judy Blume, Gore Vidal, Joyce Carol Oates, and James Michener. There were two of Tweed with J.D. Salinger, who had become something of a publicity hound since the release of the videogame version of *House of Glass*.

Tweed's desk and credenza were piled high with gaudy readettes, most of them still unread in shrink-wrap. Roger sorted through them, searching for *Cat's Cradle*. Every now and then he would find one he was certain Tweed wouldn't miss, like the latest Ursula Le Guin historical, or the sequel to *Nineteen Eighty-Four*. As he looked, he tried not to listen to the desktop, on which played the live feed from the studio up on the ninety-fourth floor. Tweed was browbeating a weary Vonnegut.

". . . fantasy, romance, thrillers—sheer vulgarity, in my opinion, and I'm not ashamed to say it. Don't you agree, Kurt, that the people who control our publishing houses ought to be ashamed of the way they have dragged American letters into the gutter, have foisted popular hacks like Kelly and Resnick, Kessel and Malzberg off on them while publishing only two Pynchon books in the past decade? Don't they have the responsibility, nay, the obligation to publish works of fiction that ennoble us?"

Vonnegut squinted suspiciously into the studio lights. "All my aliens are metpahors."

"Obviously, Kurt. I quite agree. But does it bother

you that an innocent reader, say some bright thirteen-year-old boy, might mistake your work for sci-fi?"

"Doris Lessing." Vonnegut picked up his water glass, considered it and intoned, "Margaret Atwood." He sipped.

"Rog, what are you doing here?"

As Roger spun around, he knocked over a stack of readettes haphazardly piled on top of Tweed's brushed titanium IBM File-O-Matic. He managed to snag three in midair, but the rest clattered to the floor. One of those in his grasp was *Cat's Cradle*.

"Your clueless boss is live, Bookboy." Doreen Best grinned at him from the doorway. "Shouldn't you be up in the studio getting ready to wipe his nose?"

Doreen Best flustered Roger in just about every way possible for a woman to fluster a man. It started with her looks. While not exactly beautiful, she was inarguably striking. Doreen was taller than Robert by a head. She had a dancer's long body; when she was eighteen she'd appeared in the chorus lines of Stephen Sondheim's *The Cherry Orchard* and Andrew Lloyd Webber's *Treasure Island*. Some people might have said that her neck was too long or her nose was too stubby, but Roger was not one of them. He usually tried not to look directly at her, because every glimpse seemed to sear itself into his memory and return to haunt him at odd moments, especially just as he was trying to fall asleep.

Then there was the fact that Doreen had been working for the Understanding Channel for almost seven years, which always made him feel like the total neophyte that he was. At various times she'd been on the production staffs of shows like *24/7*, *Protons and Planets*, *Pan Am Broadway Showcase*, *Yesterday Today*, *Poet's Theater*, *March of Progress*, and *Impact!*, and had even spent a few months working with Edward R. Murrow, whom the network had lured away from CBS with the promise of a weekly fifteen minutes of prime-time for *It's Bad For You,* his anti-smoking show. And, more than anything else, her attitude toward television in general and the Understanding Network in particular flustered him. Sometimes she seemed too cynical about TV's momentous enterprise, which Roger believed—no, *knew*—nothing less than the cultivation of the human spirit. And when it came to the day-to-day of the UN, she was usually more interested in office gossip than the quality of the programming.

But what flustered Roger most about the glamorous Doreen Best was that she seemed to be taking an interest in him.

Now she crossed the carpet moss to where he stood goggling at her and gently tapped his chin, encouraging him to shut his open mouth.

"Let me try again, Bookboy, this time in English." She pressed a finger into his chest. "You are *here.*"

His heart leapt to his throat.

She pointed toward the ceiling. "Tweed is *there.*"

He swallowed it again.

She folded her arms over her chest. "Why is that?"

"He's not clueless," Roger mumbled, and stabbed at the mute button on Tweed's desktop. It made him uncomfortable whenever Doreen mocked his boss, even if he agreed with every brickbat she hurled at Tweed. Tweed may have been an inconsiderate asshole, but he was doing the most important work a man could do, bringing civilization to the great unwashed of Florida and Ohio and Montana.

"He just doesn't always think things through," said Roger at last.

"Are you stealing his stuff again?" She stopped to pick up one of the readettes and glanced at it. "Oh, you better leave *The Cat in the Hat Comes Back* if you know what's good for you." She tossed it carelessly onto the File-O-Matic and lowered her voice into an uncanny imitation of Tweed. "A classic *bildungsroman* in the tradition of Goethe's *The Sorrows of Young Werther* and Twain's *Huckleberry Finn.*"

"Don't, Doreen," he said uncomfortably. "I shouldn't be listening to this."

"Then come out with me tonight," she said. "I have something I want you to see."

"It's tomorrow morning, actually." He checked the clock that hung over the doorway. "Twelve fifty-eight." He gathered the rest of the fallen readettes. "I need to get back to the studio before they sign off."

"But after you finish helping Tweed pat himself on the back, your time is your own, right?"

"What is it that you want from me, Doreen?"

She sat down in Tweed's chair, kicked off her shoes, and put her feet up on his desk. "I was hoping for your immortal soul, but I'd settle for a slice of innocence."

Roger concentrated fiercely on her stockinged toes, afraid that his gaze might slide up her calves and perhaps stray past her knees. "What would you do with it?"

"I'll think of something," she replied with a leer.

"Put your shoes on, Doreen. This is an office, not your living room."

"You know what your problem is, Bookboy? You're too serious." She slipped one shoe on, then the other. "But maybe that's why I bother with you."

"And why do I bother with you?"

She scribbled something on a sheet of Tweed's notepaper, folded it, and tucked it into Roger's shirt pocket. The touch of her fingertips through the thin material made his neck muscles go tight. "Meet me at the Pneum-A-Pod on forty-eight," she said, as she walked past him. "Twenty minutes." She paused at the door. "Bring your sense of humor. You do have one, don't you?"

"Of course I have one," he said heatedly.

"I was starting to wonder. Dust it off once in a while."

"We're in a deadly serious business, uplifting the public."

"Deadly, right." She waved over her shoulder on her way out.

He waited almost a minute before he opened the note.

You don't have a choice, it read.

Roger and Doreen lay side by side in the Pneum-A-Pod as it hurtled on a cushion of air through the Eighth Avenue tunnel. Through the clear walls of the tunnel, Roger might have seen the lights of the city rushing beneath them, if he hadn't been staring into Doreen's eyes.

"What I believe is that ratings reflect our mission," he was saying. "According to the May sweeps, the UN has more viewers than Fox and CBS combined. And if the World Chess Championship hadn't gone to fourteen games, A&E wouldn't even have come close to us."

"The only reason so many people watch us is that there isn't anything on TV that's more fun," Doreen responded. "Uncle Ralph makes sure of that."

"Uncle Ralph? Are you talking about Ralph Nader?"

"Right—the Secretary of Television," she confirmed. "The man who knows what's good for you—or else."

"Are you seriously suggesting that the *Pan Am*

Broadway Showcase isn't fun? Don't we run Shakespeare and Aristophanes every week? Didn't we just have a Moliére Festival?"

She made a lemon face. "There are more things in heaven and earth, Horatio, than are dreamt of in your philosophy."

She had never quoted Shakespeare to him before. Roger tried not to let her see that he was impressed. "But where are we going?"

"You've been cooped up in the Tower for too long, Bookboy," she said with a smile he didn't quite understand. "Wake up and smell the gutter."

"I've never been in this part of town before." Roger glanced uneasily at the garish lights that blinked and throbbed around dim doorways and dark windows. "Where are we going?"

"What difference does it make?" asked Doreen. "You're out on the town with a sexy girl on your arm. Stop thinking and enjoy."

"Don't talk like that."

"Why not?" she said. "This is the real world, Bookboy. You know," she added confidentially, "'even Harvard professors leave the ivy-covered halls and blow off a little steam from time to time."

"It's the buildings that are ivy-covered, not the halls," he corrected her.

"Roger, come down off the sixty-fourth floor. The air is too thin up there for life."

"Why do you keep belittling our work?" he asked, "Television is the greatest invention of the century, maybe the greatest since the invention of fire."

"You never heard of penicillin, I take it," she said sardonically. "Or Botox."

"Antibiotics are certainly wonderful breakthroughs, but they save sick people. Television saves *everyone*.

Surely you've seen movies from the pre-television era: Abbott and Costello talking nonsense about who was on first base, private detectives walking into a hail of bullets and never getting hurt, Hoot Gibson and James Cagney being held up as examples of American manhood."

"There were good movies too, you know," said Doreen.

"But nobody watched them, so they stopped making them. Nobody wanted to know that Frankenstein's monster spoke perfect English and had a soul; they just wanted to be scared into mindlessness. Or James Bond. Here's a secret agent, a covert agent, and he can walk into any bar in the world and someone is sure to say 'Shaken, not stirred'—and no one objects or guffaws. Movies dumb the public down; it's up to television to pull people back up." Roger could feel his adrenaline flowing as he warmed to his subject. "Same thing with popular literature. Before people like Tweed came along, junk like sci-fi and thrillers and romance dominated the bestseller lists. Now thoughtful essays and avant-garde poetry get the readerships they deserve."

"Just because books are bought doesn't mean they're read," said Doreen. "I think Stephen Hawking proved that years ago." She paused in front of a double door painted a lascivious shade of red. The humming neon sign above it read *All Night Long Lounge.* "What if people just want to escape?"

"From what?" he asked, genuinely puzzled.

"From the culture Tweed and acolytes like you are forcing on them."

"Ridiculous!" he snapped.

"Speaking of ridiculous, we're here." She gestured at the door. "I want you to see this show."

"What is it?"

"Something very funny."

"Well, the network can always use more humorists. Mort Sahl is getting a little long in the tooth, and Lord Buckley and Severn Darden both died a few years ago."

"Well, Woody Allen *did* apply for a job with us. So did Nichols and May."

He sniffed contemptuously. "Too lowbrow."

"But people understand them," she said. "How many people do you think understood Lord Buckley, or Ken Nordeen's *Word Jazz*?"

"Our job is to *make* them understand."

Her eyebrows arched and for a moment he thought she might laugh at him.

"Let me amend that," he said hastily. "Our job is to expose them to such things, and give them the cultural tools to comprehend and appreciate what they're seeing and hearing."

"I was wondering what our job was," she said, and as happened so often when they spoke, he had no idea how to answer her.

A well-dressed couple walked past them and entered the club, and Doreen turned to Roger. "So, we can stand here arguing all night, or we can go in."

"Wait," said Roger. "How much is this going to cost?"

"Nothing," she said. "They know I've been scouting the talent here, and I told them I'd be bringing along a consultant tonight."

Roger didn't know whether to be relieved or disappointed. If this was just business, then he'd have to lower his expectations. But if it was just business, why did she keep flirting with him? He opened the door and held it for her.

They passed through and were immediately greeted by the doormanbot, who was wearing a gorilla suit.

He greeted Doreen warmly and allowed them to pass through. A skimpily clad hostess (which, decided Roger, was just one tiny step more acceptable than a scantily clad hostess) escorted them to a table very near the small stage.

Soon a scantily clad waitress approached them and asked for their orders.

"I'll have a Manhattan," said Doreen.

"And the gentleman?"

"Just coffee," he said. When both women stared at him, he fidgeted uneasily and added, "I have to have my senses about me if I'm evaluating talent. One drink and I'll probably miss half of the subtleties and nuances."

"He'll have a martini," announced Doreen. As the waitress walked off, she said to Roger, "Not to worry. These people check their nuances at the door."

"Then why are we here?" he asked earnestly.

"Just relax and we'll discuss it later."

The drinks arrived, and Roger took a sip of his martini. He tried not to make a face as it went down. It was the drink of the masses, and he found himself wishing for a '48 Chardonnay, or possibly a '51 Dom made entirely from grapes raised on the north slope. (In truth, his tastebuds couldn't tell the difference between Dom Perignon and Two Buck Chuck, but that, he knew, was merely because they weren't yet properly educated. He watched all three of UN's wine shows religiously, and he by God knew good from bad, even if his mouth didn't—another gift of television to the drab, empty lives of its audience.)

Suddenly the lights dimmed, and a fat man in a sad sack suit sidled nervously onto the stage. He had a receding hairline and bulging eyes almost as big as ping-pong balls. He goggled at the audience, as if he expected that they might start throwing things at him.

For a long moment, he said nothing. The room went quiet as well. He shuffled from foot to foot in the spotlight in front of a microphone. Roger thought maybe he had wandered onto the stage by accident. Then he crooked a finger between the collar of his shirt and his neck, loosening his tie.

"I get no respect," he said. "I took my wife to a fancy restaurant on her birthday and I made a toast. 'To the best woman a man ever had.' The waiter joined me."

The room exploded into laughter.

"My wife and I were happy for twenty years. Then we met."

A man at the next table doubled over and banged his head against the tabletop.

There followed another ten minutes of one-liners, none of them new, and none, in Roger's opinion, the least bit funny. The alleged comedian complained about his wife, his kids, his doctor and his dog, a sad litany of abuse and misunderstanding.

"They actually pay this man to stand up there and spout this drivel?" whispered Roger.

"They not only pay Rodney Dangerfield to perform," replied Doreen, "but you'll notice that every table in the house is full."

"But he belongs in a saloon a century ago!" said Roger. "This whole act is about how stupid he is."

"Everyone laughed," she said. "Doesn't that mean anything to you?"

"It means we've got our work cut out for us," said Roger grimly.

"Nothing else?" she persisted.

"Should it?" he asked, confused.

She looked pityingly at him and sighed. "No, I suppose not."

"So can we go now?"

"This is just the opening act," said Doreen. "We're here for the headliners."

"If I have to sit through anything else like this Dangerfield, I'm going to need another martini," said Roger, signaling to the waitress.

The drink arrived. Roger was just lifting it to his lips when the place erupted in such a deafening roar that he almost spilled its contents.

"What is it?" he asked, looking up.

"The stars of the show," said Doreen.

Two old men strode onto the stage. One, tall and handsome, carried his age well. He strode confidently to the microphone and began crooning a melodic tune. Meanwhile the other shuffled out among the tables, picking up customer's drinks and sniffing them, looking down women's dresses and mugging shamelessly every time his partner hit a high note. He might have been skinny once but now had gone to fat. He seemed to move with difficulty.

"What do you think of his voice?" asked Doreen.

"Well, it's sure as hell not *La Traviata*."

"I didn't ask what you thought of the song."

"How can I tell about his voice if he won't sing an aria?" replied Roger.

"Not everyone sings opera, and not everyone *likes* opera," she noted.

"Not everyone likes coming in out of the rain," he shot back. "I don't see your point."

Just then the fat man with the uncertain step seemed to slip on something. His arms windmilling wildly, he caught himself by sitting briefly on the lap of a woman with enough blonde hair to stuff a pillow, then rolled off her to onto his knees and rested his head on the shoes of her date. The slow-motion pratfall sent the audience into paroxysms of laughter.

"Hey Lllaaadddyyy!" He stared up at the blonde

with a grin. "Don't worry, lady. I'm all right, but your boyfriend needs a shine."

The comedian clambered gracelessly to his feet, pawing at the woman as he did, then crossed his eyes and started complaining about the singing in a high, whining voice.

"If you think you can do better, Jerry," said the singer, "go ahead and try."

"You bet I can, Dean!" whined Jerry. Then, to the audience, "I'll murder the bum."

He began singing, horribly off-key, and the audience began laughing again.

"Ladies and gentlemen, if you think that's bad," said Dean, "you should hear it in French."

"My God!" muttered Roger. "This is what passes for entertainment in this place!" He turned to Doreen. "I can't take any more of this. I feel like I'm losing my mind. I'm dizzy. I have to get some air!"

"All right," she said unhappily. She left a tip on the table and then led him through the maze of people and chairs until they reached the exit.

"That was dreadful!" he said when the world stopped spinning around him.

"Those are the most popular acts in New York, Roger," said Doreen. "Maybe there's something wrong with *you*."

He stared at her. "This is all some kind of practical joke, right?"

"No," she said seriously. "I intend to use whatever clout I have to get the network to hire them and start a variety show."

"We already *have* a variety show, in case it's slipped your mind," said Roger. "We've had St. Martin-in-the-Fields Choir, Allen Ginsberg's Poetry Slam, Pilobolus, the Kronos Quartet . . ."

"Roger, we're giving the people what *we* think they

should have," said Doreen. "I think it's about time we started giving them what *they* want."

"They don't *know* what they want!" Roger shouted. "A baby doesn't want to stop suckling at its mother's breast. A two-year-old child doesn't want to learn to use a toilet. A six-year-old doesn't want to go to school. We teach them to accept things for their own good, and thanks to television and visionary men like Nader and Murrow and, yes, Tweed in his limited way, we don't have to stop teaching them just because they've grown up and left school."

"You left out one important thing, Roger," she said.

"Oh?" he replied. "And what is that?"

"The element of choice."

"Do you give a child the choice between touching a live wire and not touching it?" asked Roger.

"We're not talking about children, Roger," said Doreen.

"All right then, what if you're right?" said Roger. "Have you ever seriously considered that?"

"What do you mean?"

"What if you're right?" he repeated. "What if you gave the unwashed masses their choice?"

"It would be a good thing," said Doreen. "There's room on television for everything."

He shook his head. "If that audience tonight was typical, then Martin and Lewis and Rodney Dangerfield won't share time with Mort Sahl. They'll share it with dumb weekly shows about dippy housewives and teenaged hippies and country hicks outsmarting city slickers. Dance bands and crooners won't share time with Pavarotti and Domingo; they'll shove them into the shadows and their places will be taken by more tuneless music, aimed at the least sophisticated tastes. And worst of all, the news shows will be unable to hold an audience unless they start covering beauty pageants and diet fads and crimes no one has any reason to care about."

"That's the silliest thing I ever heard," said Doreen.

"The bad always drives out the good," answered Roger. "Why do you think I keep working for a mean, self-centered son of a bitch like Tweed? Because he's what stands between us and Dangerfield. Can't you see that? Ed Murrow is what stops the Super Bowl from being more important than the war in Uruguay. We have a sacred mission to uplift and educate."

"Jesus, you really *are* brainwashed, aren't you?" said Doreen. She sighed deeply. "I'm sorry I wasted your evening, Roger."

He took her home, and, for the first time in months, didn't have the urge to kiss and paw her. In fact, suddenly the thought of touching her made his skin crawl.

Which was probably just as well. After he reported her to Chairman Nader and the others, there was no question that she would lose her job, and at least now he wouldn't feel guilty about it.

His decision made, he made his way to his apartment to watch the late-night opera and ballet, resisting the urge to look up and see if his halo was visible.

DARK WINGS

Lisanne Norman

"**S**low down, Weis," Jensen said quietly from his seat next to the burly pilot. "There's no rush. The weather's worsening. We can finish the survey to-morrow."

"I wanted to finish scanning this sector before heading back to the settlement," muttered the other, banking sharply to the left to compensate as a gust of wind caught their scouter side-on.

Moments later, like a cork from a bottle, they shot out of the small valley into the plains, only to be caught again by the swirling blizzard.

This time, Jensen was flung back against his seat as Weis fought the controls, trying to force their craft back on course.

"What's ahead?" Weis demanded. "How close are the Splitback Mountains?"

"Too damn close," said Jensen, forcing himself up against the gees so he could reach his console and check their erratic course against what they had charted of the landscape below and around them. No point looking out the windscreen; all they could see was the swirling white-out of the storm. "We need to get above this weather and head back now, Weis."

Weis snorted. "Yeah, right. Like I'm not trying! I wanna get off this dirt ball and back into space even if you don't!"

"Pull up! Now! Starboard!" Jensen said urgently as the mountains suddenly loomed closer on his nav screen.

Again Weis yanked on the controls, banking sharply to the right as he pulled the small craft's nose up.

Engines whining as the hull creaked and groaned in protest, Jensen clutched the armrests and, against all reason, willed the small scouter upwards while mentally trying to hold the hull together. He didn't need to hear Weis's low, repetitive swearing or the sudden blaring of the proximity alert to know they were in real trouble.

Then, with a shriek of tortured metal, Jensen felt the scouter grasped as if by a giant hand and flung against the mountainside.

Consciousness returned by degrees, but he had no inclination to move. Some sixth sense told him if he did, he'd discover that every part of his body hurt. Besides, he was comfortable right now, and his insulated flight suit was keeping him warm. Then something tickled his nose. He wriggled it, trying to dislodge whatever it was, but the tickling persisted. Reluctantly, he raised his arm to brush it away, but his hand only flopped unresponsively against his face.

Shock surged through him then as he remembered the crash. He struggled to sit up, panicking when he found he couldn't. It was only as he opened his eyes and realized that the scouter was lying canted to one side that, with an effort of will, he sat still.

Now fully conscious, he began to take stock of his

surroundings. His seat had semi-reclined into the crash position and the harness was all that was holding him there, and yes, every muscle in his body ached as if he'd been pummeled, but there was no sign of blood on his white winter fatigues. So far, so good. Now for his hands.

Lifting them up, he peered at them through half-closed eyes, expecting the worst, relieved when he saw they were unhurt, just numbed by the cold.

He turned his head, looking for Weis. The pilot lay inert in his seat, either out cold or dead, he'd no idea which. Almost subconsciously he noticed there was no blood visible on him either.

"Weis?" His voice cracked as he tried to call out. Licking his lips, he tried again, only to have his words swept away by the wind.

Wind? Inside the scouter? He frowned, confused, trying to make sense of what was happening. Then, beyond Weis, where the port hull had been, he saw the open gash. Through it, the blizzard was howling, coating everything in a layer of snow.

He wrapped the harness round one arm, and with his other hand he began hitting the harness's release stud. It took several attempts, his numb hand being as much of a hindrance as an advantage because he felt no pain . . . yet. Finally it gave, and as he began to slide out of his seat toward the main console, he was able to check himself.

Turning round and grabbing hold of his chair arm as well, he hauled himself up until he got a foothold on the side of the console between the two seats. Then he reached for his pilot.

Beneath a frosting of snow, Weis's face had a bluish-white tinge that was far from healthy. Reaching out to grasp him by the front of his padded flight suit, he noticed his own hand was the same bloodless color.

"Weis! Wake up! We crashed."

The other began to move sluggishly, his hand going up automatically to brush the snow off his face before his eyes even opened. Jensen let him go, squatting back on his heels.

"What . . ." Weis groaned and began to move.

"We crashed," said Jensen, slithering off his perch and down to the main console.

Hitting the emergency beacon, he prayed that the backup power unit hadn't taken any damage.

Weis sniffed audibly, then, hitting his release buckle, catapulted himself out of his seat into Jensen, sending them both flying against the starboard bulkhead.

"Fuel," he said succinctly, scrambling to his feet and reaching down to haul Jensen up by the collar. "Tank's gone. We gotta get outta here."

"Damnit, Weis . . ." Jensen staggered as Weis released him, biting back a groan of pain as he rubbed the back of his head.

"She could go up like a torch any minute. Can't you smell the goddamn fumes?" Weiss demanded, grasping the dangling harness and pulling himself up onto Jensen's seat, then onto his own.

Jensen followed, trying to ignore the pounding headache and the pain in his hands now that the circulation was finally returning to them. Snow made the surfaces slick and he slipped more than once, but finally he made it to the gash in the hull through which Weis had disappeared.

Grasping hold of the rough edges, he yelped in pain as the bitterly cold metal burned into his hand. Pulling free hurt even more. Dazed from this fresh pain, he stood watching as the blood welled up from the torn flesh into the hollow of his palm.

"You retard! Why didn't you put your gloves on first like I did?" Weis demanded, hauling him bodily from the crashed scouter out into the darkening night and the full force of the blizzard.

"The ship's not going to blow!" Jensen yelled, staggering through the deep snow in Weis's wake as he was hauled along. "We must have been unconscious for over an hour!"

Weis said nothing, only increased his pace until they rounded a snow-covered rocky outcrop that offered some protection from the worst of the blizzard; then he stopped.

Jensen jerked himself free, and, unfastening one of his thigh pockets, reached inside for a field dressing. The wind had dropped and he could actually hear himself think.

"Give it here," Weis snarled, looming over him and snatching the pack. Moments later, the dressing had been slapped over his palm and hastily tied in place. "Now put your headgear and gloves on! Didn't the Company teach you tekkies nuthin' about survival out here?"

The analgesic in the dressing hit his system almost instantly, bringing relief from the pain and sealing the wound. From his other pocket, he drew out his gloves and face mask.

He was angry, bloody angry if truth were told, at the way Weis had been treating him right from the moment they'd taken off from the valley settlement.

"Yeah, they taught me," he said, fitting on the earpiece and mic set, then the face mask. Activating the mic, he reached behind his head for the hood, pulled it up, and secured it, then turned his attention to easing his hands painfully into the mitts.

"But they didn't teach me how to survive a kamikaze pilot and being thrown against a bulkhead and landed on by him!" he added when he heard the click of Weis's mic going live.

Weis's laughter nearly deafened him, and the slap on his back sent him sprawling into the outcrop.

"You're OK, Jensen." he said, throwing him the end of a piece of fine rope. "Here, tie that 'round you and let's get moving before the shuttle blows. I wanna reach those caves we scanned in the valley just before we crashed. We can hunker down there till the storm passes, then signal the *Deigon* for a pickup."

Jensen stopped dead in the middle of tying the rope and looked up. Toggling his goggles to infravision, he shoved his hood back.

"What the hell you doin', man?" Weiss demanded.

"Shut up. I heard something."

"You heard something? You heard the . . ."

"I said shut the hell up!" Jensen snarled, moving a few feet away from him, back around the outcrop. He had heard something, and now he was scanning the white-speckled swirling darkness for a clue to what it was.

His hearing was legendary on the *Deigon*—he could hear a dog whistle as easily as any dog.

"There it is again," he muttered, swinging around to face the direction they'd come from. It was high-pitched—had to be to carry over the banshee howling of the wind—and like nothing he'd ever heard before as it rose and fell in pitch before stopping abruptly. It came again, this time only a short burst, and from the opposite direction.

A flicker of red at the edge of his sight drew his attention back to the direction in which the shuttle lay. He grabbed hold of Weis's arm, shaking him.

"Look! Over where the shuttle is!" he said. "Movement!"

"Can't see a damned thing in this blizzard," said the other. "Let's get moving now before the shuttle . . ."

The ground beneath their feet began to tremble, gently at first, then more violently as a plume of flame even Weis could see erupted high in the night sky. Just as suddenly, it was gone, and as the mountain under them heaved and bucked, they were tossed to the ground like unwanted children's toys.

Jensen lay there, arms cradled over his head, even though he knew it would be no protection.

"This region isn't volcanic," he muttered, more to himself than Weis.

"Tell the goddamn mountain that!"

The ground beneath them gave one last heave, then was still. Slowly he moved his arms and pushed himself into a kneeling position.

"Tell me there was enough fuel on the scouter to cause that," he said, turning to watch as Weiss scrambled up.

"I can't, and you know it."

He got to his feet, dusting the snow off his flight suit and pulling his hood back up. "I'm going back to look at the scouter."

"You're mad," said Weis. "You'll not catch me goin' back there after that!"

"Then wait here," he snapped, losing patience with the burly pilot.

"Jensen, don't go," said Weis grabbing him by the arm. "Some things it's better to ignore."

"What the hell are you talking about?" he demanded.

The large man hesitated. "The locals were saying the mountain's haunted."

He snorted derisively. "And you believed them?"

"You said you heard somethin', saw movements before she blew!"

"I didn't see ghosts!" Then it came to him, what his subconscious had been trying to tell him for the last five minutes. "Whales! It sounded like whales."

"Now who's talking rubbish? Weis demanded. "There's no whales five thousand feet up a mountain!"

Ignoring him, Jensen set off back the way they'd come. There was a mystery here and he aimed to solve it. As soon as he stepped out from the shelter of the outcrop, the wind howled around him, grabbing at him, trying to thrust him back. Doggedly he pushed on, keeping his head down, putting one foot in front of the other, following the tracks they'd left.

"Jensen, damnit! Come back! You can't go off on your own in this weather! You didn't even tie the rope round you!"

Jensen had reached the crash site before Weis caught up with him.

"Jesus Christ," said Weis reverently as he came to an abrupt stop beside him. "The mountain ate it!"

Where the scouter had been was a ridge of bare rock some fifty feet long and as tall as a man. Of their craft, nothing remained.

Not a superstitious man by nature, even he was shaken by the sight before them. "I see it," whispered Jensen, taking a tentative step forward. Something lying in the newly fallen snow, glowing faintly, caught his eye and he stopped to pick it up.

As he did, he heard the call again, this time a longer and more plaintive cry that got rapidly louder. Grabbing the object, he stood up in time to see something rushing toward him out of the night.

Weis yelled out a warning and dove for him as he stood rooted to the spot, staring in disbelief at the almost invisible shape hurtling toward him. At the last moment, it veered to one side. His cheek was brushed by something soft yet bitterly cold moments before Weis catapulted into him, knocking him back against the mountainside.

The call sounded again, urgent this time, and from the opposite direction. He'd no sooner swung his head to the right than he heard it answered from the one on his left—both sounded very close by. Looking wildly from side to side, Jensen tried to pinpoint their locations. From the one that had come at him, he'd gotten the impression they were human-sized, but what he saw was insubstantial—they had no visible heat source.

He flicked his goggles back to normal sight. Now he could see something—a pale fluttering shape within the swirling snow. . . . No, two, they were together! They were silent now, but he could sense an urgency in their movements as they seemed to edge closer to them.

"What the hell's going on?" demanded Weis, breaking his concentration. "What came at you?"

He pushed himself away from the rock face. "We have to leave!" he said.

"I'm not moving till I know what's out there, and neither are you!" said Weis, pulling him back with one hand while waving his pistol menacingly in an arc in front of them.

"Put the goddamn gun away," snarled Jensen, hitting Weis's arm down. "Whatever it is, it isn't dangerous to us! If it was, we'd be dead already."

They called out again, sharp, plaintive bursts of sound as they fluttered closer then backed off again as if afraid to get too close.

"They know what a gun is," Jensen murmured.

"I can't see a thing in this blizzard," snarled Weis.

"We have to leave, Weis," he said again as behind him, the rock began to tremble slightly. In the distance, he heard a sharp crack followed by a dull rumbling that rapidly began to get louder.

"Avalanche!" he yelled, looking up as he tried to pull away from Weis.

*   *   *

With a shout of terror, Jensen sat bolt upright, gasping for breath. It was pitch black, and he could hear his heart beating loudly. Sweat began to run down between his shoulder blades, coating his body in a slick film, making his T-shirt stick uncomfortably to his back.

Reason told him if he could sit up, he wasn't still buried under the avalanche, but reason had little to do with the nightmare of being buried alive that he relived each night.

The light flicked on, making him blink owlishly.

"Another nightmare?" asked a sympathetic feminine voice. "That's the third this week. Want me to get you something to help you sleep?"

"No," he said, rubbing shaking hands over his face and through his sweat-soaked hair, pushing it back from his eyes and forehead. Tonight's dream was proving more difficult to shake off. "I'm fine. Just leave the main light on."

"You know I can't do that," she said regretfully, stepping into the room. "Power is still rationed in Landing, but I have brought you a spare bedside lamp. It runs off a small atomic cell."

He glanced up at her as she walked across to his bedside and placed the lamp on his night table.

"Touch the base to turn it off or on," she said, demonstrating before turning to check that his left leg was still held firmly in the traction unit.

He lay back among his pillows, watching her. Something was different tonight.

"Tell me again how you found us," he said abruptly.

Keeping her back to him, she gave a small laugh as she busied herself tucking the blankets around his uninjured right leg.

"I tell you this every night. We picked up the signal from your scouter before it exploded, and a party of the men went out to rescue you. You were extremely lucky, you know. There was a ledge just above you that took the brunt of the avalanche. You were only buried under a few feet of soft snow, and somehow you'd managed to push an air hole up to the surface."

Her laugh sounded forced, unnatural.

"How's Weis? When can I see him?"

She said nothing at first, just finished straightening the bed. "You need to sleep, Jensen, otherwise your leg will take longer to heal."

Straightening up, she turned to face him, a bright smile on her lips. "We'll talk about that tomorrow, shall we? Once you're rested."

"What's happened to him? I want to know now!"

She hesitated, the smile fading. "It seems the blow to Weis's head was more severe than we thought at first. I'm afraid he died a few hours ago."

"What?" He sat up again, staring at her, hardly able to believe what he was hearing. "But you said he was fine . . ."

"It was very sudden," she said, turning to leave. "Dr Kingston will be in to see you again tomorrow. He can answer all your questions."

"I want to know now!"

"In the morning," she said firmly, turning out the light and closing the door behind her.

"Damnit!" he snarled, reaching for the lamp and hitting the base to turn it on. It wasn't bright, but it did push back the darkness immediately around his bed.

Why had the Company left them on Kogarashi instead of taking them back to the *Deigon* to be treated? None of the colonists had wanted them there; in fact, once they knew the Company had sent them to scan the mountain range at the back of Landing, they'd been as near hostile to them as they could be.

His instincts were telling him there was something wrong about the whole setup, that even the nurse was hiding something from him. It was a hell of a time to be stuck flat on his back with a broken thigh!

He froze, hearing a small sound from behind the drapes off to his right. Slowly, he turned his head.

"You better have a good reason for . . ." he began quietly.

"There's nothing wrong with your leg now," she said, pushing the curtains aside and moving closer to the light so he could see her. "They're lying to you. And your friend isn't dead. He escaped."

He scanned her face, taking a moment or two to recognize her. She'd been at the town meeting when they'd been asked to explain why they were there. What was her name? Avana! That was it.

Small, her long, fair hair now drawn back in a single plait, she was clad in the ubiquitous jeans and sweater of the colony. He knew he was focusing on irrelevancies, but what she was saying, after the events of the last few days . . .

She moved closer, walking around the bottom of his bed to his injured side, then stopped. Seeing a flash of metal in her hands, he uttered a wordless cry, lurching forward to stop her.

The knife flashed, slicing through the cables holding his leg up. Released, it fell to the bed. He braced himself for pain that never came.

"I told you," she said, leaning down to sever the bindings on the cast that encased his leg from groin to foot.

"Hey!" He grabbed her hand, holding it firm against her attempts to pull free. "What the hell do you think you're doing?"

She stopped struggling, eying him up and down. "They certainly don't choose you Company men for brains, do they? Mind you, you are quite cute, though. Nice green eyes. I'm taking off the cast; what do you think I'm doing?"

The compliment threw him for a moment, until he realized it was what she'd intended. "My leg's broken . . ."

"What makes you think that? Does it hurt?" she demanded.

He stared at her, taken aback by her vehemence.

She took advantage of his loss of attention and pulled free, her knife quickly slipping under the remaining fastenings and severing them.

"Stop!" he hissed, instinctively jerking his leg away, then wincing as the blade grazed his flesh. "Damnit, woman! You don't have to slice me up to prove your point!"

Slipping the knife back into its sheath, she stood, hands on hips, and regarded him dispassionately.

"If you don't believe me, look at the palm of your left hand."

"Why?"

"You hurt it, probably on the side of your scouter. There was a dressing on it when you arrived here."

He closed his hand into a fist, determined not to do what she wanted. "What does that prove?"

"So don't look then. You can fly a shuttle, can't you?"

He frowned, thrown again by her sudden change of topic. "I can, but what has that to do with anything?"

"The *Deigon*'s left. The Company believes you both died in the avalanche."

"What?" Stunned, he sank back against the pile of pillows.

"They won't be back for another ten years, 'cause winter's just started here."

"They can't have left. . . . Why would they think we're dead?"

"Because the town told them you were."

He felt a tug on the cast and immediately turned his attention back to her. "Dammit! Leave my leg alone!"

"Only if you look at your hand," she said, continuing to work her way up the form-fitting cast, pulling the sides apart.

"All right! Just stop!" he snarled, unclenching his hand and turning it over to examine. There wasn't a mark on it.

Nothing made sense right now, but somehow, what Avana was telling him seemed more credible than anything he'd been told since he and Weis had crashed on the mountain.

"How?" he asked, leaning forward to take hold of the top of his cast, where it was against his groin, and pull the sides apart. If his hand could have healed that quickly . . . He had to know if his leg had been broken.

"I'll tell you if you help me," she said, reaching out to help him.

He batted her hands away and pulled the cast apart. "I can manage."

She pouted briefly. "You're spoiling my fun."

Ignoring her comment, he stared at the pink jagged line on the top of his thigh, the one that hadn't been there a few days ago.

Her hand reached down, one brown finger lightly tracing its length. "That's where the broken bone came through. Not bad for only three days. You might find your leg a little painful for another day, so be careful," she said, her tone very matter-of-fact.

"I want to know what the hell is going on here, and I want to know now!"

"I'll tell you when we're in the air," she said. "The nurse will come to check on you again shortly. You do want to be gone by then, don't you?"

"Help me get this off," he said, suddenly making

up his mind and releasing her. He began pulling at
the cast again.

"That's not the way," she said, stopping him. "Roll
over on your side, with your back to me. I'll cut it
down the center, then it'll just fall off."

He looked at her suspiciously for a moment, watching as her face lit up in an elfin grin.

"What, don't you trust me? I'd never take advantage of a man in his sickbed . . . unless invited."

"You're mad," he said with feeling, rolling over, but
turning his head so he could watch her.

"Not mad," she said, pulling out her knife, all trace
of the grin now gone. "Just different."

"I'll need my clothes. Do you know where they
are?"

"In the closet over there," she said, nodding her
head toward a corner of the room.

The repaired tears and the rubbed patches of cloth
on his insulated fatigues were impossible to miss.
Thoughtfully, he ran his fingers over them. No one
could fake that kind of damage. What she'd told him
must be true.

"Nothing gets thrown away in Landing," she said,
uncannily following his thoughts. "Everything's reused.
Hurry up. Much as I hate to lose the rather pleasant
view of you in your shorts, we must leave now."

He glanced at her again, trying to work out how
old she was as he balanced himself on his good leg
and started pulling the one-piece on.

She moved closer, ready for him to lean on as he
put his full weight on his injured leg. There was an
ageless quality about her, but this close, he could see
the tiny signs that she had left the first flush of youth
behind—laughter lines at the edges of her eyes and
frown ones between her eyebrows.

"I'll answer all your questions later, when we're in the air," she said, holding up the top of his fatigues for him, taking the weight so he could push his arms into the sleeves.

"Lady, I'm going nowhere with you till I get some answers," he said, pulling up the zipper and sealing the protective flap over it.

Shrugging, she turned away. "Then you can stay here and I'll try to fly the shuttle myself."

"That's insane, especially in this weather!"

"You keep saying those words," she said, frowning. "I assure you if you come with me, you'll find out that I'm perfectly sane. Now, are you coming or not?"

Knowing she had no intention of telling him anything until she got her own way, he followed her to the window with an exclamation of annoyance.

Outside, though there was no sign of snow on the ground, it was bitterly cold. The night sky overhead was only partially clouded; every now and then the crescent moon swam into view, illuminating the village that was Landing.

Almost immediately, they'd stopped behind the generator shed belonging to the medical facility, where she'd hidden her own winter gear—brown fur jacket and hood and plain fur-lined trousers that tucked into the matching boots she wore.

"They'll be cold," he said, picking up her jacket as she began hauling the pants over her jeans.

"You don't know much about Danu, do you? Furs like these are better stored outside. Helps them keep their thermal properties."

He held the jacket for her as she shrugged herself into it.

"Follow me, and keep to the shadows."

She led him round the outside of the village, darting

into the shadows of the buildings whenever the moon lit up the sky.

"The place is deserted. I thought you said Weis had escaped. Doesn't look to me like they're looking for him or guarding anything."

"They aren't. They expect the mountain to kill him," she said shortly, as they waited in the lee of one of the communal buildings for the moon to disappear behind the clouds again.

"The mountain? Why the hell would that kill him?" Even as he said it, he felt a shiver of uncertainty run through him.

"How much do you remember about the crash, Jensen?"

"Everything, of course! The wind slammed us into the mountain and the actual crash knocked us out."

"Then what?" she asked, turning round to look at him.

"We got out and . . . walked away from the scouter before it blew up." Even as he said it, he knew that wasn't right.

"You saw or heard something else, though, didn't you? You must have."

Her brown eyes regarded him seriously as he tried to remember that night.

There had been something more, he was sure of it, but the harder he tried, the more it seemed to slip away from him.

"I can't remember," he said, angry and frustrated with himself. "You know what it was, so tell me!"

"I can't," she said, turning away again. "You have to remember it for yourself."

The moon disappeared behind a large cloudbank, plunging them into darkness.

"Let's go!" she whispered, starting to run out across

the last open space to the building where the shuttle was stored.

Safely inside, she switched on the lights, almost blinding them both after the darkness outside.

"Won't they see the lights?" he asked, blinking and rubbing his eyes.

"No," she said, pushing her hood back and taking off her mitts. "It's the middle of the night, and the building has no windows."

Satisfied, he did the same as he walked over to where two squat grey vehicles took up most of the hangar space.

"You've got two shuttles?"

"We had three but we lost one in the first year."

Jumping up on the running board at the nose of the nearer one, he thumbed the opening mechanism. The door slid back, allowing him a good view of the cramped bridge.

"These are ancient," he said. "They should have been scrapped fifty years ago."

"The Company isn't exactly known for its altruism toward its settlers," she said drily. "We're grateful to have even these. This one is fueled and ready to go. Can you fly it?"

"In my sleep, darling," he said, turning back to grin at her. "In my sleep." For the first time since the crash, he felt confident of his ability to handle the situation.

Time seemed to slow as he watched her mouth drop open and her eyes widen in fear. Then something cold and hard was pressed against the back of his neck.

"You ain't goin' nowhere, Jensen. I'm taking this shuttle. You just step back down onto the ground and back away."

"Weis! They said you were dead."

"Well, they were wrong. Move it!" Weis snarled. A hefty shove in the middle of his back sent Jensen stumbling off the running board, down to the concrete floor.

"Weis, what the hell are you doing?" he demanded.

"Same as you, but for different reasons. There's aliens out there on the mountain, that's what you saw and heard, and they're controlling the settlers, twisting their memories till they believe what they want! I got me some of Landing's explosives, and I aim to stop it, not warn them we've found out the truth!"

"Will you listen to yourself, Weis? Aliens? Mind control? That's wild talk. We've thirteen colonies now, and not one world has had any life more intelligent than a mouse on it!"

"They made you forget, Jensen, but they couldn't wipe my memories." Weis gave a short, bitter laugh and reached up to touch the scar that ran from one temple, across his forehead and out of sight into his cropped hair. "See, I got lucky. A rock hit me on the head, made it impossible for them to mess with my mind. As for that woman, I wouldn't get too cozy with her; the rest of the village is afraid of her, she's important to them."

"Don't be a fool, Weis. Even if what you say is true, you can't possibly kill all of them! At worst you'll start a war . . ."

Avana pushed past him. "Weis, you're wrong," she said, taking a few slow steps toward the shuttle. "It's not what you think. There's no mind control, no danger to us."

"Come any closer and I'll shoot you," said Weis, pointing the gun at her.

"You don't know the whole truth," she began, taking another step.

"Avana, no!" said Jensen, lurching forward for her as Weis let off a warning shot.

It hit the concrete just in front of her as he grasped her around the waist and swung her out of the line of fire. He felt her stiffen in shock, then relax back against him.

"Enough talk! I'm outta here!" snarled Weis, stepping back and closing the shuttle door.

"You OK?" Jensen demanded as he put her down, then dragged her with him to the back of the hanger, well clear of the shuttle's exhausts.

"Yes."

"He's lost it," he muttered, pushing her down behind some packing crates. "That blow to the head did some serious damage."

The shuttle's engines roared into life, drowning out anything else he was going to say.

He leaned over her, putting his mouth to her ear. "Now what? This is going to wake the whole damned village."

The shuttle rose into the air, the whine of the engines getting louder and louder until suddenly it shot forward.

Jensen flung himself of top of Avana as they heard it crashing its way through the closed doors. Splinters of wood rained down around them.

"Can you get off me now?"

Hearing the pain in her voice, hurriedly he rolled off her. "You sure you're all right?" he asked, helping her up.

"I'm fine, just landed awkwardly," she said, but there was a drawn look about her face he didn't like.

"We need to stop him," she said. "The villagers will help us now; they wouldn't have before."

"You don't seriously believe there are aliens out there, do you?"

She motioned him to silence, stepping out from behind the crates as the first of the villagers rushed in, half-dressed and brandishing a shotgun. Jensen joined her, determined that whatever happened, she'd not face it alone. He recognized Nolan, the leader of the small colony, instantly.

"Is this your doing, Avana?" Nolan demanded, coming to an abrupt stop when he saw them. "What's he doing here?"

"It was Weis, Nolan. He was hiding in the shuttle. He's taken explosives . . . gone looking for . . . them." Her voice trailed off as the hangar began to fill with more of the angry colonists.

"You had to tell him, didn't you?" demanded the woman next to Nolan. "Just had to meddle again!"

"I told him nothing except his leg was healed."

"Be quiet, Kate," said Nolan, lowering his gun. "You're missing what's important here. Weis has gone hunting them with explosives."

"We have to warn them. Jensen is taking me," Avana said.

"You were going there anyway," accused Kate. "That's why you let him out!"

"She's been Called again, hasn't she?" said another woman from the rear of the small group. "I told you not to stop her going last time, Nolan, but you had to listen to Kate!"

"No one wanted to take her, Mary, you know that," muttered one of the men.

"I'm not going near them again, and you can't blame me seeing as no one else volunteered," said his neighbor.

Jensen was growing angrier by the minute as he listened to them degenerate into squabbles.

"It wasn't my decision," said Nolan, stung by the accusation. "You all voted for it at the town meeting!"

"I warned you there'd be trouble," said Mary, pulling her fur jacket tighter around her and pushing to the front. "Not only did you break the agreement, but you stopped Avana from going to them. You, Llew, have no backbone!" she said, turning on the youth. "They've never done us harm, only helped us. Now this Weis is going to try and destroy them. Just what do you think they'll do about that?"

"I have to go now," said Avana, trying to pitch her voice to carry over those of the villagers. "I need to warn them."

"Just a goddam minute!" said Jensen, raising his voice so it did drown them all out. "I want to know what the hell's going on here! Who's this *them* you keep talking about, for starters?"

Silence fell abruptly as they turned to face him, suddenly remembering his presence.

"Well?" he demanded again when no one answered.

"The yukitenshi," said someone quietly from the rear of the group.

"That's Company talk," another said derisively.

"Snow Angels, the Sidhe, Children of Danu, call them what you will," said Mary. "They live up in the mountains and mostly keep to themselves, thanks to Avana. They don't scare me! I'm not forgetting to keep the old ways!" She glowered around at the dozen people gathered in the hangar.

"Snow angels? The Sidhe?" said Jensen, more confused than before.

"Llew, Conner, get the shuttle fueled up and ready to go," said Nolan abruptly. "You're right, Mary, we should never have stopped Avana from going the last time they Called her. Fetch food for them, three days' worth."

"Mark my words, Nolan, you'll live to regret this!" said Kate. "Because it was right for you thirty years ago doesn't mean it is for us younger ones! Let him kill them . . ."

"Come with me, Kate," said Mary firmly, grasping the younger woman by the arm and forcefully escorting her from the hangar.

Nelson turned back to Jensen and Avana. "Is there anything else you need? There's comm units and face masks as well as ropes and other rescue gear on board."

"A med kit, please," Avana said. "And sensible winter gear for Jensen. I had some for him in the other shuttle."

Jensen watched the sudden activity, aware of a dull ache beginning behind his eyes. Doggedly he kept focused on the one fact that currently posed the most danger.

"You're serious, aren't you? There really are indigenous natives on Kogarashi."

Nolan looked questioningly at Avana.

"He's forgotten, like the others did," she confirmed. "We call it Danu, Jensen."

"We don't rightly know what they are, Jensen, but they do belong here," said Nolan.

"Why didn't you tell the Company? These are the first aliens we've ever come across! We made laws against colonizing a world that's already inhabited by intelligent life!"

"We didn't know at first, and by the time we did, it was too late. The Company had sunk too much into setting up our colony. Besides, what do we tell them? I told you, we don't know what manner of beings they are." Nolan glanced obliquely at Avana. "You'll understand when you see them."

"How do you know these are the first aliens mankind has met?" said Avana. "None of us trusted the Company enough to tell them."

"Colonization is a ruthless business, Jensen, you should know that."

He did, but to think that any company would commit genocide just to remain on a colony world . . .

"I'll need weapons," he said tiredly, rubbing his aching temples. "For Avana too. Weis isn't going to be easily stopped."

"We aren't aiming to stop him directly," Avana said. "We need to warn them first. Our advantage is he doesn't know where they live, and I do. Nolan, I'm going to wait inside the shuttle. Don't let him do any lifting. That leg of his may be healed but it's still weak."

The half-hour it took to get them fueled and provisioned was revealing for Jensen—what the colonists refused to say about Avana and the aliens told him as much as what they did. He taxied out into the moonlight, then began to accelerate away from the village.

"What's that?" he asked as they flew over a ring of small boulders just to the west of the village. "A Zen garden?"

"You could say that. It's the ring."

"Any painkillers in your medicine kit? I've got the mother and father of all headaches," he asked as a stab of pain made him wince.

Avana stirred. "There should be. I'll go look."

"See if you can find something I can eat now," he added, checking his bearings on the small nav screen and heading out toward the mountains. "I don't think they fed me much over the last three days. You should have something too—you're looking pale."

Cramped though the bridge section was, there was a reasonable-sized cargo area behind them. As he listened to Avana rifling through the various bags that had been stowed there, he began to relax a little for the first time that night. On the Doppler screen, it showed exactly what Nolan had predicted—clear weather across the plains and into the lower foothills; then they'd hit a storm worse than the one that had caused him and Weis to crash. He planned to land and weather it out, just as Weis would be forced to do.

She came back, sitting down in her seat and stowing the drinks in the armrest console before handing him a couple of pills. When he'd taken them, she held out a regulation non-spill mug.

He was surprised to find it was hot coffee.

"We have a small coffee plantation on the foothills," she said, handing him a sandwich, then buckling herself in.

"I think it's time you told me our exact destination," he said before taking a bite.

"It's close to where you were before—the small valley just off the plateau. There are some caves there. You must have seen them on your scans."

"Yeah, Weis wanted a good look at them. Is that where your aliens live?"

"It's the entrance, yes. I know about the blizzard, but get us as close as you can before stopping."

"What are they like?" he asked, glancing over at her as she nibbled on a granola bar.

"You know what they're like. You saw them."

"If I did, I don't remember, so humor me and tell me."

"Do you know what the Sidhe are?"

"Stop answering me with a question every time I ask you something! You promised me answers, Avana."

"I am answering you," she said, taking a mouthful of her drink. "Do you know what the Sidhe are?"

"Mary told me something of them."

"They're supposed to be one of the original inhabitants of Eire, or Ireland. It was said they were angels, fallen ones, too good to go to hell and too mischievous to go to heaven. A few besides me have seen them, but all they see is a ghost of what they truly are—a flicker that is hardly there."

"And you can communicate with them?"

She gave him a long look. "They communicate with me, but I am learning."

"Doesn't sound very friendly."

She smiled. "You'll see."

"Is it because of them that you all refused to map the Splitback and scan it for minerals?"

"Who said we refused? We lost the scanning equipment when we lost the shuttle."

"You're sure about that?"

"Yes. I'm tired, Jensen. Let me rest a while," she said, folding her arms across her lap and shutting her eyes.

"You were on that shuttle, weren't you?"

"What makes you think that? Do you really think I am that old?"

"It's the only way you could have met these Snow Angels."

She said nothing for a minute or two then murmured, "Jensen, don't ask me a question unless you really want to know the answer."

He glanced over at her again, seeing the high cheekbones, the slightly upturned nose, and the pale braid lying against the dark fur of the jacket, comparing her to Mary. There *was* no comparison—how could he have thought they were the same age?

"Who rescued us, Avana? Was it them or your people?" he asked suddenly.

"Later, when we land, I'll tell you," she said.

"It was them, wasn't it?" he demanded, feeling his blood run cold, but Avana said nothing, just lay there, her breathing slowing as she slept.

* * *

Her sleep was not restful. Jensen watched as she moved fretfully, muttering words that even his good hearing couldn't identify. They were deep in the storm now, almost at the caves when she suddenly sat bolt upright.

"Hoshi! The mountain! Watch out!"

"What the hell?" he muttered, adrenaline rushing through his system as he pulled the scouter back on course. He glanced at her, seeing her staring out the windshield, eyes wide open in terror.

"Avana." Attention still on the nav screen and looking ahead of them, he reached across for her shoulder, shaking her gently. "Wake up, Avana."

She shuddered, blinked, then looked around her, hand reaching up to grasp his as her gaze came to rest on him. "I'm sorry, I had a bad dream."

"You sure did. It aged me ten years at least," he said, trying to make light of it as he squeezed her hand comfortingly before returning his to the controls.

He risked a glance at her, seeing how gray her complexion had become as she began to shiver uncontrollably. With a sinking feeling in the pit of his stomach, he realized she was in shock.

"Dammit, Avana! Weis shot you, didn't he? Don't try to deny it!" he said as she opened her mouth to speak. "Why the hell didn't you tell me?"

"You wouldn't have brought me and I had to come."

"Your life is more important than this!"

"The whole colony depends on me. I have to go— they Called me," she said, wiping her sleeve across her sweating forehead. "It's only a flesh wound."

He swore, volubly and descriptively, cursing himself most of all for missing the signs she'd been hit. "Don't lie to me, girl! I know the symptoms. Where did he hit you and how bad is it?" he demanded, his attention now torn between her and piloting the craft through the rapidly worsening snow storm.

"My arm, and I don't know how bad," she said, her voice quavering a little. "I put a pressure bandage on it when I came into the shuttle."

On the scanner, he saw a flat area ahead and changed course for it. "I'm taking the shuttle down. You need treatment now, Avana."

She sat forward, looking at his nav screen. "Just a bit further, please," she said. "We're almost there. They'll heal me. I only need to . . ."

"No!" he snarled, starting to descend. "I'm not risking your life!"

"Jensen, please," she whispered, sitting back and hunching herself around her injured arm. "I've had worse, trust me."

"No, dammit! You're the only sane thing on this godforsaken planet!"

The landing was not one of the smoothest; he had to break hard on the maneuver jets as the shuttle began to skid on the glassy surface, but they were down and safe.

"It's too dangerous here, Jensen! My blood will bring them to us! Weis could be nearby . . ."

"Blood? Great, they're vampires as well," he muttered, releasing his harness and instantly going to her side.

She laughed faintly as he undid her harness and scooped her into his arms. "Not vampires. It's the life-energy in blood—makes it easier for them to find me in a blizzard."

He carried her to the cargo area, sitting her down on one of the crates secured there, resting her back against the hull. "Where's the med kit?" he demanded, shaking her as her eyes began to close.

"Don't you dare fall asleep on me, Avana!" he said harshly.

Her eyes flicked open and she looked around. "In the bag there," she said, pointing to one secured against the opposite bulkhead.

He fetched it, then began to strip her out of her jacket. Now he could see the burned hole on the inner side of her sleeve. Flinging her jacket around her shoulders, he let her lean back again. Squatting beside her, he lifted her injured arm.

She'd pushed her sweater sleeve up before placing the pressure pad over the wound. Thankfully it had acted as a basic tourniquet, but she'd still lost a lot of blood. Reaching for a fresh pressure pad, he ripped the wrapping off, laying it aside before carefully removing the old one.

The energy blast had clipped her on the inside of her upper arm, vaporizing an area about four inches wide and over an inch deep. Much of it had been cauterized, but there was still a slow seeping of blood and fluids. He thought he saw the glint of bone. Swallowing hard a couple of times, he hastily covered the wound with the new dressing. This was beyond his ability to treat except with the most basic first aid.

"Bad, eh?" she said, watching his face.

"Not good. The beam was wider since it was deflected up at you. Avana, we need to get you back to the settlement," he said, carefully binding the dressing in place. That done, he took the scissors and began cutting through the rolled-up sweater. "You've lost a lot of blood."

"Just take me to the caves, Jensen. They'll heal me. I've had worse, believe me."

"You're too weak . . ."

"Jensen, *listen* to me! We have to go on. If Weis

succeeds, they'll come for the colony, especially after they prevented me from going last time I was Called. There's energy drinks in the pack where the med kit was. Help me back to my seat and give me one of them," she said, getting unsteadily to her feet. "It'll keep me going till we reach them. Trust me—trust them."

He got to his feet, reaching out to catch her jacket as it slipped from her shoulders.

"This will be the death of you, Avana, and I don't want that," he said, helping her put the jacket back on. "Why should I trust them?"

"Because they've saved you from death already, Jensen, as once they did for me. And they've Called you—the first time they've ever asked to meet anyone but me," she said, her hand touching his cheek.

Memories began to return then, of a fleeting, feather-light, bitterly cold touch on his cheek, of humanoid shapes fluttering in the blizzard, crying out in voices as haunting as those of the whales; of being drawn from the avalanche and clasped firmly in strong arms, while lips as cold as ice touched his, breathing life and health back into a body wracked by pain.

He pulled her close, almost crushing her to him in his need to know what was real. She was his touch-stone, his only anchor on this alien world.

"You've remembered," she whispered, her lips brushing his. "They saved you, healed you, then brought you to the ring at Landing for us to find. Take me to them, Jensen. We're closer to them than Landing."

"I'll take you, but don't you die on me, Avana!" he said, covering her face in kisses, driving back the memories of the coldness with her warmth. "Promise not to leave me," he said, reluctantly letting go of her to carry her back to her seat.

She chuckled. "I'll do my best." She stiffened suddenly, grasping hold of his arm. "They're here! Take me to the door and open it!"

He hesitated, scared to the depths of his soul, yet thankful at the same time. Through the windshield, he saw movement, white shapes within the swirling snow, and heard again their plaintive song. Turning, he walked to the door, letting her reach out to open it.

Heart racing, he watched it slide back, fearful of what it would reveal. Nothing waited for them, only the darkness and the snow. It took all his courage to step out of the shuttle and down onto the icy ground.

A sudden downdraft of air and snow swirled into his face, temporarily blinding him. He heard the sound of large wings beating the air, and felt the weight of Avana in his arms lessening.

"No!" he cried out, trying to grasp her tighter, blinking furiously to clear his vision. "She's mine, not yours! You can't have her!"

Then she, and the sound of the wings, were gone.

Frantically, he searched the darkness for her. "Avana!"

Suddenly one of them stood not ten feet from him. She was everything Avana had said they were—tall and slim, her long hair and skin as pale as the snow around them, and beautiful in a way that was truly unearthly. The more he stared at her, the more she seemed to elude his senses. Her whole body shimmered and flickered as if she was not quite there. She stepped toward him, cocking her head on one side, gesturing to him. He couldn't pretend not to understand; the gesture for *Come* was universal.

"Oh my God, you're real," he muttered, backing off until he felt the hull of the shuttle behind him.

Come. This time he heard it inside his head. The mental voice was as unearthly as the song had been.

She came closer, her steps slow and measured, her body swaying elegantly. With another shock, he realized she was naked save for a simple short kilt.

He closed his eyes, only opening them when he felt her hands encircle his waist. Vertical slitted eyes of pale gray gazed back at him as she drew him close against her cool body. She might look insubstantial, but she was real.

A shadow fell over them and the sound of the slow beat of wings filled his ears. He felt his feet leaving contact with the ground and clutched her desperately around the waist. He'd barely time to register that she was covered in a soft fur before the cold winter wind was whistling past his face, making his eyes sting. Instinctively he turned his head, finding his face buried, not in fur, but soft, downy feathers.

The wind dropped and all he could hear was the beat of her wings. Risking a glance, by the faint luminesence that seemed to surround her, he saw they were traversing a wide tunnel.

A shot rang out; she faltered, her wing-beats becoming irregular.

"Weis, no!" he yelled, clutching her more tightly as her flight became erratic. "Godamnit! They're friendly!"

Suddenly the cavern was filled with the sound of many wings and harsh singsong calls. Strong male hands grasped him, ripping him from her embrace, talons jabbing uncomfortably through the hide of his jacket into him. He was flown to the other side, then dropped unceremoniously to the ground.

Scrambling to his feet, he looked up. Overhead, the cavern was a shifting mass of glowing, flickering white shapes, weaving between each other and calling out with harsh, singsong cries of anger.

"He has explosives!" he yelled. "Avana and I, we came to warn you!"

The calls died down to a sound like the faint buzzing of angry bees.

He took the life of one of us. The voice, its tone harsh even inside his mind, came from behind him. *Injured our Envoy, Avana. He must suffer for this. Be grateful you were Called to be her mate.*

He spun around, finding himself facing a group of four aliens, one of whom held Avana. He tried to move, to call out to her, but something, or someone, held him motionless.

Once again he felt the downdraft of wings beating on his face as the fallen one was gently laid at the feet of the tallest.

Jensen stared at the body. Now that she was dead, the glowing aura that had suffused her in life was gone, as was the flickering quality. Now he could see her clearly. There were no wings, and the opalescent feathers that covered her whole body were now a dull, lifeless gray. Anger welled up in him for the loss of her life, and Weis's senseless violence.

She will rest where she fell, as is our way, said the tall one, stepping forward and stretching out his hand over her lifeless form.

The ground began to tremble, gently at first, then more harshly until a fissure formed under her body and slowly she sank into it. With one last rumble, the gap closed over her.

As he watched, Jensen knew how their scouter had vanished.

Held between two males, Weis was brought forward.

Once more the cries rose in pitch, but from Weis, there was no sound. Released, the burly pilot stood there, as unable to move as Jensen.

You took the gift of life from us and used it to harm our Envoy and kill one of us, said the tall one. *Our rule is a life for a life. Yours is now forfeit.* He gestured to one of those beside him. *Tyril.*

Beyond shock and fear, Jensen watched as Tyril stepped forward and stood in front of Weis. Wings that were not wings unfurled and gradually, the pearly white glow that surrounded Tyril faded, grew darker until his wings were shot with an angry dark red. Then, reaching out, Tyril touched Weis.

The man seemed to crumple, to fold up on himself and shrink until finally he fell to the ground. Jensen felt a shiver of fear course through him: he had no doubt at all that Weis was dead.

What of the village? Tyril demanded, turning back to his leader, wings furling and unfurling in anger. *They broke our agreement, Nephil, kept the Envoy from us!*

Yet here she is, and the Man we Called, sent by them with a warning, Nephil replied.

Then let me visit them, remind them not to neglect the agreement!

I will consider it.

No! Leave the village! They did you no harm! he yelled mentally, praying they could hear him.

Nephil swung his head toward him briefly before turning back to look at the one holding Avana. *Heal our Envoy.*

Jensen watched, helpless, as the one holding Avana bent over her, touching his lips to hers, infusing her with his life force. Gradually, the glow that surrounded him faded, making him appear more solid, until Avana began to stir. Lifting his head, he set Avana down on her feet.

She inclined her head to him. "Thank you, Caer," he heard her say.

Be more careful, little sister. You have great value to me.

"I'll try, Caer."

Turning to the leader, she once again bowed her head. "Thank you, Lord Nephil, for coming to our aid."

Nephil gestured to his left and as she moved there, Jensen found himself staggering forward as whatever compulsion had held him motionless was suddenly lifted. He ran to her side, anxious to know for himself that she was well again.

"I'm fine," she said, taking his hand.

Caer, take them within. I will decide the fate of the Landers now.

"Don't harm them," she said as Caer joined them. "They only prevented me leaving out of fear for my safety."

Tyril frowned, his aura darkening slightly in anger. *This is not your concern. Go with Caer. They must be taught to value what you sacrifice for their benefit.*

"They sent us to warn you . . ." Jensen began.

Go!

Avana pulled him close and whispered, "It's not wise to argue with him in front of his people."

"But the colonists . . ."

"Will survive," she said as they followed Caer out of the cavern and down the adjacent tunnel. "Danu's Children are not fools. They each depend on the other. It just takes one visit each generation for Landing to realize it's better to keep the agreement."

"What's this agreement you all keep taking about?" In the distance ahead he could see a faint glow and already the air was beginning to feel warmer.

"The first year we were here, they stole some of our cattle and developed a liking for beef. Now, in return for leaving them alone, we leave some milk and cheese out for them, and give them the occasional side of beef. They also keep an eye on our herd beasts grazing on the lower slopes. They're omnivores like us and eat mainly the mountain deer and goat-like creatures native to Danu. I also teach them about our art and literature in exchange for learning about them. Primarily, they're teaching me how to heal. The headache pills I gave you earlier were one of their recipes."

"Why am I here?"

You were Called, as she was. You can learn our ways and be a mate for her, said Caer.

Avana's face flushed and she looked away from him.

"You were one of the original settlers, weren't you?" he asked, choosing for both their sakes to ignore what Caer had said.

"Why do you need to know?"

"A question isn't an answer."

"Yes, I was. I was the only survivor of the first shuttle crash. They hadn't had chance to meet any of us till then, so I was brought here to be healed. They soon realized I could understand them and began to exchange learning with me. Time isn't the same inside the mountain, Jensen. I think it's because they don't quite live in the same dimension as us. What was weeks for me, when I went back to Landing, had been years there."

He digested this for a few minutes. "Then the reason my leg was healed was because I was here."

"You were missing for three months. That's why Nolan told the *Deigon* you were dead. We thought you were."

"And being Called?"

"Means staying with them for some time as students, and helping me find a way to stop the Company from finding out about them."

He glanced at Caer pacing elegantly beside them, imagining how the Company would want to either exploit these people, or anger them to the point that war ensued. Beings with mental powers, access to a new dimension where time ran at a different rate from the world outside; he could imagine how salable a commodity this would be for any company, let alone theirs.

"Do they know what's at stake?" he asked, looping his arm around her waist and drawing her in against his side.

"Oh yes. That's why they call me their Envoy, Jensen. They're preparing me—us," she amended, "to speak for them and defend their rights."

"Sounds to me like a good way to spend the next ten years."

MY FATHER, THE POPSICLE

Annie Reed

Jodi thought she was an orphan until one sweltering Thursday night in late June when she received *The Letter* from Billingsly, Wendham & Owens, attorneys at law.

That's how she always thought of it after that. *The Letter*. Wasn't that how you were supposed to think about things that changed your life? All capitalized and important?

At first she thought it was a joke. She'd just worked a double shift at Hot Dog on a Stick in the new mall south of town. She was dead tired, and sick of the smell of lemons, corn dog batter, and hot grease. Her head hurt from where she had to pull her hair up under that stupid striped hat, her shoulders ached from all the fresh lemonade she had to mix, and to top it all off, the air conditioning had been out on the bus ride home. To say the bus had been fragrant was the understatement of the century. She was in no mood for jokes. Her roommate Harry had a pretty twisted sense of humor. A fake letter from an attorney was just his style, but tonight it wasn't funny.

"I ought to rip him a new one," Jodi muttered as

she opened her front door. "Hear that, Harry?" she said to her empty apartment. "I ought to rip you a new one."

Not that Harry was home yet. Harry worked as a bartender at the only gay club in town, and tonight he was on swing shift. Whether he could hear her or not, after a day spent swallowing the snappy comebacks she wanted to make to clueless customers whose IQ wasn't much higher than the hot dogs they ate, muttering about Harry's lack of humor sure as hell made her feel better.

Still, the envelope did look kind of authentic. Hmmm. . . .

Jodi dropped her keys and the rest of the mail on the coffee table. It was all junk mail flyers and offers for credit cards neither one of them could afford, so it didn't much matter where she left it. She plopped down on the couch she'd rescued from a secondhand store, slipped off her sensible, style-free shoes so she could stretch her toes into the carpet, and ripped open the envelope.

She skimmed through the introductory stuff. *Dear Ms.* blah-blah-blah *I represent* more blah-blah-blah *bankrupt estate*. The word *assets* caught Jodi's eye, but the word that brought her up short was *father*.

What?

If this was Harry's idea of a joke, it definitely wasn't funny. He knew she had no sense of humor when it came to her family, or lack thereof.

She ended up reading *The Letter* three times in a row, each time with an ever-increasing shakiness in the pit of her stomach, not to mention a growing sense of unreality.

The Letter wasn't the easiest thing to understand. Jodi had managed to finish high school—barely—but there had been no money left after her mother died

for college. She made enough to pay rent and keep
herself fed, but higher education was out of the question. The letter writer sounded like he had degrees up
the wazoo and wrote to impress. *Way* out of Harry's
league. But Jodi did understand enough of the letter
to realize that she'd been wrong. She wasn't an orphan
after all. She did have a father.

He was just frozen solid.

Billingsly, Wendham & Owens, attorneys at law, oc-
cupied the twelfth floor of a fourteen-story office
building of gleaming chrome and glass. It took Jodi
three buses and nearly an hour to get there, and if it
hadn't been for the letter in her purse, she would have
turned around and gone home without even stepping
inside.

Jodi didn't know which was more intimidating—the
building or the idea of meeting with an attorney. Even
when her mother had died, there'd been no attorneys
involved. Jodi's mother hadn't owned much of anything. Jodi just kept paying the rent on their small
apartment until the memories became too much and
she realized she could move somewhere else if she
wanted to. She had no one left to tell her she couldn't.

She rode the elevator to the twelfth floor with three
other women, all dressed far better than Jodi could
afford. She'd worn her best pair of jeans and the only
semi-dressy blouse she owned. She clutched her small
purse as if it might fly away and leave her any minute.

The elevator ride was swift and quiet. No one in
the elevator looked at anyone else, not even covertly
in the mirrored walls. The doors opened directly into a
reception area with a black marbled floor and indirect
lighting. Jodi had to concentrate to keep her voice
from shaking as she gave the receptionist, a girl probably no older than Jodi, the name of the letter writer—
Artemus Owens, Junior, Esq., whatever that meant.

The receptionist took Jodi into a conference room with dark walls, thick burgundy pile carpet, and the same indirect lighting. A huge, dark wood table with a top so polished it looked mirrored dominated the room. High-back, black leather chairs surrounded the table. Jodi felt like she was sinking in black tar when she sat down.

The room was probably meant to soothe clients with an impression of old money, like in some of the movies Jodi had seen, but all it did was remind her of the little chapel in the hospital where her mother had died. Only here the room smelled like stale coffee instead of burning candles.

Mr. Owens didn't keep her waiting long. Jodi had been expecting someone old. Weren't old guys the only ones who got their names on the letterhead and sat around in offices like this? Artemus Owens, Jr., looked like he was thirty—maybe—and he wasn't even wearing a tie. He had dark hair and kind eyes and looked like he could have been a manager at one of the stores in the mall, only nicer. He even shook her hand like she was a grownup.

"I understand you're here about the Cryonomics bankruptcy," he said as he sat down. "What can I do for you?"

"About this letter." Jodi pushed the letter toward him across the glassy surface of the conference table. "I don't get it. Does this mean my father's alive?"

Mr. Owens glanced at the letter, looked up at her. "Well, not exactly 'alive' in the accepted definition of the word. He's been stored at the Cryonomics facility for the last ten years."

Stored? That made her father—her *father*; god, how odd it was to even think that she actually had a father—sound like some unwanted piece of furniture locked away in a storage shed.

"I still don't get it. What does 'stored' mean?"

Mr. Owens tented his fingers on the table in front of him. "You don't know about any of this, do you?"

Jodi shook her head. At least his voice was kind. He didn't make her feel like one of her high school teachers when she'd given a wrong answer in class. "I didn't even know I had a father," she said. Jodi's mom had never mentioned him, not that she wanted to share that gem with a relative stranger.

Mr. Owens pushed a button on the phone and asked someone named Shirley to bring in two bottles of water. "And one of those Cryonomics brochures we have in the file.

"OK, it goes like this," Mr. Owens said to Jodi. "Cryonics is the process of preserving people who are dying so that at some unknown time in the future they can be defrosted when technology exists to cure whatever's wrong with them. Some call it science, others call it desperation. Cryonomics made a business out of it, although not very successfully, as it turned out. The specifics about the process and the company are in the brochure Shirley's bringing in."

Jodi actually knew a little bit about cryonics. She and Harry had Googled Cryonomics, and in turn cryonics, after he'd come home from work.

After she'd whacked him on the arm when he wouldn't stop laughing.

After he'd realized the letter was serious.

"That's . . ." Jodi shook her head. "That's just science fiction. I mean, it was in one of those old television shows my mom used to watch. Nobody really believes that stuff, do they?"

"At the time Cryonomics filed for bankruptcy, they listed twenty-three individuals who'd submitted to the procedure. Your father was one of them."

Twenty-three frozen corpsicles. And here Jodi

thought religious cultists were gullible. Her father had done this? Why hadn't her mother ever told her? Had she even known?

"I didn't know," Jodi said in a small voice.

The conference room door opened, and one of the women from the elevator brought in the water and a thick booklet. Mr. Owens pushed one of the bottles and the booklet across the table to Jodi along with his letter. She started to thank the secretary, but the woman had left the conference room as silently as she came.

"Do you have an attorney?" Mr. Owens asked her. His voice was still kind.

Jodi shook her head. "Do I need one?"

Not that she could afford to hire an attorney. Not on what she made frying corn dogs.

"You might want to look into it. I represent Cryonomics, so I can't represent you. The reason I sent you this letter is to advise you that your father's body, for lack of a better word, the trust fund he set up for its continuing care, and the machinery he's stored in are considered assets. The bankruptcy court views Cryonomics as a high-tech mortuary, essentially. The bankruptcy trustee is going to require Cryonomics to liquidate its assets. Do you understand what that means?"

Jodi understood maybe one word in three. All of a sudden she felt like the dumbest kid in the class.

"Just tell me what I'm supposed to do," she said.

Whether she'd do it or not . . . well, there was something to be said for not having a parent around—a living parent, anyway—to tell her what to do.

"I can't tell you what to do," he said. "That's what you need an attorney for, to help you figure it out. But I will tell you this. Cryonomics is going out of business. Cryonomics has been storing your father's body, but they're not going to be able to do that anymore."

He took a long drink out of his water bottle. Jodi wondered if he did that on purpose, to give her a chance to figure out what he meant. He didn't have to. She got it. This time she knew what he was going to say before he said it.

"You're going to have to figure it out on your own. What to do with your father. Before the court decides for you."

"You mean they'd let him thaw?" Harry said. He shivered, only partly for effect. "That's just disgusting."

Jodi and Harry sat on the couch devouring a half-and-half pizza, Jodi's side black olive and mushrooms, Harry's side sausage and onions. They usually only had pizza once a month, but tonight made twice in one week. Jodi felt the emotional upset of finding out your father was a popsicle in a pressure-controlled tank was a sufficient reason for splurging.

The Cryonomics brochure lay open on the coffee table next to the pizza box. She'd studied it until she thought her brain might explode.

"I don't know what to do," Jodi said. "I mean, it's my father, right? I can't just let him die."

"Technically, you know, he's already dead."

"He didn't think so."

"How can you know that?"

She pointed at the brochure. "Kind of obvious, Captain Oblivious. He must have bought into this whole idea."

It still sounded like a scam to her. Paying someone to store your body in deep freeze after you died just on the off chance that you *might* be cured someday.

Not that California wasn't chock full of odd cults and scam artists ready to prey on the gullible, but this had to top everything Jodi had ever heard about.

Then there was that whole paying thing. As far as Jodi knew, her father had never paid one cent to help support *her*. Help pay her way through college. Help her get the hell out of Hot Dog on a Stick.

And another nasty thought—did he even know she existed?

How could she decide what to do with a complete stranger, even if they were related by blood? Not every father was a *father*. Hers certainly wasn't. Did she really owe him any of this angsting over his future? If he even had a future?

"You could just walk away," Harry said, like he'd read her thoughts.

Harry was weird like that sometimes, like he was the sorta-kinda brother she'd never had. Maybe when you didn't have a family, you created one.

"But then there's all that money," Harry said, voicing the other nasty thought Jodi had been trying to ignore.

Trust fund, Mr. Owens had said.

Jodi might not know legal stuff, but she knew that trust fund meant money. Her father had set up a trust fund to keep himself frozen for as long as it took. That must mean a lot of money.

"I don't think I could walk away from all that money if it was me," Harry said.

Harry didn't walk away from much, actually, but Jodi loved him anyway.

"It might not be anything," Jodi said. "The company is going bankrupt. That means they're not making any money. Maybe he didn't leave enough."

Harry ate another bite of pizza. "Only one way to find out," he said around a mouthful of sausage.

Jodi put her piece of pizza back down in the box. "I'm not going back to that lawyer." Mr. Owens might have been an okay guy, but she still felt like he'd talked down to her at the end, and she wasn't about to go back.

"So don't," Harry said. "Listen. He told you the company listed the trust as an asset, right? Well, if it's listed, that means it's got to be part of the court's records. All that stuff's public record."

Harry had dated a reporter for the local newspaper a few months ago. The guy had tried to impress Harry with how important his job was, but it turned out all he did was report births, deaths, court filings, and an occasional human interest story so dull it usually put Harry to sleep. But Harry had learned more about how the court system worked than Jodi ever would. What would it hurt to look? At least then she'd have some idea what, besides her father the popsicle, was at stake.

"You feel like driving me up there?" she asked.

Harry patted her on the arm. "That's my good girl," he said, and finished off the last of his slice of pizza.

Jodi just looked at hers.

My good girl.

Wasn't that what a father was supposed to say?

The bankruptcy court was in one of the crumbling old buildings downtown, one complete with marble columns covered in decades of pigeon droppings, not that far from the law offices of Billingsly, Wendham & Owens. Jodi felt a little more self-assured this time venturing into the world populated by lawyers. Maybe because she had Harry with her, and he'd actually worn what he called his straight clothes—khaki slacks, a navy silk polo shirt, and freshly polished loafers. Nothing like blending in with the natives.

Jodi let Harry guide her through the maze of room after room of files and paperwork. Harry explained that most of the documents were on computer, but there was a per-page charge for even looking at the files online. This was supposed to save the court staff from wasting time dealing with paper files and the public. But Harry just had to flirt with one of the clerks, a pretty girl he had no interest in, to get her to bring the appropriate file for his "sister" to look at.

"Just one of my many useful bartending skills," Harry whispered to Jodi after the clerk left with a little giggle.

It took a while for them to find the right document in the huge Cryonomics bankruptcy file. If Mr. Owens was getting paid by the word, he was making a mint on this case.

After forty-five minutes of diligent reading, Jodi finally saw the name that had been in Mr. Owens's letter—Andrew Sommersby. Her father's name. Jodi hadn't even known his name until she read it in *The Letter*. Now here it was again in an official court document. Jodi's last name was Carnahan. Her mother's name.

"Wow," Jodi said. "He's really there."

She realized that up until this moment, she'd still thought that this was some kind of big joke. But here it was, in the court's own file. She didn't think anyone played jokes with a court.

Her father's name was on a chart with twenty-two other names. Each name listed a date of interment and next of kin. Jodi's name wasn't listed next to her father's, but her mother's was. Someone—maybe the clerk—had handwritten "deceased" next to her mother's name.

"Have you found anything on the trust?" Harry asked.

Jodi shook her head. It had to be here somewhere, right?

Three pages later, Jodi found another chart, this one listing all the trusts. Twenty-three trusts, twenty-three frozen people. None of the trusts was named Sommersby. None of the trusts identified the person it supported. How was she supposed to tell what her father would have named his trust when she didn't know anything at all about Andrew Sommersby?

Jodi scanned the list again, frustrated.

Next to her, Harry let out a low whistle. "My good God, will you look at that? he whispered.

She looked at the column Harry was pointing at, the one she'd been ignoring in her search for the right name. What she saw were rows of numbers. Lots and lots of numbers. Numbers with more zeros than Jodi had ever seen in her life.

She felt the blood drain out of her face.

Her father's trust could be any one of the ones on this page. And any one of these trusts could fund not only four years of college, but probably graduate and post-graduate school too, not to mention a nice house and a car of her own.

Holy shit.

Did this mean she was rich?

Jodi dialed Artemus Owens's phone number from a pay phone in the courthouse lobby. She tried to ignore the way her fingers trembled and her stomach clenched around the soda she'd had in Harry's car.

Harry stood next to her, leaning in to listen.

"About this trust fund," she said once Mr. Owens answered the phone. "Does it belong to Cryonomics?"

She heard Mr. Owens let out a deep breath. "That would depend on the terms of the trust document. You realize I can't advise you."

Jodi rubbed her forehead. She wished her hands would stop trembling. "I know that," she said. "I just need to know whether the whole thing belongs to that company, or whether, you know—" She took her own deep breath. "—it might actually belong to me because he's my father."

There. She said it.

Harry gave her a little hug.

"Figured out how much is at stake, did you?" Mr. Owens asked. He didn't sound upset. In fact, Jodi thought she could almost hear the smile in his voice.

"Yeah," Jodi said. "So, does it?"

She heard a rustle of papers on the other end of the line, then the tapping of computer keys.

"Well, I can tell you this," Mr. Owens said. "It's public record, and you could probably have found out for yourself if you'd kept reading what you've obviously looked at. Cryonomics is only claiming income from the trust as an asset. In other words, the trust earns money, and that income is what the company's been using to maintain your father. The figures are annual estimates, rounded to the nearest dollar."

"Wait." Jodi was having a hard time comprehending what he was saying. "What's on the chart . . . that was only *income*?"

"Yes."

Jodi dropped the phone. She thought Harry might have caught it before it hit the floor, but she couldn't focus on that. All she could see were numbers followed by lots of zeros, and that wasn't even the real number.

Her father must have been a millionaire. At least.

And he'd never provided anything for her mother, or for her.

She walked away from the phone, leaving Harry to deal with Mr. Owens. All of a sudden she was too angry to talk to anyone.

Her father had left her mother to deal with a life of penny-pinching and never having enough to make ends meet. A life of macaroni and cheese dinners, and coupon clipping, and keeping the heat at sixty in the winter just to save on the electric bill.

Jodi knew exactly what she wanted to do.

Let the bastard thaw.

"Calm down," Harry said.

He'd run after her only to find her pacing by the side of his car.

"I want him to die," Jodi said. Apparently too loudly and with way too much venom if the wary look she got from an older couple passing by on the street was any indication. "Do you know what he did to us? How we had to live? While he—what, dreamed about his nice little fantasy where he gets to be resurrected so he can ruin someone else's life?"

Harry opened the car door and herded her inside. She jammed the seatbelt closed, then pounded her fist on the dashboard.

Harry glared at her as he got in the driver's seat. "Just because you've found out your father, the popsicle, is a tightwad, that's—"

"Corpse. He's a corpse who doesn't know it yet."

"Okay. Have it your way. He's a corpse. That still doesn't mean you can take it out on my car."

Jodi took a deep breath. Harry's Mustang Cobra was his pride and joy. Most of his bartending tips went toward his car payments.

"Sorry," Jodi muttered.

"Besides, he's a rich corpse. And you're his only next of kin, right?"

She shrugged. "I guess so. Or at least I'm the only one Mr. Owens could find. But I don't want his money. I don't want anything to do with him."

Harry raised an eyebrow. "Oh, honey, of course you do. Don't be ridiculous. If you didn't want the money, we wouldn't have made this trip, would we?"

She picked at a hole in her jeans instead of answering. This wasn't her best pair. It was her second-best pair, and they weren't supposed to have holes in the legs.

Harry started up the car and pulled into traffic. Jodi sat quietly in the passenger seat trying not to think about anything at all. Couldn't she just go back to the way things were a couple of days ago? At least then she'd been poor but not quite so angry about it. And she didn't have such a big weight on her shoulders. No matter how angry she was at the former Mr. Andrew Sommersby, he still was her father, absent and irresponsible or not.

After a few minutes she looked out the window expecting to see familiar streets on the way back to their apartment. What she saw was an on-ramp to the interstate.

She turned toward Harry. "Where are we going?"

He glanced at her, then went back to watching the traffic.

"It's your day off, right? Well, if you're going to let him thaw, you might want to meet him first," he said.

What?

"Sit back and enjoy the ride," Harry said. "We're going to Cryonomics."

For a high-tech company, the Cryonomics building

looked like little more than a standard warehouse with once-fancy landscaping and a snazzy front office. Jodi could see the resemblance to the lushly depicted building in the company's brochure, but clearly impending bankruptcy had taken a toll on nonessentials. Like watering the lawn.

Or paying for staff.

One harried-looking middle-aged woman looked up from a desk piled high with paperwork when Jodi and Harry walked in the front door. Cardboard packing boxes with open lids surrounded her desk like a fort. She was in the process of shoving papers into a shredder.

"Lawyers frown on that sort of thing," Harry said over the whine of the shredder.

"What?" The woman pushed up her glasses and turned the shredder off, then glanced at the papers in her hand. Understanding dawned on her face. "Oh, this stuff." She waved it at them. "I don't think we need to preserve the office football pool from 1998 for posterity. Amazing the amount of junk you collect over the years."

She put the papers down on top of another stack on her desk. The woman looked sad, Jodi thought, like she was saying goodbye to an old friend. Jodi wondered if she was losing her job too. Probably, if the company was closing.

"Are you from the bankruptcy trustee's office?" the woman asked. "I don't have the final figures for you yet. The judge gave us until next month.

"No," Jodi said. "I'm . . . uh . . ." How to say this. "I'm the daughter of one of your clients. Andrew Sommersby. Your attorney contacted me."

The woman blinked, then she smiled. "I didn't know Andrew had a daughter. I'm Willomina Hardy."

"Jodi Carnahan. Rachel's daughter."

Willomina shook Jodi's hand, and then Harry's. "Excuse the mess," she said. "You're the first relative who's come out to visit. Everyone else has just made arrangements through the mail, or through their lawyers."

"Arrangements?" Jodi asked.

"For transfer of their loved ones to a new facility." Willomina pushed at her glasses again. "That is what you're here for, isn't it? Have you found a new place for your father?"

Jodi shook her head. "I'm sorry, but . . ." She took a deep breath and started again. "I didn't even know I had a father until two days ago."

Willomina put a hand to her chest. The gesture seemed as old-fashioned as her name, and definitely out of place in a cryonics company. "Oh, dear," she said. "Surely your mother told you."

"Jodi's mother passed away several years ago," Harry said. "I don't think she knew about this either."

"Oh dear," Willomina said again.

She stepped around the packing box fort to make her way to a file cabinet. The cabinet was locked. Willomina took a key from around her neck and unlocked it, opened the second file drawer, and took out a large file pocket.

"I'm sure your father put down your mother as next of kin," Willomina said. She rummaged through the folder, found a slim manila file and opened it. She flipped to a page in the back, then nodded her head. "Yes, here it is. Next of kin—Rachel Carnahan. Relation . . . oh." Willomina paused. "Ex-wife. How unusual."

She spent a few more minutes looking through the file. Jodi stood next to Harry, arms wrapped around herself, and waited.

Now that she was here, Jodi was less sure about

pulling the plug on her father. It was one thing to think about it miles away with anger to fuel her decision. It was something else again when faced with the reality of Willomina and her old-fashioned concern.

"Well," Willomina finally said. "Your mother is listed not only as next of kin, but also co-beneficiary of his trust. You say she passed away?"

Jodi nodded.

"Were you appointed her executrix?" Willomina asked.

Jodi frowned. That sounded official. "I don't understand."

"The executrix of her estate, dear. Were you appointed executrix by the court?"

"We didn't have anything. When she died, it was just her and me. No lawyers or courts." Jodi felt small, like she'd felt when it first hit her she was alone in the world. "It was just us."

"Oh, dear."

Willomina took off her glasses. They hung off a chain around her neck, cushioned against her ample breasts.

"Well, I'm no expert at this, but I'd say your mother had quite a lot, actually, when she died. You might need to see a lawyer after all, dear."

Another person telling her to get a lawyer. "And pay him with what?" Jodi asked, frustrated with the whole thing. "I don't have any money!"

"That's not exactly true." Willomina took something else out of the file. "I can give you a copy of the trust document. Have your attorney contact us, and let us know what arrangements you'll like made for your father."

Jodi waited while Willomina made the copies. This was what she wanted, wasn't it? To know?

But it wasn't all she wanted.

"Can I see him?" Jodi asked, her voice soft, barely audible over the sound of the copier.

Willomina frowned at her. "You can't really see him, dear. Our tanks don't have viewing windows. We've always thought it was better if the family remembered their loved ones the way they were. It can be upsetting to see someone after they've been preserved."

"But that's just it. I never met him. I don't have any memories of him."

"You never . . ."

For a minute Jodi thought Willomina was going to say "oh dear" again, but she didn't. Instead she reached into the folder and pulled out a video cassette tape.

"Then I think it's about time you met your father, don't you?"

The viewing room, as Willomina called it, was a small, private theater with four rows of plush seats and a screen only a little bigger than some of the new flat-screen televisions Jodi saw at the mall. Jodi sat alone in a seat in the back row. She'd asked Harry to stay with her, but he said she should meet her father by herself for the first time.

"Next viewing, I'm right there," he said, and he'd gone out the door with Willomina, leaving Jodi alone with a remote control.

She took a deep breath of stale air. Heart pounding, she pushed *Play*.

The screen came alive with a shot of the Cryonomics logo, the same one Jodi had seen on the brochure, followed by a simple white on black title page with her father's name—Andrew Sommersby.

And then there he was.

Jodi was amazed that he looked so young. On

screen, he looked little older than Artemus Owens. Shouldn't a father be old?

Andrew Sommersby had Jodi's straight black hair, her thin face, and the same cleft in her chin boys had always teased her about. He had deep circles under his eyes, and his skin had a pallor to it. Jodi remembered what she'd read about cryonics—everyone who elected to undergo this process had an incurable illness. Her father had recorded this tape when he knew he was dying.

"Hello," the Andrew on the tape said. "I'm Andrew Sommersby. I'm told I have to leave a video record of my wishes just in case someone wants to challenge my election to have myself cryonically preserved. So here's the official part."

He looked down at something, probably a printed form, and read what sounded like a canned statement. Kind of like how Jodi had recited the Pledge of Allegiance in school. She'd said it so many times the words lost their meaning.

"Now, that's over," Andrew said. He looked back up at the camera. "I can't imagine anyone challenging my wishes. Rosie—"

Jodi's breath caught in her throat. Her mother's nickname had been Rosie.

"—you don't even know I'm ill, do you, sweetheart?"

Andrew sighed on tape. It was such a forlorn sound, Jodi felt her chest grow tight. *I'm not going to cry,* she told herself. She never cried. Not anymore.

"I know you'll never see this, but I want to explain a few things to you. Probably more for you than me, but you know how I am. Belt and suspenders, you used to say. Belt and suspenders. That's probably what this is all about, when you get right down to it. Belt and suspenders in the age of technology."

On screen Andrew coughed, a raspy, painful sound. He paused to take a drink of water.

"I wish you could see the future as I see it, Rosie dear, but that was another thing we disagreed on. You always saw the technology of the future as fiction. I saw it as science waiting to happen. Just think of it. All the things we read about, all the things we grew up watching on television together—they're all just waiting to be invented! Can't you feel it? Don't you want to experience that? See it take shape and form and substance? I know I do, but then again, I've always been the dreamer too. Odd combination, a dreamer who's a belt and suspenders guy. But I don't deny I'm an odd duck in a world full of swans.

"I hope you're happy in your life. I've done what you asked when we divorced. I've stayed away from you. I've tried to send you money, but you always send it back. You were a proud woman. Independent as hell, as passionate as a man could ever want."

Jodi felt her cheeks blush. She wondered if she should watch any more of the tape. She almost felt like she was reading a love letter not meant for her. But her father's next words took her breath away.

"I've stayed away from our daughter too, like you asked me. It's the hardest thing I've even done, and there have been many times I've watched her and wanted so desperately to walk up to her and say 'Hello, I'm your father,' but I didn't. I wanted to be a part of her life. I admit a part of me hates you for taking that away from me, but that's how much I love you. You have always been the love of my life. My only regret—*only regret*—in doing this is that you won't be there when I wake up. Maybe my daughter will be, with children of her own. I promise I won't intrude on her life. But a man can want to live to see his grandchildren, don't you think?"

Jodi felt tears prick at her eyes again. On screen, Andrew held his hands out wide.

"If I can't have that," he said, "what have I done all this for? I've amassed a fortune thanks to a bit of ingenuity and good luck, but without living to see my grandchildren, what really have I done?"

Andrew rubbed at his face with one unsteady hand. It took him a minute before he looked back at the camera.

"So here, in my own words, are my wishes. I believe the technology will exist one day, maybe one day soon, to revive me and cure me of the cancer that's invaded my bones. I wish to live to see that day. I want to be around to buy my grandchild a balloon in the park, even if he never knows it was his grandpa, and maybe ride in a car that floats above the ground. I want to see my daughter grow into an old woman, see her happy and healthy and loved as much as I loved my Rosie. And if that's not enough of a last will and testament, I don't know what is."

The camera held on Andrew's face for a moment, and then the screen went black.

Jodi put her head in her hands and cried.

The new apartment was twice the size of Jodi's old place. She missed Harry's techno music and his dirty dishes in the sink. He still came over at least once a week, and they ordered half-and-half pizza for old time's sake. Tonight Harry brought it with him, along with a six-pack of imported beer.

"We're celebrating," he said, hugging Jodi after he put the pizza on her new dining room table.

"It was just an A," she said.

"An A in psychology," Harry said. "When did you ever get an A in any 'ology' class?"

Never. Science had never been her strong suit, but

she'd been unusually motivated the last six months. She had the rest of the year to go before she had to declare a major, but she was seriously leaning toward some sort of bachelor of science degree. She might even go to law school. Wouldn't that be a hoot?

"Picked up your mail," Harry said, dropping it next to the pizza box. The latest issue of *Popular Science* landed on top.

These days Jodi read everything she could about life sciences, particularly any advances in nanotechnology. The people at the Institute for Cryonics told her the best chance for revival of cryonically preserved people was in the area of nanotechnology. Science fiction meets science fact. Given what she knew about her parents, that was about the best way to describe her life.

She'd taken Willomina's advice. She'd left Cryonomics and made an appointment with a lawyer specializing in trusts, shown him the document Willomina had given her, and let him earn his $300 an hour figuring out a way to keep her father in his tank and let her have something of a life for herself.

Jodi's lawyer had earned every bit of his hourly fee. Andrew Sommersby had been transferred to The Institute for Cryonic Research and Studies in southern California, a non-profit foundation, where he was still happily frozen as he wished. Jodi had enrolled in college and kissed Hot Dog on a Stick goodbye.

Harry opened two beers and handed one to Jodi. "What shall we toast to?" he asked.

Clinking bottles to an A seemed kind of lame. Even if it was an A in psychology.

"I've got it," Jodi said.

She touched her bottle to Harry's, the clink of glass loud in her new apartment.

"Here's to giving a little boy a balloon," she said. "And the look on my father's face when he does it."

DESTINY

Julie Hyzy

"I am not building a shuttle," Gran said, irritated.

"No?" I asked with a tiny bit of hope.

"I'm modifying one I have."

She must have seen the look on my face then, because she laid her warm, freckled hand on my arm and winked.

As Gran refilled my iced tea, a breeze kicked up and rushed through my hair. A little bit cool on this otherwise warm afternoon, it made me glance over to Emily, who sat on the whitewashed planking of the porch. Gran had given Emily plenty of cookies to share with the doll perched on one dimpled leg. To give myself opportunity to process Gran's comment, I moved over to Emily to feel her arms. She was warm enough for now.

Back at the table, I took a deep breath. "Tell me more about this modification."

"Now . . . you ask that like you've got a pain somewhere," Gran said, grinning. "Look at you, trying so hard to smile, kinda gritting your teeth, your eyes all worried."

I wanted to argue. But she was right.

Gran grabbed me by both arms and made me look at her. I could feel the strength in those skinny little hands, see it in her bright blue eyes.

"I have a project I'm working on," she began, slowly, the same way she used to explain things when I was five. "And it's something I don't want just anybody to know about."

"But the doctors said . . ."

"Those doctors," she said with a sniff, "think they're so smart. One of them came nosing around here. Can you believe that? Don't they have anything better to do with their time than spy on old ladies?" Gran sat back, shaking her head. "They caught me, too," she said, looking more bemused than angry, "out in the workroom. Had to come up with something, so I told them I was studying sculpture. Ha! Thought I fooled them. Guess not."

"No . . . I guess not . . ."

"Come on then. You're the only one I wanted to show, anyway."

The workroom was a long walk from the house through a dandelion-strewn field. It was slow going, with Emily stopping every few feet to pick up the dried weeds and blow them to the wind. I grabbed her hand to pull her along but Gran bent down and plucked one of her own.

"Make a wish, Emily!" she said. Together, lips pursed, she and Emily scattered their wishes to the wind, and then turned to each other with twin grins of uncomplicated joy. I watched the seeds take wing on the breeze and tried to remember wishes I'd made when I was Emily's age. How many of them hadn't come true?

As we got nearer, Emily noticed humming and pulled me along, eager to see what was making the noise behind the door.

Gran's eyes glittered as she stood before the keypad.

"Are you ready?"

I bit my lip. "Sure."

She tapped in a code on the entry keypad. In answer the door whooshed open. Dust danced, fairy-like, swirling through sun rays that fell in from the skylights above. I watched the motes hover, then land gently on the silver contraption that stood before us.

"Yay!" Emily said, clapping.

Gran hadn't been too far off when she picked sculpture as her cover story. Shiny metal flanges almost obscured my old playhouse. Gramps used to tell me it was a shuttle, and as a child, I'd spent endless hours inside, hoping it could fly me backwards in time so I could meet my parents. Now, graceful curves shaped like twisted flames engulfed the cab and reached skyward. I released the breath I'd been holding as I walked around it, unsure of what it was, now. And yet, something about it . . .

I pointed at the back end. Completely redone, and fitted with jets, wires, conduit. "What's this?" I asked.

"A multiphase conversion catalyst."

"Speak English."

"Your grandfather and I invented this catalyst, years ago." She grinned, rocking back and forth on her heels. "This little dohicky makes it possible to propel the shuttle and its occupants into another dimension." She gave a little half shrug. "Theoretically."

I almost couldn't speak. "This isn't a real shuttle, Gran. This is my playhouse . . . I hoped someday it would be Emily's."

Her eyes were clear, her expression bemused. Not at all what I'd expect from someone clearly losing touch with reality. "I believe this creation has the power to take us exactly where we want to go."

"Us?"

She shrugged. "I'm hoping you'll come with me."

I didn't know what to say for a long time. Finally, all I could do was ask, "Why?"

Gran pointed.

I ran my hand over the hull. Carefully lettered on its side—*Destiny*.

My eyes asked the question; Gran tut-tutted. "Now don't you go thinking that I've gone out of my head. Think about it some, honey. Gramps and I decided long ago that people who really care about each other should be together. But then he died. Too soon." She shook her fist at the sky, "Too soon, you hear me?" She made a funny face then, and I thought she might cry. Instead, she turned with a smile as big as the object before us. "I know he's waiting for me, but he'll have to wait just a little longer because it's a bit more difficult with only one person working."

I didn't know what to say.

Gran wasn't finished. "I'm going to be with your grandpa. We'll be together again, forever, this time."

"But Gran, that means you'll die."

She wagged a finger at me. "Now that's where assumptions'll get you into trouble."

The doctor's diagnosis flashed before my eyes. I tried to mask my reaction, but I knew that Gran had read my mind. She stopped right there and made what I used to call her "mad face."

"You know I'm not crazy," she said.

I must have squirmed, because Gran continued, a bit vexed. "Gramps and I had it all figured out, honey," she said. "Death is just existence in a different dimension."

Then she grinned and grabbed Emily's hand, "How would you like some ice cream?"

*   *   *

"I'm worried about Gran."

Don sat at the kitchen table, head bent, reading. Watching him, I grabbed a mug from the cabinet and banged the door shut a little louder than necessary.

The top of his head moved back and forth as he followed the words on the page before him, and he pushed his too-long brown hair out of his eyes. Don was one of those people who never learned to track the written word without moving his head, a habit that hadn't bothered me years ago. Now, it was one of many that drove me insane.

I closed my eyes for a moment and breathed in the fresh-brewed aroma of the coffee warming the mug in my hands. *Give me strength.* A tentative sip stung as the liquid trailed a path down the back of my throat. The warmth felt good, very good.

Don was fiddling with his bottom lip, squeezing it till it formed a tight "U," and studying a brochure he'd brought home. The same brochure that had been too important for him to put down earlier when Emily stood on tiptoe to give him a kiss goodnight. He'd said, "Uh-huh," and absently patted her brown curly head. "Daddy's busy."

"Don?"

He made eye contact, but his mind remained on the glossy paper in front of him. I could almost see the struggle going on in his head: *Keep reading? Or talk to her?*

Talk won. Barely. His eyes were so glazed that I felt like he *hadn't* stopped reading—that he was still poring over the copy now tattooed on my forehead.

"We gotta get one of these."

"Get one of what?"

"Here," he said, "it's new."

He turned the brochure for me to see, but when I tried to pick it up, Don held a corner, as if it were something very precious and he was afraid to let go. With obvious reluctance, he loosened his grip. "Where's my coffee?" he asked as he stood.

I fluttered my hand upward toward the counter in a vague gesture that after four years of marriage meant *get it yourself.*

Nice brochure. Whatever they were selling, it had to be expensive.

I started to skim, and in a moment, raised my eyes to meet Don's. He was hovering with a huge grin on his face. I gave him my best "you gotta be kidding" look.

The brochure was for Sensavision. The newest toy on the market for grown-ups so bored with the reality of their lives that they looked elsewhere for stimulation. This gizmo boasted a room-size screen with gears and sensors, speakers and cameras, aromabytes and atmospheric enhancers. Stressed? Hedonistic spa programs glittered to life, ready to soothe your troubles away. Ache for excitement? Design your pleasure. Physical, mental, sexual. Unparalleled virtual-sensory experiences guaranteed.

"We can't afford one of these." I said.

"We can, if we borrow from your trust fund."

"No." I said. "Not again. Gramps set that fund up for me years ago, for my future. And what have we done with it? Borrowed so many times I can't count. We need that money for Emily's education. And serious stuff."

"There's plenty there," Don said, stressing the word "plenty." I think his teeth were clenched.

"There won't be at the rate we're going. You bought that hover-camper last year and we've never even used it. I don't think Gramps had campers and

Sensavisions in mind when he put the money away for me."

Don's expression fell. He pulled the paper back to his side of the table with a huff and bent over it again, elbows on the table, face in hands. He started to read again, mouthing the words even as he maintained a pout. With his stubbled pink cheeks pressed firmly into his palms, his mouth was pulled up at the corners showing the bottom half of his teeth. He mumbled something I couldn't hear, then said, "You got what you wanted."

"What did I get?"

Don stopped and with a deliberate movement, turned his eyes upward toward the stairs and then back down at his paper.

It took me a moment. "Emily?" I asked. "You didn't want the baby?"

"Didn't say that. Just saying you wanted it more," he said, not meeting my eyes. "And I want this more." Hitting the brochure with his finger for emphasis, he caused a wrinkle. He smoothed out the paper with care.

A long minute passed.

When he did look up, he grinned. "They take credit."

Dr. Andrews called me again Monday. Grin missed another appointment.

I agreed to talk to her.

"My aches and pains are my own," Gran said when I tried. "I can handle them. A few visits with those pill peddlers and I'll be ready to pull the plug myself."

"Gran," I reminded her, "you're not hooked up to anything."

"Not yet." She wiggled a finger at me, "But there's a reason behind the expression 'doctoring up.' They want to change me. Or worse, to put me away. And I won't have it."

The Triage Trio, as Gran so eloquently called them, kept in contact with me. They asked that I report to them anything strange in Gran's behavior, any indication that it was time to take action.

"What kind of action?" I'd asked.

Their answers made me cringe. Maybe a cranial implant would do the trick, maybe a short admittance to a holo-home. Maybe permanent admittance. They spent lots of time singing the praises of one particular holo-home. The best in the business and, after all, isn't that what Gran deserved? This place, they insisted, would be virtually indistinguishable from her current home. And virtual commitment was their preferred method of treatment. She'll love it, they said. Guaranteed.

But would the holo-emitters be able to capture the sun on the hyacinths? I wanted to know. The hyacinths were Gran's favorite.

They suggested I visit the place, to feel better about sending her there.

They'd done their homework: I had to give them that.

Emily wiggled out of my arms and ran through the holographic house, calling, "Gannie!"

"She's not here, honey," I said. Yet.

How, I asked, had they managed the detail? The picture I'd painted when I was five was there, the awards Gran had won were there, even the smell of the baking cookies that permeated the room. Yes. They'd gotten that right.

Casual but prim, the woman in charge of admissions smiled, showing perfectly straight white teeth. Her nose crinkled like a ferret's. "There's no rush, you know. We can keep your grandmother's house on our digital file indefinitely. We want you to be comfortable with your decision."

"How did you do this?" My mouth was open, but I was too overwhelmed to be embarrassed.

"We sent an operative to her home," she stage-whispered, though only Emily and I were there, "posing as a realtor needing information for a neighbor. Took digigraphs of the whole house. Did we get it right?"

She giggled, knowing full well that my answer was, yes, perfectly.

So why did I feel like crying?

Safely tucked in bed by eight o'clock, Emily went right to sleep. I poured myself a cup of tea and sat down to read, thinking that a good book would help me relax. When Don walked in moments later, I was surprised.

"You're home early."

"Yep."

Don always went straight to bed or sat in front of the teleview when he got home. Right now he was standing in the family room doorway with his hands behind his back.

He'd gotten a haircut.

"These are for you," he said all in a rush, and thrust a bouquet of roses at me.

"But . . ."

"Happy anniversary."

"Don," I said, taking the flowers, "our anniversary was in May."

"I know that. But remember how hurt you were that I forgot?"

I didn't remember being hurt in the least. He'd forgotten every anniversary except the first one, and frankly, I'd gotten used to it.

He knelt before me and took my hands in his. Too startled to think, I let him. He was still good-looking. His brown eyes twinkled and his mouth curved into the smile that I fell in love with so many years ago.

Encouraged, he took my book, closed it, and sat next to me. Tentative, his fingers stroked my forearms with light touches, moving upward in slow circles. He cupped my chin and kissed me, softly. My eyes sought his as we parted. What could have caused this change?

He pushed my hair behind one ear and pulled me close. "Tell me what's new with you and Emily," he said.

And so, with my head on his shoulder, I told him about the doctors and their diagnosis, and worries about Gran. I left out the part about the shuttle, which was tricky, but I sensed that he wasn't analyzing my story too thoroughly anyway, probably because there was so much to catch up on.

We sat there for a long time and I talked. It felt wonderful. I turned to look at him. That sparkle in his eyes was what did it for me. I leaned forward and kissed him on the lips, happy to feel the tingle again. The tingle I'd thought was gone for good.

When I described my visit to the holo-home, Don started to ask questions. Yes, it looked just like Gran's house. Sure, she could have an outdoor and an indoor world. She could even plant flowers. Could she change the program? No. That would be up to me. The goal was to make her feel as though she was truly at home and not in an artificial environment. State of the art? Absolutely. Expensive, too.

He made a passing comment about wanting to see

this holo-home, and in my naivete, I jumped at the suggestion.

"That would be great, Don. You have no idea what it would mean to me to have you see it too. I mean," I shook my head, my hands making helpless gestures, "it just doesn't seem right to send Gran to one of those places. You know?"

I should have known better.

Don grinned. "Yeah," he said, "I would love to see one of those things. They're supposed to be just like that Sensavision I want, only better."

"Sensavision."

"Now that you got your chance to talk, I thought maybe I could tell you some more about the Sensavision." He reached into his back pocket, displacing me from his shoulder, and pulled out another brochure, different than the one we'd argued over. "You're gonna love it, I just know."

I was dumbfounded. He continued, oblivious. "Y'see what a nice time we had tonight, with me home? I'd be home *every night* if we had one of these. Wouldn't you like that?"

Sitting up, I grabbed the flowers. "Is that what this is all about? You trying to look like a sweet and thoughtful husband so you could romance me into buying one of those?"

His eyes told me he was confused by the question. But his shrug told me more.

I threw the flowers to the floor. "You fooled me. I'll give you that. Here," I went to the banking console and inputted the code that transferred funds from my trust account into a debit disk. He watched me, the whole time, his eyes alert, not contrite. I waved the silver disk at him. "Buy the stupid thing. But don't ever pull a stunt like this again."

*   *   *

The next day we sat in Gran's kitchen.

Emily sat at my feet, and I sighed with pleasure. For the past hour, she'd been pressing Gran's door chimes over and over. Programmed to play Emily's favorite song, "Whatsa Whatsa," they'd been the hit of the morning. I was relieved she'd finally gotten bored with the game.

Gran sat down next to me, "So. What are you going to do about it?"

I bit my lip. Complaints about Don had just fallen out of my mouth. I usually tried to keep marital discord safely under wraps, but today something had snapped. And now Gran knew it all.

"Marry in haste, repent at leisure, isn't that how it goes?" I asked. I was kind of kidding, kind of not.

Gran snorted. "I married your grandfather knowing him only two months," she said, her blue eyes telling me an important point was about to follow. "And a finer man, a better lover, there never was."

Settling in for a "talk," Gran continued. "We knew. We both knew that no matter how many years we had together, no matter how many thousands—no—millions of moments we had—they were never going to be enough. A lifetime together was just going to be the start. And we knew that right off."

She looked at me. "So it isn't that you married young, or quick, honey. It's that you married someone who couldn't make you the center of his world." Offering me her ever-present cookies, she added, "I'd move on, if I were you."

I hadn't expected that. I took a pink sprinkled cookie from the plate, even though I didn't want one. "What about Emily?" I asked, "She deserves to have a father." I looked over at my daughter, singing to her doll, crumbs covering both their faces.

"You think Don's the best one for the job?"

There it was. "Why didn't you say anything before?"

"No one could have talked me out of marrying Edwin. They had no right. If you would've asked, I would've given my opinion. But you didn't, so I kept my mouth shut."

Not for the first time since my consultation with the doctors did I question *their* sanity. Gran was the most lucid person I knew. I needed Gran's company. I craved her advice, her insight. These were not the rantings of a crazy woman.

If it weren't for that shuttle thing.

She handed Emily a photo imager just like the one she'd let me play with when I was little. "Take lots of pictures for Grannie, Emily." Then she dug into her pants pocket. "Here," she said.

It was a debit disk.

I didn't understand.

"Take it." She shook it a little, tapping my arm. "There's enough here to cover what you took from your trust. And then some."

"But . . ."

"I don't need money where I'm going." She grinned and sipped her iced tea.

"Don?"

He nodded, his eyes glazed, fastened in rapt attention to the scene playing out on the Sensavision before him. "Oh!" he said. "Ah!"

Leaning in the doorway, I watched him.

The Sensavision, nine feet tall and twelve feet wide, took up nearly an entire wall of our family room.

Though it stood two-dimensional, Don was standing on the bridge of a futuristic spaceship. It looked a lot like the one from the sci-fi television show he liked to watch. He wore a uniform of sorts. Several people around him, similarly clad, smiled up with looks of bland adoration and called him "Captain."

I looked at the far wall out the spacecraft's window where stars went on endlessly. Yeah, Don was sure imaginative if this was the best he could come up with.

A hiss, a puff and one of the hidden modules released some experience-enhancing aroma. I wrinkled my nose, not knowing what to expect.

I sniffed, then smiled.

Cinnamon.

This stripped-down version of the Sensavision was all I'd been willing to buy. Don wanted the top of the line model, but I'd finally put my foot down.

Aliens appeared on the bridge. Angry, green monsters, with bright yellow fangs. The entire crew jumped up from their stations to fight.

I watched my husband pull a knife from his pocket. The weapon didn't belong in this time frame, but Don must have wanted to hold something real. I recognized it as one of many from our kitchen drawer. He dodged a light-beam and then charged the hologram alien who'd fired on him and whose round silver eyes quivered in fear. The warrior screamed in pain even though Don's blade only glanced the being's upper arm. In a blink, I understood. The Sensavision, loyally programmed, had adjusted the knife's trajectory and the holographic soldier lay dead on the floor, pierced fatally through the heart.

"Haaaaaaaaaah." My husband released a long breath, and dropped his shoulders.

"Don?"

He turned, eyes blazing, and advanced on me. I stepped back. "Hey," I said, attempting a light tone, but failing to keep the panic from my voice. Although the soldier at his feet wasn't real and the aliens' weap-

ons weren't real, the blade Don held, and my fear,
were.

He launched himself at me, knife high and ready
to strike.

I screamed.

And, just like in stories, he blinked. For a moment,
ever so brief, he looked sheepish. Then, as he lowered
the weapon, his mood changed. The Sensavision froze.

"Don't ever do that!" he yelled.

"Do what?"

"Interrupt me. You always ruin everything."

A burst of anger skyrocketed in my chest. My mind
exploded with white light as I fought for control. "Me?
Ruin things for you?"

"Look," he said, still furious, "I work all day. This
is my way to relax. All I ask is that I get a little
uninterrupted pleasure here. At least I'm home. Most
guys go out on Saturday nights. Can't you just go . . .
do something?"

I opened and closed my mouth twice. "You aren't
here," I said. "You don't know anything about anything around here. You have no time for me. But you
have time for this—thing." I shot my hand toward
the Sensavision.

He sat down hard on the chair behind him. It gave
a high-pitched whoosh. "You want to talk? Fine. All
the fun's gone now anyway. Whaddyawanna talk
about?"

In that instant I realized how futile it would be to
discuss my concerns about Gran with him. And so I
said the only other thing that was on my mind.

"We have no life together, Don."

Did I expect him to sit up and take notice at that?
I suppose I did. When he shrugged and said, "So?"
my legs went a little limp. I sat down on the couch.

A few hours ticked by. But it was only seconds.

Don stood up. "OK. So, are we done talking?"

"Yeah." I said. And I went to go check on Emily, because that's all there was to do.

Gran and I took Emily to the very same playground that I'd scampered through in as a child. We watched her go up to a bigger girl, about five years old, I guessed, and start talking. Soon they were both giggling. Emily's brown curls and other girl's straight blond hair waved in the breeze and got in their eyes as they played a rhyming game that started them skipping in circles.

On the bench next to me, Gran said, "She makes friends easily. That's a gift."

I watched them.

She kept her eyes on Emily. "You always did, too. Make friends easy. Adjust."

I stared at the sky, but a question nagged. "What if it isn't Gramps? Out—there, I mean."

Gran gave a half-smile that I caught out of the corner of my eye. "I've considered that. Had to."

Emily was dancing now. She'd did make friends easily.

Gran was looking right at me. "And what if it isn't? I'll be disappointed, to be sure. Very disappointed." Her bright blue eyes clouded, and for a moment she looked just like she did the day Gramps died. "But there's a place out there that's different from here. Do we look unusual there? Don't know. Can we taste, smell, hear, see, touch? Don't know."

She laughed. "All I know is that I'm willing to go see. To find something—more. It isn't my time yet. I'm not going to just sit here and wait to die. And if your grandfather's there, all the better. But it isn't a deal-breaker."

I understood. All of a sudden. It surprised me. She

was doing everything in her power, taking the necessary steps to unite her with Gramps. I was here, doing nothing, staying with Don. So which one of us was crazy?

"The only thing that could keep me here," she said as she grabbed my arm, "is you and Emily. You two are everything to me. And if you don't want me to go, I won't."

She gripped harder and looked at me intently before she spoke again.

"I'd even go live in one of those virtual homes if it made you happy."

Emily and I ran up to the holo-home with some last-minute enhancements for the program. With Gran's debit disk in my pocket, I was prepared to prepay all the necessary fees. The disk would ensure years of uninterrupted care. Gran and Gramps had amassed a fortune in their day, and there was plenty in the bank to cover every cost, even after the debit disk ran out.

When I got back, I finally sat down with Gran. We talked, we cried, we tried to make sense of it all. And she agreed to go to the holo-home the next day. When I told Don about it later that night, he wanted to be part of it, and his cooperativeness made me suspicious.

"You'll be there?" I asked. "You sure you want to?"

"Will I get to see it? The holographic house?"

"Of course," I said. "But why do you care? You have your Sensavision."

"Yeah, but I want to see the top-of-the-line version." He winked at me. "And you've got full control over her money now, don't you?"

Gran and I arrived exactly at two and sat on hard orange chairs in the brightly colored lobby to wait for

Don. Gran was holding a bouquet of fresh-cut hyacinths. Her head bent; she took a deep breath.

"Are we doing the right thing?" I asked.

She didn't answer me.

Don arrived late, but he clapped his hands, and said, "Let's go!" when he got there.

The resident liaison, Alice, led us to the eighteenth floor, chatting about everything and nothing at the same time. My mind raced. Could I do this?

Emily liked the elevator. She pressed her face against the glass and watched the world slip away beneath us. Don watched the numbers change on the readout and avoided looking at me.

My first thought when we reached eighteen was that there had been a mistake. Before us was pure white. It was luminous and beautiful, but I didn't understand until Alice pressed a few buttons on her handheld control. Two doors appeared. The one on the right, Alice told us, was for the maintenance crew access. Don looked at the control she held and raised an eyebrow at me. He didn't look at all displeased.

He mouthed the words, "She won't be able to get out?"

"She'll never notice," I whispered, moving closer to him. "To her, it'll feel like she can go anywhere, do anything, see anyone. What would happen if all the poor demented souls here could come and go as they pleased?" I asked, then added, "Gran's not one of *them,* of course."

"Yeah, right," he said with a snort.

I pointed toward the remote. "They're giving me one of those for when I want to visit."

"And behind this door . . ." Alice opened it with a flourish.

Gran's house was there, even better than before. The sights, the sounds, the smells, all perfect.

Even Don was impressed.

"Wow," he said, "wow."

Alice whispered, as she backed out the door, "I'll leave you to settle in here."

Gran stayed near the door. She looked a little shell-shocked. Emily stayed with her.

I led the way to the kitchen. Don followed, his mouth agape.

"What do you think?" I asked him.

"Way more sophisticated than what we have at home."

"Fully self-contained." I pointed to near-invisible sensors on the ceiling. "Those pick up the resident's life signs. Just to monitor health. Otherwise everything is completely private. State-of-the-art."

He gave a slow whistle. "I'll say. What I wouldn't give to have this technology for my Sensavision."

"Speaking of which, I had one installed in the spare bedroom." I walked in that direction.

"For your grandmother?" he said, giving a short laugh. "What a waste. She's never going to use it."

He followed me. This room was larger than the real one at Gran's house and I'd had it stripped bare of all décor. All four walls held Sensavisions. And since this was a holo-home, I tried not to think of how this was just a holographic image of holographic screens, because it hurt my head to make sense of it.

"I have a surprise for you."

I flicked the "on" switch. Before us, the spaceship's bridge shimmered to life. No cinnamon in the air; this time, I smelled the metallic freshness of a brand-new vessel. Space stretched out before us and aliens suddenly appeared, ready to fight. A blue-jumpsuited officer walked in and locked eyes with Don. "Captain," he said, "we're under attack." He handed Don a weapon.

Don looked at me, then the scene, then at me again.

"I want you to have something to keep you busy," I said, in my best conciliatory voice, "while Gran and I get ourselves together."

He smiled then, and for a moment, heartbreaking in its brevity, I saw a flash of the man I married.

"Have fun," I said.

But he didn't hear me say goodbye.

Back at the front door, Gran took my hand. "Are you okay?" she asked.

I nodded, thinking about the playhouse—how many hours of enjoyment Gramps and I had had with it when I was little, and how much fun Emily would have with it now. Gran had been right all along. That little pretend shuttle really did have the power to transport us to our destiny.

And I held Emily tight as the three of us rode the elevator down.

COLD COMFORT

Dean Wesley Smith

"Houston Space Center, do you copy?"

I sat in the big command chair, leaning back, listening to nothing as the time lag between the asteroid belt and Earth played out. The time lag wasn't as bad as it used to be during the early days of the Martian missions, thanks to some new developments in laser communications cutting through a close-warp space, but it still took some time. About four seconds each direction from this far out. Nowhere near as slow as the speed of light, thank heavens.

Although, at this point, it didn't much matter.

I glanced around at the five empty chairs in the big control room of Asteroid Six, code-named Klondike after the gold rush back in Alaska. After all, that was what we had been out here to get. Minerals, from gold to anything else worth mining, to make part of this exploration profitable. I always knew that someone would get rich off of mining these asteroids, and we had proved that to be true, but now it wasn't going to be me.

The big room with its six chairs facing six large control panels smelled of burnt wires and felt far too hot.

Usually it smelled of cooking mixed with a faint odor of Captain Carry's socks. Even with the faint burnt smell, the environmental instruments on the board in front of me were telling me everything was still all right in here, as much as it could be, considering.

The room felt even bigger than normal, with me being the only one left. I was used to this room with two or three people in it at all times. I kept thinking that one of them would come in and say something. After months together, I had gotten used to the constant interaction with the others. Now I missed it and wanted it back.

"Go ahead, Klondike. How are they doing out there, Ben?"

The voice was Devon Daniels, the day shift voice of Mission Control, and one of my best friends. He had stood up for me as my best man when Tammie and I got married twenty-two years ago. We had come up through the space program together in the late 1980's, flying missions to both the moon and Mars. Together, we had helped establish the first bases on both places. He'd been grounded because of a bad lung condition after his sixth Mars trip, and I had planned on joining him on the ground after this mission. Now he was lucky he wasn't on this mission. He'd be just as dead as the rest were and I was soon going to be.

I took a deep breath. "Can we go to visual? And get some recorders on this, some extra ones? I got a lot to download."

I sat back, waiting as they brought everything online at Mission Control, thinking over the last two hours. I had been asleep, off shift, tucked in my bunk when the grinding crash had snapped me awake.

Our pilot, Toby Terhume from the European Union, had been scheduled to land us on an asteroid with a number for a name that was longer than a worldwide phone number. We were to do the same tests we had been doing on other rocks for the last two weeks. It was the tenth such landing. Standard procedure. From what I could tell, he misjudged the timing on the spin of the thing and instead of landing the Klondike on the rough surface and clamping on, the ship hit, tipped over, and then bounced.

And we bounced hard.

We lost Kevin Chin because he was also off shift and it was his cabin that just happened to be the one that got hit by a large rock jutting out of the asteroid. The automatic controls sealed off the rest of the ship, but it was far too late for Chin. We all figured his body was going to have to ride in there until we got back.

I had liked Chin. He was young, this being his first real mission. he didn't deserve to die like that in his sleep.

It didn't take long for the rest of us to discover what else was wrong. The collision had damaged some relays to the engines and they had to be repaired. Outside.

Until they were, we were just more floating debris in this field of debris, with no way to move out of the way of drifting rocks.

The five of us remaining were all heavily experienced on outside work, so we drew straws and I got the short one, meaning I'd man the controls while the other four went out to get the work done as fast as possible.

We told Mission Control what we were planning and they agreed that time was of the essence.

They had only been out there less than five minutes when an asteroid on my screen appeared out of nowhere, a rock the size of a small house, spinning slowly.

I tried to warn them. But with our speed and the rock's speed, it happened fast. Far too fast. It scraped all four off the outside of the ship like so much crap off a shoe. If the engines and side thrusters had been working, the computer would have automatically moved the ship just a few feet out of the way as it had done hundreds of times in the past two weeks.

Instead, that nasty grinding sound of my friends dying would be something that would haunt my last hours.

Suddenly, I was alone, farther from Earth than any human had ever been, drifting in a field of debris without power, or any way to get power that I could figure out. That last rock had pretty much taken out a good part of the port side of the ship, leaving me with air and environmental systems in the control room and the galley only. I suppose I could say I was lucky to have survived as well.

I didn't feel lucky.

I had enough to eat; I had enough oxygen to breathe for months. But in this mess of swirling rocks, I wouldn't last that long. I'd be lucky to get through the conversation with Earth.

Again, I didn't feel lucky.

"We're set up, Ben," Devon's voice came back on strong; then a picture flickered into place.

I clicked on my uplink, then without a comment ran the recorded events of what had happened.

I sat and stared at Devon's face for a few seconds as he just waited for the time lag; then he got my video uplink transmission and his face went white.

For a moment, I thought he was going to be sick as he watched. I knew exactly how he felt. There had been a camera on all four of them out there. What had happened was not something anyone would want to see in the news services.

And besides that, they had been my friends. And Devon's friends.

After a short time, I punched a few buttons and sent the next compacted data streams toward Earth. "Telemetry on the ship's status being fed now."

At least they would know exactly what happened and why.

I gave them everything, downloaded it all, to show everyone back at Houston Control just how screwed I was. That way they wouldn't go off half-cocked trying to come up with some harebrained scheme for me to fix this mess.

There was just nothing to fix.

I might die at any moment from some stray rock. Or some weakness in this cabin's walls caused by the two crashes. Or I might live until my food and air ran out. I was betting on a stray rock taking me out very shortly.

"Give us a few moments to look over all this," Devon said, his voice barely holding back the emotion I could see in his eyes.

Then he cut the link and I was alone again.

"Hope I'm still here," I said into the silence of the big control room.

At least some of the cameras and sensory equipment were still working on the outside of the ship. That way I could see what was going to kill me. I think someone once called that a cold comfort.

I tested the main computer and it seemed to be up and running as well, so I worked to plot my course as best I could in relationship to the big rocks we had charted. Banging off two different rocks like a bad game of billiards could send a ship going in some very strange directions, and the Klondike had been no exception.

After about ten minutes, I had figured out that at

least I wasn't going to go head first into any of the bigger asteroids for at least a few months. In fact, the last impact had sent the Klondike upwards and slightly out of the main debris field. So it was going to have to be a small piece of rock that finally took me out. And there were far, far too many of them just in my neighborhood for even our best computers to try to track.

I might see it coming. Maybe two, three seconds ahead was all.

The connection to Houston remained blank, so I stood and moved around, stretching my muscles as best I could in the zero gravity. My magnetic boots held me to the deck, so, as I had learned over the years, I used that force to work against doing my exercises.

I wasn't sure why I was doing that. Just force of habit, I suppose.

What else could I do while waiting to die?

Poor Tammie. I could see her long, brown hair, her big eyes, her small but wonderful smile. I had been gone almost more than I was home over the last two decades. From what I could tell, she had lived the life perfectly, keeping her own interests in teaching, sharing in mine when I was there, saying goodnight to me every night, no matter how deep into space I was, or what she was busy with.

A perfect astronaut's spouse.

She never really mentioned, and we never really talked about, the fact that I might not come home. It was just understood, part of my job.

I suppose I took her for granted far too much. The job of exploring space had always come first for me. The adventure was what I loved. I had to admit I had let the marriage just coast along. When I got home after this trip, I had planned on making up for that.

Too late.

I finally sat back down and stared out the forward viewport, watching the shadows of the dark rocks turning slowly, blocking out the background stars as they moved around and past me.

It was like a bunch of ghosts moving through a very dark night. Only these ghosts were real hard. And real deadly.

May 23, 2008. This would be a day that would be remembered as a footnote in the history of space exploration. All six of our names would be put up on the big golden obelisk sitting on the mall beside the United Nations building. It was a fantastic way to remember the dead. It was over thirty stories tall, yet no more than seventy feet across at the base. Standing back on the UN Plaza, staring up at it, the entire thing seemed to be reaching up for the stars. On its sides near the base, in large block letters, it held all the engraved names of those who had given their lives in the adventure of space.

Unless someone else died while I was sitting out here waiting, I would be the three hundred and twenty-sixth name on the memorial.

I knew exactly where my name would be. I had stood under those names many, many times, remembering all my friends who were on that memorial.

I had no doubt Tammie would stand there as well. I always felt it was too bad we had never had children. Now I was glad. I would never want to put a son or daughter through what Tammie was going to have to go through.

It took Houston a good twenty minutes before they got back to me. Guess when there was no hope, time suddenly lost its importance.

"Ben," Devon said. My friend's face looked drawn

and older, far older than he had looked just a half hour before. "I don't know what to say. I'm sure you know the situation."

"Yeah, I know it," I said. "Got any friendly neighborhood aliens with spaceships to stop by and pick me up? I could use a lift."

After the few seconds' timelag, Devon would smile at my corny joke, since we had both loved that story, published when we were kids, of an alien rescuing a stranded astronaut. Where was a good alien when you needed one?

"We're seeing what we can do," Devon said. "And don't give up hope just yet. We're still working on this."

"Sure," I said. "Has it got out to the press yet?"

"No," Devon said. "We've kept a lid on this for the moment, and no one's paying any attention. It was just a regular day for you guys out there."

"Yeah, real regular," I said. "After you guys finally figure out that my goose is cooked, I'd like to talk to Tammie."

"Copy that," Devon said, nodding, as if my request didn't just go in. "We'll be back in a half hour."

With that, the screen again went dead.

"He sure trusts that I'm still going to be here," I said out loud. My voice echoed in the empty control room.

I sat back and stared out the front port at all the twisting shadows cutting out the stars and then blinking them back on as they moved past, a slow-motion light show.

I glanced at the clock that told me what time it was in Phoenix where Tammie and I lived. Five in the morning. She would still be asleep. What horrible news to wake up to.

We had built a wonderful home on top of a rock

ledge overlooking the green fairways of a private golf course that wound through the rocks and cactus in the valley below us. Actually, Tammie had built it while I was on one of my Mars runs. And I didn't play golf, but that scene was so beautiful, I had decided I liked the place.

I commuted to Houston, being home on most weekends when I could and when I was on the ground.

Last time I was home, Tammie said she had learned how to play golf, had been taking lessons. She said she really loved it. I had planned on joining her on the links after this mission, although, to be honest, I just couldn't see myself being happy doing nothing but that. I wanted to move into test piloting some of the new suborbital planes being developed.

I stared out the viewport. I just hoped all the drifting shadows out there gave me enough time to at least say goodbye.

Suddenly, a very large shadow seemed to block out all of the stars in front of the viewport. I could see nothing in the pitch black, and the brains back at Mission Control had just never thought that headlights on these ships were worth the expense.

Looks like I wasn't going to get to say goodbye to anyone.

I braced myself and held my breath.

Nothing happened.

The shadow remained in front of me, covering every star as if someone had just put them all out like candles on a cake.

Then there was a slight tingling in my arms and legs, and the next moment I found myself standing, facing my best friend.

Devon was sitting in a huge, ornate throne that seemed to fill a very strange, very massive chamber covered in ornate drawings and strange lights of red and blue and purple. It felt like you could put a basketball court in the space and still leave room for a lot of spectators around the edges.

He was wearing the same clothes he had been wearing on the communications link.

And he was the only one in the chamber besides me.

I stood there, staring, trying to grasp what I was seeing, but my mind felt numb.

Nothing made sense, nothing felt right. Even the air smelled of great age, not burnt wires.

"Sorry it took so long, buddy," he said, smiling. "We had to make sure the situation really was as bad as it seemed."

"I'm dead. It doesn't get any worse."

My voice sounded just damn silly and was swallowed like so much silence in the massive chamber.

"To the rest of the world, yes." Devon said. "The Klondike, in about two minutes, will be completely destroyed by the impact from a four-meter wide asteroid."

"But . . . ?"

I stared around, trying to figure out a pattern in the strange lights, then back at Devon, the pitiful question sort of hanging there.

"But what's all this?" Devon asked, indicating the vast chamber around us. "This is the *Peace-Maker,* on loan to us for missions like this from the aliens everyone in the tabloids refer to as the Grays."

I nodded. "Now I know I'm dead. Or being gassed by some environmental leak."

"Well, this is the future we always wanted," Devon said, laughing. "Remember as kids how we used to dream about going to the moon, going to Mars, exploring out here and beyond? And finding friendly aliens to help us along the way? Well, they found us."

"Roswell?" I asked, shaking my head at the stupidity of my question.

"Actually far before that. Roswell was just an accident with one of their small training ships as we were trying to learn how to fly them."

"Come on, Ben," I said to myself. "Wake up. You've got to wake up, check the gas levels. You're hallucinating."

"Yeah, I didn't believe it either," Devon said. "But the truth is, you're alive, but to everyone else, you are officially dead and you can no longer show yourself to anyone. You'll either live and work at Area 51 or on the base on Titan."

"Titan? We have a base on Titan?"

"Actually, the Grays do, and they let us use parts of it. The Grays will be returning for their next visit to our system in twenty-three years, and we'd like to impress them with our progress. You're going to be a great help to us. We need some experienced test pilots for some new deep spacecraft we're testing."

I wanted to slap myself, but didn't. This was one hell of a hallucination for a dying person.

Devon reached out and touched something in the blank air in front of him, and half the wall to my right vanished, showing me the blackness of space and the Klondike floating there. I could see the extensive damage from the two impacts. For such a proud ship, it looked very, very sad and small and helpless.

"Coming in from the right," Devon said, his voice clearly upset by what was happening and what had happened to the rest of the crew.

I stood there, transfixed, watching what I was sure was my own death as the shadow seemed to appear out of nowhere suddenly, then smashed into the Klondike, ripping it apart and sending pieces swirling off in many different directions.

"You are now officially dead," Devon said, his voice soft. "I just wish I had gotten here in time to save the others from real death as well. But we thought the repair plan would work."

I stared at him, my mind still not grasping this, but I had one question that just pissed me off if anything about this dream was real.

"How come, if we have this, we let people like me go out into space on ships like that? How come we let them die?"

"Because we have to," Devon said. "The Grays only lent us this one ship. We have to fight our own way out into space, prove that we can survive out here, that we belong out here, and that takes growth and sacrifice. We have to pay the price."

"Five good men just paid a very heavy price," I said, disgusted.

"Yes, they did," Devon said. "And all six of you will have your names on the memorial in ten days, in a very large and impressive service. But what you learned out here won't go to waste. As you discovered, there are vast riches out here, more than enough to keep the space program going for another hundred years, until we finally figure out how to reach the stars and find even greater riches."

I glanced down, suddenly realizing my feet weren't sticking to the floor.

"Artificial gravity?"

Devon nodded. "We don't know how it works, but we know it exists and is possible, so there are a thousand scientists around the planet working on it in different ways."

"You came from Earth?" I asked.

Again he nodded. "I was beamed aboard the ship

where we keep it parked in a hidden orbit, and I flew it here to get you."

"That's one fast trip. It took us two months."

"Some sort of dimensional jump engine," Devon said. "Way beyond us so far."

"Why you?" I asked.

"Mission Control figured I would be the best one to do the rescue since you were going to have trouble believing all this was real."

"No kidding," I said. "I'm still not."

"I don't blame you," Devon said.

I walked over to the wall that seemed to be open to space and touched it. I could feel a warm, almost soft metal, even though it looked like I could stick my hand all the way out into the vacuum.

"We don't know what that material is either, or even how it works."

"But I bet we're working on it," I said.

"Oh, yeah, we are, but we haven't even figured out how to analyze it yet, let alone reproduce it."

"And you say this is the only ship they lent us?"

Devon nodded. "I wish we had more. That way we could shadow all the different missions going on in space, save more lives."

I remembered my five crewmates who had just died ugly deaths. "Yeah, too bad." The disgust and anger was clear in my voice.

Then I remembered Tammie. She was going to think I was dead.

"Can I take Tammie with me to wherever I'm going next?"

Devon shook his head. "I'm afraid not. Only very specific people can know this exists. No families allowed. Besides, you need her to keep up your legacy of what you did."

I nodded. Tammie had always been the perfect astronaut's wife. She would make sure my memory stayed alive and that my death wouldn't be in vain.

"Can I at least say goodbye?"

Devon looked like I had just trapped him bluffing in a poker game. I knew that look. There was something he didn't want to tell me.

"There is a way, isn't there?"

He nodded slowly. "We've worked out a way that you can say goodbye."

Devon's hands flew through the air in front of him, seemingly touching and brushing different things that I couldn't see.

Suddenly, outside the ship, the stars seemed to blur for a moment. Then at the next instant, we were in orbit around Earth. There had been no feeling at all of movement.

I had to be dead. What had just happened wasn't possible. That was all there was to it. I had just traveled the same distance it had taken me two months before to travel, and all in a fraction of a second without feeling a thing. Dead people traveled like that, not live ones.

"We're above the Phoenix area," Devon said. "The Grays have this nifty device they showed us how to use that transports you to a place where you can hear and see and talk to people, but not actually be there. You'll stay here on the ship the entire time."

"Like a projected hologram?"

He nodded.

"And Tammie will be able to see me?"

"As a sort of ghostlike figure. If you tell her you're dead and just came to say goodbye, she'll believe you, especially when you vanish. But it's going to scare the hell out of her."

"I don't think that learning that I'm dead is going

to do her much good either," I said. "I assume others have done this before?"

Devon nodded. "This isn't easy on either you or her, but at least you have a chance to say goodbye, if that's what you *really* want."

"Why wouldn't it be what I want? She's the woman I love."

From his large, thronelike chair in the middle of the massive space, Devon looked down at me with an expression I had seen many times before. He was worried.

"You're not going to want to do this," Devon said. "I think you should just let it go and we'll beam into Area 51 and get you settled into your new life."

"Why?"

"Just let her deal with her grief on her own, in her own way. It's better that way. For both of you."

I stood there, staring at my friend, thinking about what seeing me as a ghost would do to Tammie. Devon was right. It would scare her, and the news of my death was going to hurt her more than enough.

If I loved her, I didn't need to hurt her any more.

But I did want to just see her one more time.

"I guess you're right. Can the hologram he made so that she wouldn't see me, or hear me? I'd still like to say goodbye in my own way."

Now Devon looked really pained. "It can be, yes, but as your friend, I'm suggesting you not do that."

"Why?"

Devon sighed. "Sometimes it's better to just let memories alone, leave Tammie in your mind as you know her."

"I'm still back in the Klondike, aren't I? Having a horrid nightmare?"

"No," Devon said. "You are very much alive, and

we very much need your experienced help in our program. If the Klondike had come back on its own, we were going to try to recruit you into the program. We were lucky that circumstances at least saved you."

"I don't feel so lucky."

"Let's go to Area 51," Devon said. "You have great memories of Tammie; just leave them that way and start the next part of your life."

I laughed. "You know I'm not going to, unless you tell me what is so bad that I'm going to see when I visit her."

Devon looked like the day he had swallowed his first oyster. I remembered laughing at him for an hour that night.

I wasn't laughing now at all.

Devon sighed again, then said, "Maybe you should just go take a look. You won't be seen or heard, and you won't be able to touch anything. After that, we can talk more when we're off this ship."

It was as if the area around me on the ship suddenly changed into my home. Devon had put me in the living room, and everything was as tidy as Tammie always kept it. Outside the open window, the sun was just starting to paint the tops of the rock bluffs pink. We had a fantastically beautiful home. It was too bad I was going to miss retiring here.

I looked around. Actually, this wasn't really my home. Granted, I had clothes here and all, but I had never really felt at home here. I had no sense of still being on the ship. This alien stuff was really amazing. Or my hallucination was very detailed and felt real.

"Devon?"

"Right with you, buddy," he said, his voice coming from my right and slightly above me. "Just let me know when you want to get out of there."

"Only a moment."

I headed for the bedroom where Tammie would be sleeping. I couldn't really feel my feet touch the carpet, but the memory of walking without gravity boots made me think I was feeling it. Weird, really weird.

I tried to push open the half-closed door, but my hand went right through it, so I closed my eyes and just stepped forward and into the bedroom.

I was sure I was dead; now I was acting like a ghost. What more evidence did I need?

The pink morning light was gently filling the room through the closed blinds. Our big master bed filled the far wall under bookshelves loaded with Tammie's favorite reading.

I moved about two steps toward the bed before I realized that Tammie wasn't alone. A man, a young man, was curled up against her back, like he belonged there, like he had been there a very long time.

I had already been stunned over the last few hours with five of my shipmates dying, and then discovering that we really were friends with aliens and that I was going to live.

This sight just left me cold. I wanted to care, but for some reason, I just couldn't.

I stared at my wife for a long minute, wondering why I didn't care.

I should care. I should be angry.

But the image of my five friends' deaths haunted me. Their deaths made me angry. Not this.

I couldn't care because it really didn't matter. My shipmates, my friends were dead. I was officially dead, but getting a second chance to move on to interesting challenges that I would love.

I couldn't bring her anyway.

I stood and just stared at her. One thing was clear. She looked happy, contented in sleep.

I cared that she was happy. After being married to

a man who had spent most of the last twenty years either in space or preparing for it, she deserved happiness in any way she could find it.

"How long have you known?" I asked my friend. I had a hunch that he was seeing what I was seeing with the fancy alien technology.

"A couple of years," Devon said. "I'm really sorry."

"It's not a surprise," I said. "As much as I was gone, how can I blame her?"

I moved over beside her, ignoring the guy behind her, and stared at her beautiful hair spread out over the pillow, at her cheek, at her slightly open mouth. I had been lucky to have the time I had with her, and all the support she had given me. I would miss that.

I would miss her.

But I couldn't be angry at her.

I bent over and brushed my lips against her cheek. I didn't feel anything, but her eyes fluttered a little and she sighed and then went back to sleep.

"Be happy," I said to my beautiful wife. "You deserve it."

Then I turned away.

"Get me out of here." I stepped toward the door. "I got some new ships to fly."

A moment later I was back in space.

Back where I belonged.

THE STINK OF REALITY

Irene Radford

Dr. Wallace Beebee, PhD, associate professor of biophysics at Vasco da Gama U, swept the paraphernalia atop his wife Evelyn's dresser into a shoebox. Deodorant, perfume, hairspray, cosmetics, anything with a fragrance. When the box was full he moved into the adjacent bathroom and collected shampoos, soaps, his own shaving cream and aftershave, the candle on the toilet tank. When a second box was full he slapped the lid on it, secured it with a rubber band, and took them both to the laundry room at the opposite end of their ranch-style rental home on the campus fringes.

"The *Explorers* of VDGU? A bunch of bullshit. Haven't had an original idea in fifty years," Wallace grumbled. He'd been on faculty three years, always being promised tenure the next semester, then the next, and the next, always denied because his ideas were just a little too revolutionary. Grants controlled by the university went to projects that kept corporate America happy and conservative, not to strange new inventions worthy of science fiction novels.

Every research grant Wallace applied for ended up in the hands of a more senior faculty member.

How could he and Evelyn ever hope to afford children living on the pittance the university paid untenured—and therefore disposable—professors?

Into another box, he loaded all of the cleaning supplies beneath the bathroom sink. "I'll show them something that will keep corporate America happy!"

Max, the family corgi, followed his every step, sniffing each item with extreme interest. But then the dog lived through his nose.

That's what had given Wallace the idea. The dog's nose ruled his impulses. If it didn't have a smell, the dog wasn't interested.

Wallace now knew how to give the world every smell they ever dreamed of. That meant it had to come out of the television. TV ruled America's desires. Corporate America ruled Americans through their TV advertising, creating "needful" things where no need existed.

Wallace needed tenure. Only creating the next needful thing would get him that.

People forgot that memory was more closely tied to scent than any other of the five senses. Long before he was through with corporate America, they'd know his name and remember it.

Finally, he ejected the dog from the bedroom too. He closed the door firmly against intrusion. Then he showered with an unscented soap and donned a fresh jogging suit that had air-dried on a line in the backyard. He couldn't allow any stray odors to confuse his experiment.

Later, when he knew it worked, he'd verify everything in a sterilized lab. Until then, the invention was his and his alone, carefully pieced together from a discarded and outdated mass spectrometer and a sniffer he'd purchased with his own money from the state crime lab, again outdated. He had to come up with a better name for that device.

His next generation of Beebevision would be smaller and more sensitive. When he had grant money and grad students to collect data.

Finally, all was ready. Cautiously, he made the last connection between his invention, a black cube about ten inches on each side, and the television that dominated one corner of the bedroom. The wires slid into place easily. He tightened the screws.

Holding his breath, he fed the special DVD into the player, turned everything on, and sat in his favorite recliner—carefully vacuumed earlier.

A deep organ note played and a lily of the valley logo blossomed on the screen. He'd borrowed the lily from a design on Evelyn's favorite perfume, changing it just enough to keep from violating copyright. He'd also added radiating lines indicating the flower's fragrance.

"Welcome to Fully Sensory Theatery. A Wallace Beebee Production," intoned a husky alto voice, Evelyn, of course.

Her PhD was in medieval history. Physics didn't interest her. Nothing interested her except her own discipline. He'd make history come alive for her as it never had before: through her nose.

The scene on the TV shifted to a meadow filled with spring wildflowers. A delicate floral scent wafted to Wallace from the mesh face of the black cube.

He smiled. "It's working," he whispered.

Then the scene changed again; a hot desert wind that smelled of dust, sage, and mint accompanied the pictures of Smith Rock in central Oregon. Next, another scene, a beautiful woman (Evelyn) dancing lightly in the moonlight. Her phenomenal perfume made his heart beat faster and his hormones soar.

Then the dog scratched at the door, whined plaintively, and farted.

"OK, OK, I'll walk you now before you crap on the floor."

Wallace went about his evening chores and put the bedroom back to rights, whistling a happy tune and smiling hugely.

"My, aren't you in a good mood!" Evelyn exclaimed when he kissed her soundly upon going to bed that night.

His smile continued well into the next morning. As Wallace walked to his first class he sniffed the scent of freshly mown grass and bright spring flowers with new appreciation. He detected hints of gasoline from the mower and oil in the fertilizer spread among the flowers. That nearly destroyed his happy mood. He might have to find a way to filter his gadget. He wasn't sure how. Yet.

Two weeks later, Wallace attached his little black cube, reduced to four inches on each side, to a different television. This one sat in the university conference room habituated by the tenure committee. Or "God" as most untenured professors referred to it. Life or death in the academic community rested in the TC's hands.

Wallace made his careful presentation, then switched off the DVD at the end of the third scene, careful not to let the fourth begin. He wanted to hold that one in reserve for emergencies.

"As you can see, *and* smell, ladies and gentlemen, this new invention has tremendous commercial as well as academic potential." He then read Evelyn's notes about how she would use it to bring history alive.

"Frivolous," Dr. Pretentious declared.

"Impractical," chimed in Dr. Beta.

"Demeaning," finished Dr. Shallow.

"Is biophysics even a recognized discipline at other universities?" Dr. Pretentious asked rhetorically.

And that was the crux of the matter for the TC. Never making a decision until they knew it would be applauded by other universities, never hiring anyone who didn't have at least two other offers, denying tenure to any but the most staid and conservative candidates.

"Tenure denied." If Dr. Pretentious had a gavel, the old fart would have pounded it. Instead he gathered up his thick file on Wallace Beebee and retreated.

Wallace hit the play button on the remote. Pictures of Max, fresh from the bath and still stinking of wet dog fur, filled the television screen. He wiggled and yipped and farted, then dropped a big dump right in front of the camera programmed to pickup every hydrocarbon in the air.

"Well, I never!" Dr. Shallow declared. She held a lace-edged hanky to her nose and literally ran out of the room.

"Hmm, Max got into the garbage again. He smells a little like coffee grounds and egg shells."

Wallace stayed on at VDGU for another year. His applications to other universities were rejected or stalled in committee. He didn't have enough publication credits. He didn't have enough experience in academia. His work was too controversial.

He didn't apply for tenure again at VDGU. He and Evelyn made do with their meager salaries and postponed having children once again. She was denied tenure in medieval history because of her association with Wallace.

They postponed having children once again.

Secretly Wallace worked on his invention in the garage at home. Honing, refining, miniaturizing. Paying for every part out of his own pocket. Then, at last, he had what he needed: a commercially viable version ready to roll off the assembly line.

If he could just sell it. He had to sell it. Evelyn was pregnant despite their precautions. They desperately needed the money.

Strange, he'd detected a change in her body chemistry before she even suspected her pregnancy. Working with his invention every day, testing, honing, had sensitized his own nose almost as much as it had the gadget.

Sixty query letters to various electronics companies resulted in exactly one invitation.

He took most of his savings and bought a round-trip ticket to Kansas City, Missouri, the corporate headquarters of a major televangelist, Dr. John Baptiste Feelwell. (Wallace suspected the man's PhD in applied religions was as fake as his toupee.) A dozen suited executives and ad men filled the smallest of their conference rooms. Wallace's entire house could have fit inside it and still had room left over.

Wallace caught a whiff of musky cologne that attempted to mask a man's body smell. Wallace almost gagged on the intensity. He'd given up all fragrances himself and grown a beard so he wouldn't have to use aftershave. He'd gotten to the point where he could identify each individual component of artificial fragrances.

He also knew the man had had eggs Benedict for breakfast and sex within the last hour, probably with the buxom secretary who sat in the corner. Heat suffused his face. These morons were no better than the tenure committee. Angry words coiled on the tip of his tongue.

"Out! I demanded no external fragrances. All of

you out until you've rid yourself of that . . . that . . . stink."

"What's he talking about?" One of the ad men smoothed his freshly barbered hair with a manicured hand. His charcoal suit molded his lanky frame as if custom tailored. He made Wallace look frumpy and slovenly in his off-the-rack navy blue pinstripe suit.

"How can we appreciate a new dimension to life when all our noses are clogged with your artificial cologne?" Wallace loomed over the man and pierced him with the same gaze he used on stupid freshman who questioned his authority in the classroom.

The ad man squirmed in his chair.

"You might as well leave, Leland," Dr. Feelwell intoned from his place at the head of the table. "I haven't got all day and clearly Dr. Beebee will not continue until you do leave."

"But . . . but the account is supposed to be mine! How can I apply a new invention to your telecasts if I don't see it tested?" Leland protested.

"Seeing is not enough. My invention goes beyond the limited sense of sight. You must use your nose, and yours is tainted by your overpowering aftershave. You will have no part in my invention," Wallace decided on the spot.

He looked around the room at the carefully neutral yet attractive faces. No ugly people polluted Dr. Feelwell's staff—almost as if he conveyed the impression that giving money to his crusade made one beautiful.

"She will manage my invention." Wallace pointed to a small woman who'd scrubbed her face and hair free of cosmetics. Her soft dress looked freshly laundered as well. Wallace had seen her before, a lame child miraculously healed before ten million television viewers. "She respects my conditions for presenting this important innovation to the public."

Immediately, Wallace's emotions swung to guilt. He'd ruined his chances here. He'd never sell Beebevision now.

Leland eventually slunk out, but not until he'd protested and argued seniority and several other points. Wallace had to begin disconnecting his device before Dr. Feelwell put his foot down and threatened to fire Leland if he did not leave.

Once more the television screen brightened gradually. The logo of a lily of the valley with lines radiating outward opened before them. The voice, Evelyn's beautiful, sexy voice, which could enthrall an auditorium filled with bored freshman. Then the three scenes Wallace had carefully chosen to evoke pleasant emotions.

A grandmother in a kitchen wearing an apron and removing a freshly baked apple pie from the oven. Smiles broke out around the room as noses filled with cinnamon.

A scantily clad woman dancing in the moonlight with sexy pheromones wafting through the room. Two men, including Dr. Feelwell, shifted uneasily in their seats, as if their trousers no longer fit properly.

A cityscape with lightly falling snow and bright holiday lights accompanied the scent of cut fir trees and bayberry candles. The scrubbed woman sighed blissfully with childhood memories.

Pleasant smells, pleasant memories, pleasant endorphins coursing through the bloodstream.

"How does it work?"

"What will it cost?"

"How fast can we get this up and running?"

Wallace smiled and answered each of the questions with pleasure.

"A pherometric ionizer analyzes the components of each scent and embeds that analysis into the digital code of the video. It is integrated into the digital camera. A mass spectrometer modified to my specifications interprets the extra code in the DVD and recreates those molecules based upon their magnetic charge and hydrocarbon content."

"I want to see how it works before we commit."

"It's patented. No one sees the circuitry without a contract."

"What will it cost us to produce?"

"Less than one hundred dollars per unit if built into a television. Considerably more for a less sensitive unit attached separately." He grinned. "So of course every homeowner with a television more than two years old will dash out for a new unit."

Looking around the room, smelling the greed and the cunning among these people, he wondered yet again if he needed to find a way to filter the scents. All or nothing went through the pherometric ionizer and the mass spectrometer reproduced it all faithfully.

The frontmen kept at him with more and more detailed questions. But Wallace retreated behind a barrier of "patented secrets revealed only when the contract is signed and royalties agreed upon."

"How soon?" Feelwell cut through the garbled voices. "And who else have you shown this to?"

"I offer you a six month exclusive for the right price."

They met his price and doubled the modest royalty he requested for a one year exclusive. Not only could he and Evelyn afford to have the baby now, they could afford to send the child to the best universities in the world—not Vasco da Gama University.

"But we can't call it Beebevision; that sounds like something out of the Jetsons," the scrubbed woman chimed in.

"The invention is mine. It carries my name," Wallace insisted. He'd have his revenge on the tenure committee only when his name became a household word. Soon they'd be begging him to accept tenure.

But he'd show them. He'd teach somewhere else. Anywhere else.

Or maybe not teach at all, if the money became as good and regular as he hoped.

They batted around various word combinations. Wally-vision sounded wonderful to Wallace.

"It's sort of like the feng shui of television," the scrubbed woman finally added. "It completes the experience and attunes it to the human spirit. It opens the soul to revelation." Her face shone with an angelic glow.

Or maybe just the sunshine creeping in through the tinted windows.

More ideas spilled forth.

They finally settled on Sensaroma.

Wallace grumbled. He really wanted his name to become a household word. He'd have to settle for going down in history as the inventor.

And the money. Dr. Feelwell had his own television channel. The highest-rated of all cable channels. So he had the clout to get personal television units on the market within weeks. He also did many personal appearances that made use of big-screen televisions so that all fifty to one hundred thousand members of the audience could feel as if they were in the front seat of the massive stadiums and auditoriums.

Now all of Feelwell's followers would also experience Sensaroma.

Wallace had a niggle of guilt that Feelwell might be manipulating his audiences. The guilt only lasted until he cashed the first check.

*   *   *

Wallace and his wife watched the first broadcast of Dr. Feelwell produced in Sensaroma on the first augmented television unit off the production line—gratis as part of his contract.

"The odor of sanctity," Evelyn whispered. "I think we need to start going to church again. Our baby deserves to grow up knowing the truth."

Wallace was unmoved. His sensitized nose had separated out the various chemically produced pheromones and incense coming from Dr. Feelwell's television studio, and he knew how the preacher used his audience.

"I think I need to demand a higher royalty," he muttered.

Wallace turned his classes over to his grad students and hit the talk show circuit. By the end of the month, his name was on the tip of many more tongues. Sensaroma became a household word, even if his name did not.

Within the month the Secret Service, the FBI, and Homeland Security showed up on Wallace's doorstep.

"You owe it to your government to sign over the patent," their oily lawyer said, shoving a sheaf of papers at Wallace.

"Pay the royalty and you can use it any way you want. But the patent is mine," he insisted. "And so is the chemical formula for persuasion. I would think the reelection committee of our much-maligned president would be more interested in that than the military. But then again the Pentagon would more likely be interested in the patent for nose plugs and filters for our troops as they bombard the enemy with scents guaranteed to lull them into complacency."

Shortly thereafter, Wallace marketed separately a

filtering unit to a television manufacturing company outside of Dr. Feelwell's control. The FBI shut them down within an hour of going into production.

He and Evelyn bought a bigger house with no mortgage, complete with a nursery and a live-in nanny, a housekeeper, and a chef who used only natural ingredients.

The tenure committee clamped their mouths shut and refused to acknowledge Wallace when they encountered him on campus or at faculty gatherings.

The much-maligned president won a second term of office by a landslide. Few people remembered to criticize him for anything.

Wallace bought Evelyn the largest diamond ring he could find. It barely made a dent in his bank account as the royalties poured in. He also gave her the funds to produce her own documentary on life in a medieval village. She adored the project and thanked him properly.

She conceived a second child that night.

He had to have the housekeeper buy baby powder and baby soap at the health food stores to get away from artificial fragrances. All of their groceries came from there as well, so he wouldn't have to smell and taste chemical fertilizers and preservatives. He spent more and more time in the sterilized lab as body odors, deodorants, and cosmetics overwhelmed him to the point of nausea.

The day before the Evelyn premiered her movie, the tenure committee summoned Wallace before their august presences.

At last!

He dressed in his best suit, a new custom-tailored one in charcoal grey, with a subdued tie and blindingly white shirt with French cuffs and eighteen carat gold cufflinks with a tiny diamond set in the center.

He paused outside the door to the conference room to gather himself and settle his shoulders. Out of habit he sniffed, assessing his surroundings.

The acrid scent of a predator on the hunt stung his nostrils.

Where?

A surge of defensive adrenaline coursed through his system, sharpening all of his senses. His muscles bunched, ready to flee or fight. He sniffed again.

The scent was strongest at the closed doorway.

He took three long deep breaths, calming himself, forcing his mind to take over his instincts.

Yes, inside. The TC had become predatory. Life or death committee. And glad about it. They wanted to take something very precious from him. That's what predators did.

If not his life, then what? They'd already denied him tenure.

Suspicion crowded out his fear.

He flipped out his cellphone and speed-dialed his stockbroker. "They can't take the money if they can't find it."

With a few terse orders he sold all of his stock in Sensaroma and other diversified industries and laundered the money through the Cayman Islands.

The dumping of a large amount of the stock might create a slump in the stock market. But soon the numbers would rally as investors rushed to buy a piece of the most amazing innovation to come on the market in decades.

Then he dialed his contact at Homeland Security. Time for some interesting facts to go into the background checks of key members of the university administration and the TC.

Time to cash in some favors for their confiscation of the filtering unit.

With renewed confidence and armored against his enemies, Wallace entered the conference room as if he owned the university.

"Our lawyers inform us that since you developed Sensaroma while in our employ as a biophysicist, the patents belong to the university," Dr. Pretentious informed Wallace without preamble.

"We will expect the signed patent transfer documents within twenty-four hours," Dr. Beta continued. "Along with royalty statements and a check for the entire amount paid to you."

"You will of course be rewarded with a small bonus for bringing such a valuable commodity to Vasco da Gama University," Dr. Shallow concluded.

"Does tenure come with that bonus?" Wallace snarled at them. His temper boiled, but he kept it under control. He had the upper hand at the moment.

"Of course you'll get tenure. Once all of the legalities are completed and there is an opening for a tenured position in your department," Dr. Pretentious said graciously.

"If I'd known I could have bought tenure, I'd have taken out a loan years ago. My lawyers will contact your lawyers." Wallace stalked out of the conference room. "And I bet my lawyers are smarter and more powerful than yours."

At the close of business that day, instead of patent transfer documents, the TC received a counter lawsuit. The TC had rejected the invention when offered to them; therefore, Wallace was free to market it elsewhere. He tendered his resignation in a separate envelope. Something he should have done when he received the first royalty check for six times his annual salary. But his need for revenge had outweighed his good judgment.

No more. He had other plans. Like founding his own university in the Cayman Islands.

The next day, Wallace left the baby with the nanny to attend the premier of Evelyn's movie. He slipped unnoticed into the back of an auditorium filled with two hundred history majors. He wore small filter plugs in his nose, the only way he could tolerate crowds of people anymore.

He took them out the moment the projection screen came to life. The camera panned across an ocean that pounded a rocky shore. Wallace smelled salt and fish and seaweed on the cold wind. The ragged coastline became the ragged ramparts of a castle. New scents assailed the audience. Mud in an enclosed courtyard. Mold on damp stone.

People clad in ancient peasant garb strolled across the scene. Their unwashed bodies, the sweat of hard labor and anxiety over daily trials and tribulations replaced the sharp, clean aroma of the open sea.

To Wallace's sensitized nose, the combination smelled like fear. He realized that for the average peasant, even in Third-World countries today, life represented fear.

No wonder so many less modern societies revolved around their faith. People needed to pray daily for survival and thank the heavens for each day they came through unscathed.

A different way of life. A different way of thinking.

He sat forward fascinated, more interested in history than ever before. This was how his invention needed to be used. His love for Evelyn increased as he began to understand her passion.

Unfortunately, her students took a different view. The sound of gagging accompanied the movie as the camera followed a woman with a child at her breast into a tiny, dark hut. The students vacated the auditorium in droves. Mud, pigs, disease, rotting food, and open sewers made them ill.

The smell of vomit, closer and more real than provided by the movie, added its own distinct aroma.

But they were natural scents, not chemical. Wallace reveled in them.

Humanity had become so detached from reality, scrubbed it clean and sterilized it, that they could no longer use their noses as they were designed to work. People didn't trust their noses like they did their eyes and ears.

And so they could be manipulated by their noses. Or they felt abused when presented by reality.

They were embarrassed by the stink of life.

"I hope total reality does not become a trend in the movies," he mused when he tried to talk to Evelyn that night about the disaster with her students.

His mind began working on how to get the filter back from the government.

"I don't care about movies. I care about helping my students relive history, to get an honest feel for life in times past so they can better understand the people and therefore the politics of the day and great historical events." She dashed into the master bathroom and locked the door. The sound of her sobs continued long into the night. Max scratched and whined solicitously at the door at frequent intervals and at last crept into his basket around dawn.

For once Wallace was almost glad that he had not become a household name.

Homeland Security did their work. The TC exploded in a scandal of bribes, sex for favors, and classroom ethics. The university chancellor himself granted Wallace tenure. A week later, Wallace accepted the position of Dean of Research and Graduate Studies along with a seat on the newly revised tenure committee.

The next night on the national news, a reporter in

the field employed Sensaroma to their coverage of the latest war involving US troops. Amongst the scenes of horror showing the wounded and dying, listening to their screams of pain and the mourning wails of the survivors, came the full array of vile odors. Blood, excrement, vomit, the sweat of fear.

Two hours later the most popular television series, a forensics drama, brought the reality of violent death and detection into everyone's living rooms. The actors investigated the death of a homeless man dead three days, his corpse ravaged by desert scavengers and insects.

Six minutes into the script, the network went black for nearly two minutes. When they came back on they played a repeat of an innocuous sitcom filmed long before Sensaroma became a part of everyday life.

Wallace called the government. "Want a major lawsuit on your hands from every television and movie studio in the country?" he asked, using a flippant tone to mask his own panic.

Much grumbling and mumbling on the other end.

"Then release the lock on my patent for a filter. Now." He didn't tell the Pentagon he'd already bought a factory and manufactured the thing and warehoused a million units with another million in production.

"No one wants to live through their noses," Wallace explained patiently to the Joint Chief of Staff. "All they want is sanitized niceness. Niceness doesn't inform. It masks, it deceives, it betrays our sensibilities. But it still leaves it open to manipulation."

"Like you are manipulating me," groaned the JCS.

"No more than you do to the public every day. Niceness makes life comfortable."

"Comfortable. Reality isn't comfortable. It never has been."

"That's why we need to pretend it is."

"OK. OK. I'll have the papers in your hands by noon."

"Make that ten. I have a world to save from the stink of reality."

YELLOW SUBMARINE

Rebecca Moesta

Life with a sixteen-year-old is never short on melodrama.

"But Mom," André groaned, rolling his eyes, "you can't expect me to drive that. It's positively prehistoric. That's what *moms* drive. I'd be laughed out of school."

"I've had that SPig for eight years now. It's reliable and I haven't noticed anybody laughing at me," I said, crossing my arms defensively over my chest.

"Maybe you just haven't *noticed,* period."

"I may be your mother, but that hardly makes me old and senile," I said, uncrossing my arms. I wiped my sweaty palms on the silvery material of the form-fitting jumpsuit I had worn to work that day. The idea of André actually having his own vehicle filled me with maternal trepidation. "You certainly don't need anything flashy. You just have to find something to get you to and from school, and to work and back."

"Maybe you don't care what you drive anymore, but this is important to me." André stopped and tried a new approach. "Please? Dad says I've earned the right to choose my own. I work hard." That was true enough. At his habitat-construction job, my son had probably logged more work hours than any other kid at Marianas High. But something inside me still resisted.

I sighed. "That's the only reason we're discussing this. Your work schedule makes it impossible for your father and me to ferry you and your sister everywhere you have to go."

"So you'll take me shopping for a minisub?" he said.

I glanced up through the clear, domed ceiling of our home, my eyes unconsciously searching the ocean for any sign of Howard's submarine returning, though I knew he wasn't due back from his fishing expedition for another day yet. In any case, I knew that my husband wouldn't thank me for putting off the inevitable.

"All right," I said, giving in. "But we'll get something used, not showy, and I'm going to insist on certain safety features. Just give me a minute to change out of my work clothes."

By the time we reached the dealership on the outskirts of Marianasville, I was much calmer. On our way past the colorful glow of habitat domes, around the kelp fields, and past the fish processing plant, André and I had discussed the budget and ground rules, and he was grinning with anticipation. I zoomed my faithful SPig right into the center of the lot and parked in the first available space. André had already donned his NEMM—nose-eye-mouth mask—and waited impatiently for me to put my gear on.

Since I didn't want to get my hair wet, I chose a full transparahelm. I popped the lower hatch and allowed André to drop smoothly into the water. I followed a moment later. The hatch closed behind us as we swam toward the first submarine that caught André's eye, a sports model Nuke Mini, a muscle sub powered by a miniature nuclear generator. The vidsticker on its window proclaimed that it could do zero to a hundred twenty in under ten seconds.

Naturally, I was appalled. The I saw the price. I gasped and quickly had to adjust the flow on my air condenser rebreather unit.

"You can't fully appreciate its features without a test drive." The voice came from behind us.

We whirled to look at the salesman in his garish plaid wetsuit. He wore a vidbadge that said, WELCOME TO SUBMARINE WORLD. I'M RON.

I activated my helmet mic. "No, thank you. I think it's out of our range, er . . . Ron."

"But Mom, why not take a test drive? It would be fun," André said with a reproachful look as if I were trying to suck all of the joy out of his afternoon.

I kept my voice calm and reasonable. I could do this. I was his mother. "There's no point in driving the ones you can't afford. Why don't we try that one?" I pointed toward a compact Waterbug.

The salesman's face fell at this much more sensible choice. The vehicle had once been red, but had now faded to a sort of rusty pink color. "It looks very fuel-efficient, and it's in our price range." I tried to sound as enthusiastic as possible. "Can you show it to us?" The vehicle was definitely ugly. Even a SPig would be a step up from it.

"You realize, of course, that the Waterbug is an older trade-in," Ron replied, forcing a smile. "It can't compare favorably to the Nuke Mini."

"My son is buying his first sub," I told him in no uncertain terms. "He doesn't need all of the features on the Nuke mini. Once he shows us that he's responsible—maybe in a couple of years—we can come back to look at a Nuke Mini, and you can help

André set up a reasonable payment plan to help him establish a good credit rating."

"Very well, then," Ron replied as the smile dissolved from his face and was replaced by a look of resignation. He led the way toward the other sub.

"Mom," André said to me over the private microphone, "I need to do this myself. It's my first time, and you're doing all the talking. It's embarrassing."

"Okay." I raised my hands in mock surrender. "I'll keep quiet. But don't forget this is for transportation, not to impress your friends."

He nodded as if he had heard the lecture a thousand times before, not just once on our way to the dealership. "I know, and it has to be safe enough to withstand a nuclear blast. I've got the whole list of your requirements right up here," he said, tapping his forehead just above the NEMM rebreather.

André was exaggerating for effect, of course. But not by much. Agreeing to let him take the lead from here on out, I made a motion across my mouth as if applying emergency water sealant.

Keeping my vow of silence, I watched as Ron of the plaid wetsuit gathered himself to launch into a full-fledged sales speech, even though I could tell he was not impressed by the Waterbug. "This minisub's a beauty, all right. She's got low usage, sturdy crash webbing, an economical smooth-spurt engine, dual rudder controls, and not a speck of wasted space." He gave me a conspiratorial grin, grown-up to grown-up, that was as false as his phosphor-glow hairpiece. "Very sensible."

I didn't answer. André peered into the vessel through its front viewbubble, then turned toward Ron and gave him an okay-just-try-to-impress-me look, and rattled off a series of questions. For once, apparently, my son had done his homework.

The salesman tried to keep up and had to make frequent reference to the datascreen on his wrist. Long before the man finished explaining the lack of warranty, the almost non-existent cargo capacity, and the inadequate max speed, I could tell André's mind was made up, so I knew that his final question was just for show. "And where do the passengers sit?"

"Ahh." Ron tugged at the collar of his garish tartan suit. "In the, ah, the interest of economy and, ah . . ." His voice trailed of. "Actually, it's a one-person vehicle."

André gave me a glance and spread his hands as if that clinched it. "I'm afraid we'll have to keep looking, then. See, I need to be able to pick up my little sister from her aquaballet lessons. I can't even take my mom out for a test drive in this thing, much less take care of Reina. At this rate, I might as well get an Aqua-Scoot. It's cheaper, faster, and even more fuel efficient, plus it has room for a passenger."

As I said, I'm a mom, and I'm not completely oblivious. André was playing both of us. I knew that one of André's primary purposes in buying this vehicle was to be able to go out on dates without wearing the protective gear and portable ACRU rebreathers that would be required on a Scoot. It was a clever stroke, of course, to mention that only with an appropriate vehicle would he be able to free up even more of my time by picking up his sister from school and lessons. I knew, of course, he had no intention of purchasing an AquaScoot, but Ron did not. And his dealership did not sell AquaScoots. I saw his face pale by at least two shades of blue-green when he realized that any chance for a commission was about to swim away.

Suddenly Ron's concern seemed to be all about safety. "An AquaScoot? With no protection from reefs, predators, and submersibles that don't watch where they're going? Besides, when you consider all the excess gear you'd need—sonic repellents, ACRU units, helmets—you would hardly save anything at all. And it's so uncomfortable. Come with me. I think I have just the thing."

Obviously, the plaid panderer finally understood whom he needed to please and was playing to André for all he was worth. "Hold on," Ron said, grabbing onto a loop on one of the continuously cycling transportation cables that crisscrossed the submarine lot. André and I each caught a loop and we were whisked away to the outskirts of the lot, where we all let go of our cables. Ron gestured with a flourish toward a sleek, flashy minisub in neon yellow. "I think that you'll find this is much more to your liking. It just came in."

I shuddered to think what the price would be. The slick vehicle was far too new to be within our price range, and maybe just a bit too sexy for my son to own. I was about to suggest that we keep looking when I remembered that I had promised to keep my mouth sealed. I decided to wait.

"Allow me to present the Subatomic," Ron said, "with twelve independent propulsion jets and eight customizable attitude jets, plus six brake rotors, complete with energy-recapture turbines. She's had some heavy usage, but for the price, this minisub is a steal. Compact and safety conscious, the Subatomic can carry the driver and three passengers—or the driver, one passenger, and a generous cargo when the rear seats are—"

"We'll test drive this one," André interrupted.

Ron obligingly cycled open the lower hatch for us, letting André enter first to get into the pilot's chair. I took shotgun, and Ron, folding himself into the rear seat, then closed the hatch again. While we all took off our masks and fastened our crash webbing, he picked up his spiel where he had left off. I sat back in my seat, which was comfortable—perhaps a bit *too* comfortable— and André punched the ignition.

"The Subatomic's TruGyro steering system," Ron droned on like an annoying commercial, "never loses track of its orientation. It boasts a wired microperiscope that shoots a tiny camera to the top of the water to let you keep track of conditions on the surface, then retracts again at the touch of a button."

André grabbed the steering gyro with both hands and hit the accelerator, throwing us all back in our seats, which quickly adjusted to support our backs and heads. A nice feature. Without slowing, André curved the minisub around toward the Test Drive area and plunged us into the Level 5 Hazard Course. A forest of wriggling fake seaweed swallowed us in darkness. I bit my lip, digging my nails into the seat's armrest. I would have cried out, but a moment later, the minisub's exterior lights winked on. The floods illuminated the course before us, while my son's face lit with an equally bright grin of fierce enjoyment.

Then, from out of nowhere, the tentacles of a gigantic "squid" reached for us. André pushed the Subatomic into a sideways spin and plaid Ron's sales speech ended with a squawk. In spite of the quick change of direction, the ride was surprisingly smooth and quiet, and the dynamic crash webbing didn't cut into my neck as it did when I made sudden maneuvers in my SPig.

Just as I began to calm down again, now that we were out of the squid's reach, the heads-up display blinked a warning signal. André tapped the brake rotors, tweaked the attitude adjustment jets on the left and lower hulls, and accelerated upward in a smooth curve as a giant coral reef loomed ahead of us. I gulped and closed my eyes, expecting a crash or the screech of coral scraping metal.

But the sounds never came. André started quizzing Ron on things like the number of spare universal jets in case one should go out (three), backup ACRU units (two portable NEMMs), and warranty (two years). Not bad for a used vehicle. I opened one eye to see that we were entering the cavern portion of the obstacle course. I quickly shut my eye again. That was when André started his negotiations—both of the cave passages and of the price.

I heard the occasional ping of the warning sensors and felt the almost instantaneous adjustments my son made in speed, orientation, and direction. In the background, André and Ron continued their bargaining while I cringed deeper into the passenger seat. It was amazingly comfortable.

"You can open your eyes now, Mom," André said, and I realized that I had actually started to relax. "We're out of the hazard course and almost back to the dealership lot."

I blinked my eyes open to see that he was right. We were almost back, and André was driving at a safe, respectable pace, observing all of the traffic laws of the sea.

"Did you hear the final price, Mom?" André said with a note of uncertain hope in his voice.

"No," I said, bracing myself for sticker shock and already preparing for the unpleasant task of talking my son out of the sub he had so obviously fallen in love with. Ron quoted me the number of credits, which was, as I had suspected, higher than the amount we had budgeted for, but not nearly as high as I had expected. It was, in fact, quite reasonable, considering the sub's excellent condition, well thought-out safety features, and luxury options. But André was a teenager. He didn't really need to start out with all those bells and whistles. In fact, it would probably do him good to start with a more humble vehicle. *I* certainly had.

Just as André was about to start his turn into the sub lot, a plump green SPig came barreling out at us. It shouldn't have been much of a problem considering that SPigs can do no more than thirty at their top speed, but its teenage driver was distracted. The young man, obviously not paying attention, had turned to speak with someone in the back seat and hadn't seen us yet.

The path of the other vessel would intersect ours dead on. I drew in a sharp breath and stifled a scream just as the other driver noticed us and began frantically trying to maneuver in another direction. But his ungainly vehicle refused to cooperate. I heard a strangled yelp from Ron in the back. André, meanwhile, seemed completely unfazed as the warning signal began to ping. I slapped my hands over my eyes, but then spread my fingers and watched in terrified fascination.

Tapping the brake rotors, André twirled the gyro steering downward and threw the upper and side attitude adjustment jets on full so that we dove directly beneath the wallowing SPig. Instead of a jarring crash that would likely have disabled both vehicles, all I heard was the tiniest squeak as the SPig's bulky rudder scratched against our hull for a bare fraction of a second.

Once clear of the other minisub, André steered the Subatomic on a slow, gentle curve back into the dealership and parked it at its original slot while I struggled to breathe normally again.

This was no time for debate. I knew what I had to do. André had wanted to make the final decision, but he couldn't afford this choice without me.

"We'll take it," I said. I glanced at André. "We'll split the cost."

The next day was Friday and, as promised, André swung by to pick up his little sister Reina from aqua-ballet on his way home from school. Howard and the rest of the submarine fishing fleet were home from their expedition with a large catch, so the four of us—Howard, Reina, André, and I—had dinner as a family for a change.

André regaled us all with the tale of the previous day's shopping expedition and test drive, as well as the story of his first day at school with his new minisub.

"You drove a good bargain, son," Howard said with an admiring chuckle. "Literally. Why don't we all go out for a spin after supper?"

"Could, uh, could that wait for tomorrow?" André said, his face growing pink. "I kind of have a date tonight."

"Who with?" Reina blurted. "Do I know her? Does she go to your school?"

Howard cleared his throat, cutting off the stream of questions. "Don't stay out too late, son."

"I won't." André wiped his mouth with a napkin and excused himself from the table. "I promised Mr. Martinez I'd have Etsuko home early."

I stared at my son in amazement. André was going out without us, on his first date alone. Howard grinned like the proud father he was. I, however, was not quite ready to let go. "Wait. What kind of date? Where are you going?" I asked as he headed for the front floor hatch where the Subatomic was parked.

He turned, grinned at me, and shrugged. "Where else, Mom? To watch the submarine races."

GOOD GENES

Kristine Kathryn Rusch

When Alden was six weeks old, the doctor called them into his office. Ro didn't want to go. She had a feeling that something was wrong. None of her friends had ever been called to a doctor's office, especially when there had been no check-up previously, no tests, nothing that would seem out of the ordinary.

Ro's husband, Gil, reassured her, but he didn't sound sincere. He didn't meet her eyes any more, and his ruddy face looked even more flushed than usual. He too knew that things were wrong. They bundled up the baby, whom Ro privately thought too small to be named after his famous great-grandfather, and went to the scheduled appointment.

The doctor's office was a different place than the waiting room. Ro had been comfortable with the waiting room. It was designed for pregnant women: large, comfortable chairs with good back support, footstools, and a gas fireplace that was in constant use in the winter. A computer in the corner constantly played information about women's health and reproductive news, and from any of the tables, waiting patients could easily access sites that pertained to childbirth and childrearing.

But the office was around the back of the clinic—actually in a different building altogether—and the waiting area felt like the waiting area of a lawyer or accountant. There was one large window with a spectacular view of the parking lot, and a less spectacular view of the lake across the street and the mountains beyond. The chairs were straight-backed with no armrests, and weren't wide enough for Alden's carrier. With some hesitation, Ro put the sleeping baby on the floor.

She leaned over and played with his curly black hair. His tiny fists were curled against his sleeper, the soft blue blanket her parents had given him tucked beneath his chin. She had no idea how this beautiful boy with his dark brown eyes, chocolate skin, and delicate features could be ill. He was developing the way he was supposed to, he ate well, although he still did not sleep through the night.

Gil paced, and somehow that reassured her: if Gil was nervous, then she had a right to be nervous too. Only she didn't tell him—couldn't tell him—one of the sources of her nervousness. She didn't want to be the mother of a sickly child. She had seen those mothers, with their vaguely frantic air despite their protestations that everything was fine and under control. She had seen the despair in their eyes, the way they clung to their babies as if determination alone could prevent whatever tragedy was ahead.

She had clung to Alden that way on the drive over, and had been ashamed of herself. She didn't even know what the doctor was going to say.

Finally, the androgynous automated voice announced that the doctor was ready to see them. The door to his office swung open, and she grabbed Alden's car-

rier, wishing once again that she was in the waiting
room at the clinic, where real people called her name
and opened the door, and gave her a reassuring smile
as they led her into an unfamiliar room.

The doctor's office smelled faintly of roses. Several
tiny hybrids lined a wall just inside. Books—old, dusty,
and obviously just for show—lined another wall. The
carpet was plush, the desk was messy, and the view
here, through the window behind the desk, was of a
small fenced-in garden, well tended. She had always
known that Dr. Wyatt was a nurturer. It was nice to
have that sense confirmed.

He looked as if he belonged behind that desk. He
wore a brown sweater with a cream-colored turtleneck
beneath it, setting off his mahogany skin. His shaved
head shone, and the single diamond he wore in his
left ear looked even more prominent than usual. As
Ro and Gil entered, he stood and took the carrier
from them, smiling down at the sleeping baby.

He ran a finger along Alden's porcelain cheek.
"Ironic," he murmured so softly that Ro knew he was
speaking only to the baby. She shuddered, thinking
that a confirmation of all she had feared. Then he
smiled at her. "Please sit."

She waited until he placed the carrier on his desk,
on the only bare spot left by the piles of paper. The
carrier was turned so that they all could see the boy.
He hadn't moved, but his blanket had. His soft breath
made a corner of it flutter ever so slightly.

"What's wrong with him?" Ro asked, unable to
wait.

Gil took her hand in his warm, strong one. She
could feel tension in both of their fingers as they
braced themselves.

"Nothing," Dr. Wyatt said.

"Nothing?" And in Gil's surprised growl, she heard

the beginnings of anger. She squeezed his hand, warning him to wait.

"That's what so wonderful," Dr. Wyatt said, leaning forward. "We did the standard genetic testing on your son."

Ro remembered. Genetic testing was required in Oregon, in all but a handful of states now, and the results were supposed to be kept private. In fact, parents could opt not to know what dangers lurked in their child's genes. Ro and Gil had taken a moderate approach: if the problem was going to be incapacitating or life-threatening they wanted to know. Otherwise, they chose to let the information come to Alden on his eighteenth birthday—a Pandora's box he could chose to open or not, all on his own.

Gil had stiffened beside her. She knew what he was thinking: incapacitating or fatal. How could Dr. Wyatt call that nothing?

"And we discovered that Alden is only infant we have seen in this clinic, indeed in this part of the state, who had a perfect set of genes."

"P–perfect?" Ro repeated. She had been so expecting the other, the bad, the horrible news, that the good news was hard to absorb.

"Perfect. No missing genes, no malfunctioning genes, no hereditary diseases. In fact, he is quite the survivor, with some extra genes that have been determined to fight certain viruses. Unless your son has an accident, he will live a long and healthy life."

Ro frowned. Perfect.

"We used to think," Dr. Wyatt was saying, "that perfect human beings could be engineered. What we didn't know until just recently was that perfect human beings already existed. They could be born into a family like yours."

Gil cleared his throat, and slipped his fingers from Ro's. He recovered quicker—or at least his brain did. It always had.

"We signed the waiver," he said. "We weren't supposed to find out anything like this about Alden."

"You signed the waiver, yes," Dr. Wyatt said, "but did you read it?"

Ro glanced at Gil. She had been in labor when they remembered the consent. He had been the one to handle the business details of Alden's birth. He shrugged. "I scanned it."

"Then you might have missed one of the clauses in the middle. It addressed this very issue."

"What issue?" Ro asked.

Dr. Wyatt smiled at her; then he leaned forward, folding his hands on the desk. She recognized the posture. It was his sincere-explanation posture. Once, another expectant mother had described it to her as his attempt not to patronize his patients.

"We have the capability of growing new organs from various cells. We do a lot of microsurgery, a lot of repair work on the cellular level before we can use some of these organs." He glanced at Alden, who was still sleeping. "Sometimes we repair genetic defects in the womb. We also do a lot of work with the new techniques, ones that involve injecting new genetic material into old cells, revitalizing them. Some of these procedures are old, some are new, but they all involve the basic building blocks of a human being."

Ro felt her breath catch. Dr. Wyatt was speaking slowly, giving them a chance to ask questions. Apparently Gil had none. She had a thousand, but didn't know where to begin asking.

"Private bio-technology companies pay a lot of money to keep cells from people like Alden on file.

We have hopes that their perfect DNA will make them useful in all areas of biological and medical sciences. There is already a use for them now."

"This is about money?" Gil asked.

"It's about healing," Dr. Wyatt said. Then he sighed. "There is more."

"More?" Ro asked.

"If you choose to have more children, any one of these companies will be willing to finance your pregnancies and the first five years of your children's lives. You have created one genetically perfect child. The chances are you will create another." His smile was apologetic. "If you don't want to do that, if you only want one child, then they would pay you quite well for fertilized embryos. In fact, you could do both—"

"Is this a joke?" Gil asked.

"No." Dr. Wyatt spoke solemnly, reassuringly. "A handful of other couples all over the country have done this already, but cases like this are very rare."

Alden stirred. His small fist grabbed the fluttering edge of the blue blanket, and he pulled it toward his mouth, uncovering his tiny feet, encased in delicate white socks. Ro grabbed the blanket and pulled it down, covering him again.

"What does the clinic get out of this?" Gil asked.

Dr. Wyatt shrugged. "A percentage. Small, actually. It amounts to one percent of the total fees paid your family."

"Plus all the payments for the additional medical care," Gil said. His anger was becoming plain. His voice was rising.

"What—?" Ro asked, loudly enough to cover him. He shot her a warning look which she ignored. "What does this mean for Alden?"

"Financially?" Dr. Wyatt said. "It means that he'll—"

"No," she said. "What will happen to my baby? Are there tests? Will he have to leave us?"

"No," Dr. Wyatt said. "At his checkups, we'll take an extra vial of blood, and send it to whichever lab ends up with his case. He won't notice a thing."

"Those are his genes, right?" Gil asked. "Do we have to give consent every time they're used?"

Dr. Wyatt looked at his long, manicured hands. "If you do this," he said, "Alden's genes will no longer be his. They will belong to the firm that buys them."

"Meaning they could do anything they want with his genes?" Ro asked.

"Yes," Dr. Wyatt said.

"Will he be prevented from using his genes?" Gil asked.

"They have a waiver for reproduction," Dr. Wyatt said. "But if he wanted to donate sperm or give blood, he would need permission. And he would need their permission if he wanted donate an organ or grow one for a family member who couldn't for some reason."

Ro shuddered. Such a decision. She had expected to make one today, but not like this.

"Would they clone him?" she asked.

"Cloning is illegal throughout the world," Dr. Wyatt said.

"But we've heard rumors—"

"No reputable company would clone anyone," Dr. Wyatt said, "although they might use a section of his DNA as a template for some infant's flawed DNA."

"How much would we get paid?" Gil asked.

"For Alden?" Dr. Wyatt shrugged. "The usual bid starts at two million dollars. It can rise from there."

"And how long would they control his genes?"

Dr. Wyatt's mouth formed a thin line. "For life," he said.

*   *   *

They did not have to make a decision right away. All they did was ask Dr. Wyatt to wait before informing any of the companies about Alden. Dr. Wyatt agreed. They were to see him again in two weeks.

During that time, they spoke to everyone they knew. Their friends had split opinions: some felt that Alden's gift should be used for the greater good; others believed that to give Alden's DNA away would be to tamper with God's plan. Their more sophisticated friends worried about the legalities. Their families worried about the restrictions.

Gil hired a lawyer who specialized in medical contracts. The lawyer believed she could negotiate a more favorable document that gave less power to the biotech company and more money to the family. She would take the case on a contingency, agreeing to work for a percentage of the final take. Gil had been satisfied with her, but Ro hadn't. When they had gone to the lawyer's office, she hadn't done more than give Alden a cursory glance. No questions about him, no gentle touches, and when he woke grumpy after a long nap, she requested that he either get quiet or be taken to the daycare center thoughtfully provided by the legal firm.

It was starting to become about money. Two million dollars would pay off all their debts, including their tiny one-story home in a distant suburb. It would pay for Alden's college, his graduate work, and, if they invested wisely, give him a nest egg, an investment that might help him as he grew older.

Ro walked through her tiny house with its unwieldy '90s kitchen with the island that always got in her way and the hooks for the cooper pots that no one had anymore, and imagined it updated, with modern appliances. She fed Alden in the living room, always chilly because of its cathedral ceiling, and wished that she could carve the space into two rooms—one of them a playroom for her beautiful son. Gil mentioned in passing, as he always did with things that were important to him, that perhaps they could consider buying a bigger house with a real yard, close to schools and public transportation. They allowed themselves to contemplate a different life.

And through it all, they fed Alden, changed him, played with him, and held him. They carried him from room to room as they dreamed their small dreams. Sometimes he giggled. Often he slept. And sometimes he cried so hard that Ro thought his heart was breaking. During those times, she couldn't understand what he needed, and she wished, oh how she wished, she could ask him what he wanted.

Because their decision would affect him in a thousand ways. It would affect everything about him, from simple acts of charity such as donating blood to large things such as his financial future. Ro did not even think about the added offer, the way that the companies would pay for more children, the way that all of this would affect their lives.

She studied everything she could find, became familiar with genes and DNA and experiment processes. She learned that Alden was one of a select group. Less than point one-one hundredth of all the children born since the human genome project had been finished were categorized as medically perfect. Of that small percentage, only a few were born in the United States each year. There was no information on families who had chosen the options she and Gil had been offered, except short mentions in various papers that people had taken those offers. Nothing about the parents, about how they made the decisions, about how they felt later.

* * *

Two nights before she and Gil were to talk again with Dr. Wyatt, she sat in Alden's room. The room smelled of talcum and baby, and was silent, except for Alden's even breathing.

They had remodeled the walk-in closet beside the master bedroom as the nursery, thinking that later they would give Alden a room farther from theirs. The nursery was small but bright, with a balloon mural on the wall that Gil had painted and matching pillows all over the floor, sewn by her mother. White baby furniture completed the look. They had modern smarthouse equipment in here and in the master bedroom, an expense that Ro had insisted on when she became pregnant. No old-fashioned baby monitors for her. She wanted the very walls to listen to her child, to make sure he was all right every moment of every day.

Still, she sat often in the rocker her grandmother had given her and watched Alden sleep. Ro did her best thinking when Alden slept. She remembered her fear of becoming one of those mothers, with a diseased child, a woman who clung to her baby hoping to give it life.

Alden had life. He had more than life. He had, genetically speaking, a life that would be healthy and full. He was the opposite of those children.

Something in that thought held her. She had come to it over and over again in the last ten days. She was approaching her child because of what he had instead of who he was, and she had always thought that wrong.

Alden was a joyful baby. Everyone said that. And they said how lucky she was. He could have been naturally cranky or energetic or listless. He could have been so many things, but he was not. He was born with a mind and a personality all his own. It was up to her—her and Gil—to help him develop those things.

She stood slowly, then walked to the crib, bent over, and kissed her sleeping child. He stirred slightly, confident in her touch. Knowing it was a light touch, a secure touch, a loving touch. He trusted her, especially now, when he could not do anything for himself. He trusted her to do the best thing for them all.

Dr. Wyatt's office door was open, and he was waiting for them. He bent over one of his tea roses, his long fingers working a particularly delicate trim. Ro watched him, seeing the gentleness, now knowing that was only a part of him.

Gil held Alden's carrier. They agreed that Ro would do most of the talking. It had been her idea, after all.

Dr. Wyatt smiled when he saw them and took Alden's carrier as he had done before. They took their places in front of the desk.

"Well?" Dr. Wyatt asked as if he already knew the answer.

"We have decided," Ro looked at Gil, who nodded at her to continue. "To let Alden make this decision when he turns eighteen. We agree with the waiver we signed. This is not a decision we should make for our child."

Dr. Wyatt frowned. "It would be better not to wait."

"Better for whom?" Ro asked. "The companies? Yes, it would. And perhaps for a few patients, too. But we are locking my son into an agreement for life, which is something medieval. We don't believe in such things, Dr. Wyatt."

"I'm sure some clauses can be waived. Perhaps you could even get a temporary agreement, something that would be nonbinding on him when he became an adult."

Ro shook her head. "This is not an emergency,

Doctor. We are willing to be contacted on a case-by-case basis in the event of an emergency, when someone actually needs Alden's help. What we are refusing is a business arrangement. We want our son to be a child first, and a commodity only if he chooses to be."

"He wouldn't be a commodity," Dr. Wyatt said.

She stared at him for a long time. "Maybe not to you," she said. "But the biotech company who bought his genes wouldn't know him. To them, he would be something that would enable them to make a profit. To other patients, he would be another tool. To us, he is a person already. And people make their own choices, and their own commitments. We're sorry, doctor."

She stood. So did Gil. Finally Dr. Wyatt did as well. He ran a hand along Alden's small face. "He is a perfect child."

"No," Ro said. "He's not. He's got good genes. That's all."

"That's plenty," Dr. Wyatt said. "Promise me you'll tell him of this opportunity when he's grown."

"You will," Gil said. "Or someone in your clinic will. We will stipulate that. We have an attorney who can draw up a document."

"It was kind of you," Ro added, "not to mention the money."

Dr. Wyatt took Alden's tiny hand in his own. "You realize how rare and precious he is."

Ro smiled. "Yes," she said softly. "We do."

ABOUT THE AUTHORS

Kevin J. Anderson has more than sixteen million books in print in thirty languages, including Dune novels written with Brian Herbert, *Star Wars* and *X-Files* novels, and a collaboration with Dean Koontz. He just finished the sixth book in his epic space opera, *The Saga of Seven Suns*. He and his wife Rebecca Moesta have written numerous bestselling and award-winning young adult novels.

Loren L. Coleman is a full-time novelist. His first novel, *Double-Blind,* was published in 1998. He has since explored the universes of BattleTech, Magic: The Gathering, Crimson Skies, MechWarrior: Dark Age, Star Trek, and Conan. His latest works are a new trilogy set in the Conan universe and co-development of a new fiction market for the Classic Battle Tech and Mech-Warrior universe: www.BattleCorps.com. Currently he resides in Washington State with his wife, Heather Joy, two sons, Talon LaRon and Conner Rhys Monroe, and a young daughter, Alexia Joy. The family owns three of the obligatory writer's cats, Chaos,

Ranger, and Rumor, and one dog, Loki. His personal website can be found at www.rasqal.com.

Brenda Cooper has published fiction in *Analog; Oceans of the Mind;* and *Strange Horizons;* and in the anthologies *Sun in Glory; Maiden, Matron, Crone*; and *Time After Time*. Brenda's collaborative fiction with Larry Niven has appeared in *Analog* and *Asimov's*. She and Larry wrote a novel, *Building Harlequin's Moon,* and her solo novel, *The Silver Ship and the Sea,* was published in 2007. Brenda lives in Bellevue, Washington, with her partner Toni, Toni's daughter Katie, a border collie, and a golden retriever. By day, she is the City of Kirkland's CIO, and at night and in early morning hours, she's a futurist and writer.

Dave Freer was born at a very early age. And then, alas, things started to go downhill for him. He was unable to maintain the status quo; despite considerable and lifelong resistance to growing up, he has found himself married to Barbara and a father to two sons—who were also born at a very young age, proving it must be hereditary. In a desperate and vain attempt to change the world and also to pay the rent, Freer turned to the writing of fantasy and science fiction. He believed they were closely related fields; both paid badly and required a great deal of intellect and very little common sense; and therefore it was something he could do. Fortunately he was wrong about the intellect it required of him, although it has taken him ten books—eight of them with co-authors Eric Flint and/or Mercedes Lackey—to figure this out. "Boys" is his eighth short story sale. When not writing Freer can sometimes be found clinging to rocks, both on the sides of mountains or in the raging sea, in the mistaken impression he is getting back to his roots.

Esther M. Friesner is the author of over 30 novels and over 150 short stories, plus poetry, articles, an advice column, and one professionally produced play. She won the Nebula Award for her short stories in two consecutive years. At present she is best known for having created and edited the five extremely popular *Chicks in Chainmail* anthologies. Her most recent novels are *Temping Fate* (Dutton/Penguin, June 2006) and *Nobody's Princess* (Random House, April 2007). She lives in Connecticut with her husband, is the proud mother of two all-grown-up kids, and harbors cats.

P. R. Frost, the author of the Tess Noncorire Adventures series, resides on beautiful Mt. Hood in Oregon. She is currently finishing up the second novel in the series. She hikes the Columbia River Gorge for inspiration, reads omnivorously, and enjoys attending science fiction conventions. She grew up in a ballet studio, performing with the Ballet du Lac, a pro/am company out of Lake Oswego, Oregon.

It's been almost exactly ten years since **Sarah A. Hoyt** sold her first short story. In the interim, she's sold over three dozen short stories to magazines such as *Amazing, Asimov's, Analog,* and *Weird Tales,* as well as an assortment of anthologies. Alongside the short stories, she's sold a dozen novels. The most notable are her critically acclaimed Shakespeare Fantasy series, her Musketeer Mysteries series, written as Sarah D'Almeida (www.musketeersmysteries.com), and her new Urban Fantasy Shifter's series (www.shifterseries. com). Sarah lives in Colorado with her two teen sons, her husband, and a varied pride of cats. Catch up with her at http://www.sarahahoyt.com.

Julie Hyzy has loved science fiction since her eighth-grade teacher put a copy of Ray Bradbury's *The October Country* in her hands many years ago. Julie's short stories have appeared in *Star Trek, Strange New Worlds* (Pocket Books), and *All the Rage This Year* (Phobos). She's also written several mystery novels, including *Artistic License* (stand-alone romantic suspense), *Deadly Blessings* (first in a series), and *Deadly Interest*. She lives with her family in Tinley Park, Illinois.

James Patrick Kelly has had an eclectic writing career. He has written novels, short stories, essays, reviews, poetry, plays, and planetarium shows. His books include *Burn* (2005), *Strange But Not a Stranger* (2002), *Think Like a Dinosaur and Other Stories* (1997), *Wildlife* (1994), *Heroines* (1990), *Look Into the Sun* (1989), *Freedom Beach* (1986), and *Planet of Whispers* (1984). His fiction has been translated into sixteen languages. He has won the World Science Fiction Society's Hugo Award twice: in 1996 for his novelette "Think Like A Dinosaur" and in 2000 for his novelette "Ten to the Sixteenth to One." He writes a column on the internet for *Asimov's Science Fiction* magazine and is on the faculty of the Stonecoast Creative Writing MFA Program at the University of Southern Maine. In 2004 he was appointed by the Governor of New Hampshire to be the chair of the New Hampshire State Council on the Arts.

Alan L. Lickiss fell in love with robot stories when he discovered science fiction. While he admires the robot vacuums that have shown up in recent years, he is still looking for the more versatile robots that can pick up his clothes first before they vacuum the carpet. He lives along the front range in Colorado with his wife and children, works a day job, and writes as much as he can in the evenings. Now if he only had a robot stenographer.

Rebecca Moesta is the author of 28 books and numerous short stories, including the award-winning *Star Wars: Young Jedi Knights* series, two original *Titan A.E.* novels, which she co-authored with husband Kevin J. Anderson, and *Buffy the Vampire Slayer* novel, *Little Things*. With Anderson, she has written an original young-adult fantasy series, *Crystal Doors*, for Little, Brown.

Born in Glasgow, Scotland, **Lisanne Norman** started writing at the age of eight in order to find more of the books she liked to read. In 1980, two years after joining The Vikings, the largest British reenactment society in Britain, she moved to Norfolk, England. There she ran her own specialist archery display team. Now living in America and a full-time author, she has created worlds where warriors, magic, and science all coexist in her Sholan Alliance Series. Her next novel in the series will be called *Shades of Gray,* from DAW.

Irene Radford has been writing stories ever since she figured out what a pencil was for. A member of an endangered species, a native Oregonian living in Oregon, she and her husband make their home in Welches, Oregon, where deer, bear, coyote, hawks, owls, and woodpeckers feed regularly on their back deck. In her spare time, Irene enjoys lacemaking and is a longtime member of an international guild.

Annie Reed is an award-winning writer whose short fiction has appeared in *Ellery Queen Mystery Maga-*

zine, three volumes of *Strange New Worlds,* and several DAW anthologies, including *Time After Time, Hags, Sirens, and Other Bad Girls of Fantasy,* and *Cosmic Cocktails.* She lives in northern Nevada with her husband, daughter, and a varying number of high-maintenance cats. In addition to science fiction, she writes mystery, romance, and women's fiction.

Mike Resnick is the winner of five Hugos and a Nebula, along with other major awards in the USA, France, Japan, Spain, Croatia, and Poland. He is the author of more than 50 novels, 200 stories, 14 collections, and 2 screenplays, and the editor of more than 40 anthologies. His work has been translated into 22 languages.

Kristine Kathryn Rusch has won or been nominated for all the major awards in the SF field for her science fiction stories. Her most recent SF novel is *Paloma: A Retrieval Artist Novel.*

Dean Wesley Smith is the bestselling author of over eighty novels and a hundred short stories. He has been nominated for just about every major award in science fiction and fantasy and even won a few, including a World Fantasy Award. His most recent fantasy novel is *All Eve's Hallows,* and he writes thrillers under a different name. He lives on the Oregon Coast with his wife, Kristine Kathryn Rusch.

Tanya Huff

The Confederation Novels

"As a heroine, Kerr shines. She is cut from the same mold
as Ellen Ripley of the *Aliens* films. Like her heroine,
Huff delivers the goods." —*SF Weekly*

in an omnibus edition:

A CONFEDERATION OF VALOR
(Valor's Choice, The Better Part of Valor)
0-7564-0399-5
978-0-7564-0399-7

and now in hardcover:

THE HEART OF VALOR
978-0-7564-0435-2

To Order Call: 1-800-788-6262
www.dawbooks.com

CJ Cherryh

Classic Novels in Omnibus Editions

THE DREAMING TREE
Contains the complete duology *The Dreamstone* and
The Tree of Swords and Jewels.   0-88677-782-8

THE FADED SUN TRILOGY
Contains the complete novels *Kesrith*, *Shon'jir*, and
Kutath.   0-88677-836-0

THE MORGAINE SAGA
Contains the complete novels *Gate of Ivrel*, *Well of
Shiuan*, and *Fires of Azeroth.*   0-88677-877-8

THE CHANUR SAGA
Contains the complete novels *The Pride of Chanur*,
Chanur's Venture and *The Kif Strike Back.*
                                        0-88677-930-8

ALTERNATE REALITIES
Contains the complete novels *Port Eterntiy*, *Voyager
in Night*, and *Wave Without a Shore*   0-88677-946-4

AT THE EDGE OF SPACE
Contains the complete novels *Brothers of Earth* and
Hunter of Worlds.   0-7564-0160-7

To Order Call: 1-800-788-6262
www.dawbooks.com

CJ Cherryh
The Foreigner Novels

"Serious space opera at its very best by one of the leading SF writers in the field today." —*Publishers Weekly*

FOREIGNER	0-88677-637-6
INVADER	0-88677-687-2
INHERITOR	0-88677-728-3
PRECURSOR	0-88677-910-3
DEFENDER	0-7564-0020-1
EXPLORER	0-7564-0165-8
DESTROYER	0-7564-0333-2
PRETENDER	0-7564-0408-6
DELIVERER	0-7564-0414-7

"Her world building, aliens, and suspense rank among the strongest in the whole SF field. May those strengths be sustained indefinitely, or at least until the end of Foreigner." —*Booklist*

DAW 8

OTHERLAND

TAD WILLIAMS

"The Otherland books are a major accomplishment."–*Publishers Weekly*

"It will captivate you."
–*Cinescape*

In many ways it is humankind's most stunning achievement. This most exclusive of places is also one of the world's best-kept secrets, but somehow, bit by bit, it is claiming Earth's most valuable resource: its children.

Julie E. Czerneda

Reap the Wild Wind

Stratification #1

In this earlier time of Czerneda's Trade Pact universe, the Clan has not yet learned how to manipulate the M'hir to travel between worlds. Instead, they are a people divided into small tribes, scattered over a fraction of their world, prevented from advancing by two other powerful races. But aliens have begun to explore the Clan's home planet, upsetting the delicate balance between the three intelligent races. Also in this time is one young woman on the verge of mastering the forbidden power of the M'hir—a power that could prove to be the salvation or ruin of her entire species...

978-0-7564-0456-7

"A creative voice and a distinctive vision.
A writer to watch." —C.J. Cherryh

To Order Call: 1-800-788-6262
www.dawbooks.com

DAW 80